Unity and Strength

A novel inspired by the contribution of
Sardar Vallabhbhai Patel

Unity and Strength

A novel inspired by the contribution of
Sardar Vallabhbhai Patel

by
Amarendra Narayan

BANYAN TREE BOOKS PVT. LTD.

Price : ₹ 695

First edition : 2017

Published by :
Banyan Tree Books Pvt. Ltd
7/31, Ansari Road, Daryaganj
New Delhi-110 002 (India)
Website: www.rajkamalprakashan.com
Email: info@rajkamalprakashan.com

Printed at :
B.K. Offset
Naveen Shahdara, Delhi-110 032

ISBN : 978-81-905401-6-2

We Are Indebted to You

The first requisite for building a strong, free India is unity and peace. We must first of all adjust our differences and behave in such a manner that there is complete harmony and peace in the country. For unity we must forget the differnces of caste and creed and remember that we are all Indians, and all equal. There can be no distinction between man and man in a free country. All must have equal opportunities, equal rights and equal responsibilities.

–Sardar Vallabhbhai Patel

Gratitude

My sincere gratitude to :

- Bapu, Dr. Rajendra Prasadji, Shri Mahadev Desai, Shri Narhari Parikh, Shri Rajivbhai Patel, Shri Rajmohan Gandhi, Shri V.P. Menon, Shri V. Shankar, Shri K.M. Munshi, Shri K.L. Panjabi and other distinguished persons whose excellent writings gave me an opportunity to understand the making of Sardar Patel and provided authentic references for progressing the work.
- Respected Padmbhushan Swami Dr. Satyamitranand Giri Ji for his interest in the book and for his blessings.
- Well known scholar Acharya Shri Dr. Krishnakant Chaturvediji, Former Director Kalidas Academy, Ujjain and Kulguru, Rajshekhar Vidyapith for his guidance, advice and encouragement.
- Famous writer and artist Shri Amrit Lal Vegad for his useful suggestions and help in improving my understanding of some Gujarati words.
- Srimati Leela Kumar Ji-daughter of Late V. Shankar Sahab for kindly sharing her reminiscences. As a child, Leelaji enjoyed Sardar Sri's warm affection. He used to play cards with Leelaji.
- Famous journalist dear Sri Nirmal Narad Ji who despite his poor health, thoroughly read the text and made very useful suggestions.
- Dear friend Shri Shankarbhai Thakkar, who described the situation of rural Gujarat during Sardar Patel's time in great detail and explained several features of the contemporary society. He gave me his valuable collection of Gujarati periodicals and took me to the library of the Gujarati

Association, Jabalpur where I found some very useful publications of historical importance.

- Smt. Dr. Sharda Mishra ji who gave very useful suggestions for improving the text.
- Shri Vipin Chandra Baveshi for his valuable help in translating many important documents from Gujarati to English and in providing very useful advice.
- Shri Ratanbhai Patel of the Bardoli Museum for his kind help in explaining the events during the Bardoli Satyagrah.
- Shri Ghanshyam Vaghela, a former Station Director of All India Radio and an alumni of the Gujarat Vidyapith for narrating his first-hand experience at the Vidyapith.
- Shri Gunjan Agrawal, for providing useful resource material and for his very valuable help at every stage.
- Sardar Vallabhbhai Patel Rashtriya Ekta Trust (SVPRET) for their kind permission to use the photo of Sardar Shri in the cover of the book. Special thanks to Shri Sanjay Joshi and Shri R.G. Acharya of SVPRET.
- Shri B.N. Patel of the Sardar Sarovar Narmada Nigam Ltd. For kindly explaining the details of the Statue of Unity project at Kevadia.
- The Sardar Patel National Museum, Ahmedabad for their permission to take photographs of Sardar Shri's statue. Special thanks to Shri R.S. Patel, Secretary and Shri Balubhai Patel, Joint Secretary and Shri S.T. Desai of the Sardar Vallabhbhai Patel Memorial Society, Ahmedabad for their help and permission to use the photographs. Thanks for other references.
- My son-in-law Kumar Vijay Prasad for sending me the photographs of Sardar Shri's statue at the Sardar Patel National Museum, Ahmedabad.
- The authorities of Sardar Vallabhbhai Patel and Vir Vitthalbhai Patel Memorial, Karamsad for their cooperation.
- My friends Thakur Subhash Sinha, Shri Vineet Mathur, Shri Rakesh Shah and Shri R.K. Mehra and Shri Amit for their help in facilitating my visit to Ras.
- Shri Sanjay Kantibhai Patel, Principal, Ras High School who gave me the details of the contribution made by Ras and

provided useful information about the visits of Gandhiji and Sardar Shri to Ras.

- Respected Dr. S.K. Hajela for his help in sending useful reference material.
- Respected Sri R.B. Upadhyayji, Dr. Aparna Tiwariji, Sri Abhijay Upadhyay Ji, Sri Sanjay Trivediji and Srimati Jyotsana Trivediji for their help at various stages of writing.
- Shrimati Sudha Trivedi for providing some Gujarati folk songs and proverbs along with their translation.
- My wife Asha, who in spite of her poor health, travelled with me to Kheda, Nadiad, Karamsad, Bardoli, Ras, Kevadia, Dandi, Ahmedabad and some other places in Gujarat associated with Sardar Patel.
- My children Ashish and Shweta; and to grandchildren Shubha and Ashirvad who though very reluctantly, allowed me to postpone my travel to Bangkok by an additional month. The allowance gave me an opportunity to complete my study of the reference material and to write the first draft of the novel. In spite of his heavy work load, Ashish read the entire text and gave some very useful suggestions.
- Respected Shri B.N. Puri and dear Shri S.K. Dhanuka for their useful suggestions for improving the text.
- Saurabh Jain, Ved Prakash Ji, Pratap, Hemant, Ajay and other friends of Amrit Offset for preparing the brochure for the book.
- Shri Ashok Maheshwari Ji, Managing Director, Rajkamal Prakashan Group and dear colleagues of Prakashan Group for their keen interest and dedicated efforts for publishing the book.

Why This Novel?

Like millions of fellow Indians, I admire Sardar Shri Vallabhbhai Patel for his tremendous contribution in unification of India. He gave us the united India in which we live.

Unfortunately, we lost him at a time when we needed him most. Had he been alive for a few more years, our India in which we live today would have been much stronger, more closely united and perhaps better managed. We all miss him very much.

Several good books have been written about the Iron Man of India-including his excellent biographies by Shri Narhari Parikh and Shri Rajmohan Gandhi, My Reminiscences of Sardar Patel by Shri V. Shankar and many others. Lot of material about Sardar Patel is also available on the internet. In spite of these, why I decided to write this book?

I wanted to understand Shri Vallabhbhai's contribution from the heart of a common farmer from Gujarat who had participated in the freedom struggle. It was very interesting to know how Shri Vallabhbhai came under the influence of Mahatma Gandhi, how he discarded his flourishing practice and plunged into the unknown labyrinths of public service.

Thereafter, the various events associated with Shri Vallabhbhai Patel shaped and unfolded his great leadership qualities. Shri Vallabhbhai began his life of public service as a fighter of peasants' and mill-workers' rights. His early contributions in the peasant movements of Kheda and Bardoli brought out the courageous leader in him. Those were the days when an average villager was taken for granted by the administration for his pusillanimity and submission to the authority. The rural masses had accepted servitude as their fait accompli. To ignite the lamp of self-respect among them, which was almost extinct, and to prepare them to wage a long struggle against any injustice caused by the mighty empire was a Herculean task.

During the Kheda Satyagrah, speaking at Karamsad, Gandhiji had said, *Shri Vallabhbhai is going through the fire and he has to undergo further tests. I am sure that we shall find pure gold from the furnace.*

Shri Vallabhbhai threw himself in the crucible and true to Bapu's confidence, emerged out as pure gold. He had found himself, Gandhiji had found a trusted follower and the country had found a great leader in him.

During the freedom struggle, a large number of people followed Mahatma Gandhi, Shri Vallabhbhai and other well-known leaders. Among them were several thousand simple unknown farmers who did not hesitate in making great sacrifices at the call of their leaders.

I have developed the novel around such a peasant family of a small village Ras from Borsad Taluka in Kheda District (Now Anand), Gujarat. Shri Vallabhbhai Patel was arrested there before the start of the Dandi Movement.

Influenced by Shri Vallabhbhai's great sacrifice and patriotism, Chamanbhai, a member of a peasant family of Ras becomes a full time follower of Shri Vallabhbhai. He participates in the various *satyagrahas* launched by him under Gandhiji's direction. Through the main character Chamanbhai, the role of Sardar Patel, his thought process, his ability to lead the masses, his practical perception of the circumstances, his personal touch and his excellent management of critical situations are described. The novel highlights several less known facts about the Kheda, Borsad, Dandi and Bardoli Satyagra has and about the integration of Princely States.

Be it controlling serious law and order problems during those turbulent times, the elephantine task of managing the migration and settlement of refugees, developing an appropriate administrative system for independent India, and above all-the integration of Princely States under very difficult circumstances-all were very challenging and precisely time bound problems which he handled remarkably well.

The indomitable Sardar gave us an India of which we are proud of. Many persons observed that perhaps no other contemporary leader would have been able to achieve the feat. Yet Sardar Patel's all dreams were not realised.

We admire his many great contributions and often ask ourselves— what can we do to fulfil *his* dreams of having a united and strong India? Perhaps, we can try to make some contribution in our own modest way, which we may feel insignificant in the beginning. But we will have the satisfaction of proceeding in the right direction. This is what the third and fourth generations of Chamanbha's family decide to do when they meet at their village home at Ras for a family get-together.

Bangkok, June 2, 2016 **—Amarendra Narayan**

Content

Part - III

[2016 and beyond...]

PART - I

[Kheda, Gujarat
Early twentieth century]

1

The golden rays of the post midday sun were fast disappearing behind the tall trees. Winter was on its way out. This was the most despised winter in the Kheda district of Gujarat in recent years. But more than the troubles caused by the unkind winter, merciless torrents of rains had devastated the crops in the entire district and had shattered the already limping village economy. The Kheda district was known for its lush green vegetation nurtured by the hard working farmers. Conveniently situated between Sabarmati and Mahi rivers, the area was known for its agricultural produce. By their persistent hard work, the farmers have been regularly enhancing the fertility of the *goradu* soil. Years of toils and sweat had earned a reputation for the Kheda land, its market value was high and so was the revenue assessment. Much value addition to the land was done by the successive generations of sedulous farmers. Although the low water table had forced them to depend upon monsoon but the farmers were used to it. The inconsistent rural economy was based upon the yield of cereals, pulses and cash crops. Tobacco was an important source of cash income. The lands of the *Charotar* tract which constituted Anand, Borsad, Nadiad and Petlad, were priced higher than the other fertile lands.

Vagaries of nature were not unknown to the district. The peasantry had faced famine in the early twentieth century. The later years were little better, and life pulled on somehow. The torrential monsoon rains of 1917 brought havoc and profound misery to the Kheda district. While the normal monsoon rain was 30 inches, that year the rainfall peaked 70 inches in the district, which washed away the sowings and created shortage of food and fodder. The rainfall continued beyond the Navratri festival. Bright sunshine in the late October revived some hopes. Unfortunately, these hopes were soon shattered. When the produce like *bajri* were left for drying in the field, heavens poured again with full might and the crops were rotted. To add to the misery, rats and pests swallowed a major portion of the salvaged produce.

The revenue rules had a provision of suspension of assessment on the basis of the crop failure. If the crop was below four *annas* then the revenue assessment was suspended in full, crop under six *annas* entitled suspension of 50% of the revenue. There was another provision in the revenue rules. If the crops failed the next year also then the entire revenue collection was remitted. However, these intricate rules had not percolated to the illiterate or semi-literate peasantry which honoured the arbitrary government orders without questioning.

Unfortunately, the plague epidemic had also been taking its toll of the human and financial resources. Several thousand people were killed in the district by bubonic plague. Medical relief was severely inadequate. The British Government was perhaps more concerned and busy about increasing the recruitment for the war and collections for the war fund.

For Jivanbhai and his co-villagers of the village Ras, goings were particularly tough in the year 1917. They were trying their best to recover from the dry season of 1915 and were hopeful of a good harvest during the current year. But good luck and prosperity eluded them! Perhaps they were destined to work hard for a huge disproportionate return. Prices were rising, cheap labour was no longer available and worse of all-the nature continued to remain unkind.

In spite of the miserable situation of the peasants, the government had pressed its claims of higher revenue. The worried and helpless peasants had resigned to their fate. Quite often they would droop their heads in utter despair-will these inexorable demands and pressure end someday? Will somebody come to champion the cause of the poor helpless farmers?

Ashabhai Lallubhai Patel had taken some initiative to represent their case to the government. He had studied at the Borsad Edward Memorial School and was a trained telegraphist. Ashabhai used to sell cotton yarn for his livelihood. This was small trading. He was more active in social work. Currently Ashabhai was away from the village but he had been assuring the people that several social workers are sending petitions to the government for relief.

Jivanbhai and his co-villagers were sitting under the *peepal* tree, idly watching the children playing in the open space and the cattle retuning home for the much needed rest. Life in the village was abysmally slow this year, the gloom and despair which enveloped the entire Kheda district did not spare his relatively better off village Ras.

Looking aimlessly at the sky, Jivanbhai said in a pessimistic tone, "God only knows when our good days will come!"

His co-villager Nandubhai, the village school master agreed, "It appears that somebody has cast his evil eyes on our happy Kheda district! Our district was known for its lush green beauty. Many visitors including the *sahebs*, have praised the trees and plantations of the area. Remember our young days-we used to spend so much time roaming around the gardens! There was no restriction on plucking fruits and other items and we never felt tired of climbing to the top of the trees!"

"Those were the golden days, Nandubhai," Jivanbhai, said. "Now things have changed. The government is not concerned about us. See the attitude of our own *talatis* and *mamlatdars*! They are rude, arrogant and tyrannical, their heads are swollen with pride. They are so unscrupulous and heartless that they will not hesitate to squeeze our dead bodies."

"We are already half dead!" exclaimed Nandubhai. He continued, "Jivanbhai, still there is a distant thin ray of hope. We know that in summer this year, Gandhiji had championed the cause of farmers in remote Champaran in Bihar where he courageously stood, with his head high, in front of the *sahebs*. Finally, the powerful government had to relent."

Jivanbhai interrupted, "Although Gandhiji is taking interest in our matter, he is very busy and we do not have another intrepid leader like him."

"Don't be so disappointed, Jivanbhai!" Nandubhai said. "When I visited my in-laws at Godhra, my brother in-law told me that Gandhiji had addressed the peasants there in the winter. Tilak Maharaj, Jinnah Saheb and Shri Vitthalbhai Patel were also present. They are trying to oppose the tyrannical rules and practices. Remember-they opposed the *veth*. Shri Vallabhbhai wrote to the

Commissioner Saheb, requesting him to stop the practice. He even published a pamphlet on the subject. I have a copy with me."

Jivanbhai agreed, "I remember that. The pamphlet was read at the *Choro*. It was written there that *veth* is illegal and should be stopped. The villagers were asked to refuse *veth*. Vamanbhai of Panchmahal and our own Asha Bhai were quite active in the matter."

Nandubhai said, "Several meetings were organised in the villages. Shri Ravi Shankar Maharaj is working in Mehmadabad and Shri Mohanlal Pandya is very active in Kathlal."

"Yes," Jivanbhai nodded. "Last year the farmers of Kathlal had appealed to the government for postponing the recovery of land revenue because the crop was less than *char anna*. But the government is very powerful and the officers are not much concerned. They are busy with collecting the war fund and speeding up the recruitment."

Nandubhai Said, "Thakkarbapa, Mavlankar Saheb, Krishanlal Bhai, Vitthalbhai, Parekh Saheb, Joshi Saheb, Deodhar Saheb and many others have visited the villages of the Kheda district and have seen that the crops have failed. They believe that the assessment made by the local officials is arbitrary and is deliberately designed to prevent award of any significant concession to the farmers. Some of them had talked to the government officials. They have met Pratt Saheb. But the officers challenged their assessment."

Jivanbhai was not much optimistic, "Nandubhai, the *mamlatdars* are pressing the *talatis* and *mukhis*, who in turn, trouble us. They are bringing all sort of coercion and are even threatening to impose *chauthai* fine upon those who do not pay. They use rough and harsh language even in front of women. They hurl filthy abuses on the innocent farmers. This is intolerable. But who will care to make a correct assessment and ameliorate our condition?"

Nandubhai said, "You are right Jivanbhai, the *talatis* are rude and ruthless. In last December, due to efforts of Shri Vitthalbhai, Shri Gokuldas Parikh and others, the government had issued orders for postponing collection from 104 villages. It was very small relief but even this was not communicated to the concerned farmers."

Jivanbhai said, "The tyranny of *talatis* is a regular source of trouble we have to live with. We all suffer from their whims. Some people have sold their cattle and land. The *talatis* are collecting not only the revenue for the current year, they are even recovering the *taqavi* given five or six years ago!"

Nandubhai continued, "Gandhiji has made his own assessment of the crop. He had sent his teams to various villages. He has himself seen the situation in Vadthal which is relatively prosperous, is conveniently connected and has many wells, yet the produce was estimated to be less than 1/8 of the normal yield."

Jivanbhai commented, "You are very hopeful! Will the haughty officers listen? Their heads are swollen with arrogance and they do not like to enter into discussion. They want to just decide as they wish! The government had made its own estimates, which are not correct. They know that if they accept that the crop is less than *four annas* then they will have to exempt us from paying the revenue!"

Nandubhai argued, "But Gandhiji is meeting *the laat saheb* other senior officers. At Godhra my relatives were telling that once he is convinced of a true cause, he will fight till end. But he will not take up a wrong cause. Remember what has he done at Champaran!"

Jivanbhai argued, "Nandubhai, at Champaran, Gandhiji had received huge support from the farmers and many respected people like Rajendra Babu, Kripalanijee, Brajkishore Babu, Anugrah Babu and others. Will he be able to get that kind of support here?"

Nandubhai said, "Why not? The farmers of Kheda are suffering a lot. They will not lag behind! They are looking for a person who can fight for them."

Madhavbhai, a co-villager was listening with interest. He was an ardent follower of the Swaminarayan sect. He was a celibate and had devoted his life for the sect. He used to frequently travel to the neighbouring villages. He said, "Gandhiji has himself examined the crop at Vadtal. His estimate was 1/8 of the normal while the government had estimated it as 75 percent."

Jivanbhai said, "The *talatis* and other officials just put whatever figure comes to their head. Who devotes his time assessing the crop in each field?"

Madhavbhai continued, "Gandhiji reported his estimate to the Collector and suggested that he should check the yield himself. Gandhiji offered to be present at the time of checking. But the Collector ignored his suggestions, went to verify the yield himself and estimated the yield at a minimum of 48 percent!"

Nandubhai commented, "His own staff had estimated the yield at 75 percent ! What a disparity-from 75 percent to 48 percent! while Gandhiji estimates it to be around 12 percent!"

Jivanbhai said, "Gandhiji may be making the best estimates but the government would not agree to him. It is a question of their prestige."

Nandubhai reminded, "Don't forget that the officers in Champaran were also adamant and arrogant but finally they had to yield."

"Our brothers at Champaran were lucky. We only have bad luck and struggle in our store," Madhavbhai lamented!

The conversation could not bring enthusiasm in the heart of Jivanbhai who had almost resigned everything to his fate. He again looked up at the sky and said, "We are not lucky, Madhavbhai. Only God can help us."

This was a good opportunity for Madhavbhai to bring their attention to his topic of interest. He said, "You are right, Jivanbhai. Let us pray God and ask His help. I will organise a *keertan* tomorrow."

Nandubhai said, "Madhavbhai, organise the *keertan*as you wish, but do not ask for donation. We have no spare money. Many people are borrowing money at a very high interest rate for paying the assessment. Don't add to their expenditure."

"Don't worry, Nandubhai," Madhavbhai said, "God will take care, it is His work. I take leave now, I have to meet some people for making the arrangements." Madhavbhai got up singing *Shriji Maharaj Mangoo Sharan Tamaru.*

2

Jivanbhai was the eldest son of Keshavbhai Patel of Ras village. Like other *patidars* of the district, Keshavbhai was a hardworking farmer and was down to earth practical in his approach. He had groomed his children in his own mould. The family enjoyed a high reputation in the village.

As the eldest son, Jivanbhai accompanied his father to the fields and quickly learned the traditional style of farming, managing the workers and the produce. The entire process was labour intensive and required personal involvement at every step. After Keshavbhai's death in 1910, Jivanbhai had to work much harder for mitigating the damage caused by the uncertainties of the nature.

Jivanbhai had two brothers and a sister. His sister Janki, two years younger to him, was married to a respectable *patidar* family of Nadiad. Her husband Mukundbhai was a grain merchant. His family business was to source cereals from various villages and after cleaning and repackaging, to sell them to wholesale traders in Ahmedabad. With their keen business acumen, Mukundbhai's family had grown their business with care. Recently the vagaries of nature had affected the business but they were making efforts to prevent any downslide by procuring the grains from the less affected areas.

Bhuvanbhai was four years younger to Jivanbhai. He studied at the local Gujarati Primary School and quickly involved himself in selling milk and milk products, specially *ghee,* which had a good market. In course of time, he developed business contacts in Nadiad, Borsad, Anand and Bardoli. He appointed commission agents at these places for selling his products.

The youngest, Chamanbhai was good at studies. Like his elder brother, he also studied at the village Primary Gujarati School.

Recognising Chamanbhai's interest in studies, Mukundbhai called him to Nadiad and got him admitted in a school. Chamanbhai completed his high school there. After schooling, he was offered a job by his brother-in-law who wanted to open a small branch of his company at Ahmedabad. The responsibility was to manage the supplies coming by carts and trains, store and send them to nearby wholesale traders at appropriate times. Chamanbhai's job involved recovering debts, depositing the amount received with money lenders and in banks, contacting concerned officials and advocates on business and legal matters etc.. The job was demanding but Mukundbhai had seen his brother-in-law's potentials. He was confident that Chamanbhai will manage the works efficiently.

Chamanbhai used to frequently travel from Ahmedabad to Nadiad and Ras. At the age of 18, he was a nice groom from a respected *patidar* family and Jivanbhai was getting several offers for his marriage. Chamanbhai was not interested in marrying at that time. He wanted to earn some money so that he can hire, and if possible, purchase a small house at Ahmedabad.

The dances of nature during the last few years had seriously affected their economy. Although Jivanbhai belonged to a well-to-do family, neither he nor his family members had adopted luxurious habits. Their life style was that of a traditional agriculturist family.

Ras, a predominantly *patidar* village, was overrated by the revenue officials. Its good name had cost the village economically. Thanks to the reputation of Ras, the original revenue assessment itself was higher in the area and now it was significantly enhanced also. The economic pressure had made the life in the village quite difficult in the second decade of the twentieth century.

Jivanbhai's brothers Bhuvanbhai and Chamanbhai used to visit their village quite often. Their business required travelling to the places concerned with their trade. Ras itself was conveniently located for facilitating such visits. Chamanbhai's family was well known in the neighbouring areas. His father was a popular figure. Their family had relations with other respected *patidar* families in the nearby villages. These contacts were very handy for both Bhuvanbhai and Chamanbhai.

Ras itself had a population of about 5000 people. Though seriously affected by famine and rains, plague and pests-the farmers were confident that with their persistent efforts, they would be able to bring back their relative prosperity. Prosperity for them meant enough for family and dependents, cash for facilitating respectable marriage negotiations and for increasing their land holdings and cattle count.

In addition to getting involved in the religious activities, the villagers were also interested in socio-political movements such as protesting *veth,* hoping that the struggle for *swaraj* will get momentum and once *swaraj* comes, all their trouble will end.

Since the villagers did not have much movement, participation in religious activities was quite heavy. Madhavbhai had selected a Saturday evening for the *keertan*. He knew that there was a considerable following of the Swaminarayan sect in Ras and neighbouring villages. He was also aware that some villagers who used to travel to Nadiad or Borsad on week days will be available in the village on Saturday evening.

The *keertan* was well attended; children were eagerly waiting for the *prasad.* Bhuvanbhai, who had reached the village just in time, asked the gathering to wait for a while. When the *prasad* was distributed after the *keertan* and children were trying to queue up again for the second round, Bhuvanbhai asked everybody to remain seated. Then he said, "I want to give you the good news that Gandhiji has finally agreed to start the struggle against the assessment. He has been ably supported by Shri Vitthalbhai Patel, Shri Vallabhbhai Patel and many other leaders. Let us go to Nadiad on the 21st March, Gandhiji will address a meeting there on the 22nd."

Several people showed interest. Some of them had participated in the crop assessment made by Gandhiji and his lieutenants.

Bhuvanbhai told him that Gandhiji and his colleagues had approached concerned officials on the matter, but their pleadings had fallen on deaf ears. Gandhiji was in Champaran, from there he was in regular touch with his colleagues about the developments in Kheda. As anticipated, the government disliked, what it called interference of the *Gujarat Sabha* in the matter. Gandhiji was the President of the *Gujarat Sabha*. The language used in government orders and correspondence was unhelping, rude and arrogant.

Nandubhai got up and asked, "Bhuvanbhai, we have heard that on the 4th February Gandhiji had addressed a meeting in Bombay about the Kheda situation. He called upon the Governor, had written to Pratt Saheb and had discussed the matter of assessment with him and Commissioner Saheb. But they are adamant."

Chamanbhai intervened, "I frequently visit the lawyers in Ahmedabad in connection with my work. I listen with interest their discussions in the bar and other places about Gandhiji. They say that Gandhiji knew that the government would not accept the assessment made by Shri Vitthalbhai, Parikh Saheb, Shri Thakkarbapa and others. That is why he himself assessed the situation in more than thirty villages and asked nagging questions to the farmers for arriving at a fair conclusion. His fellow workers assessed the crop in almost 400 villages."

Bhuvanbhai added, "The government differed with Gandhiji's assessment. Gandhiji then suggested that an independent enquiry be conducted. This was also rejected. Gandhiji is convinced that since all efforts for a fair assessment have failed, there is no other choice but to go for a peaceful struggle."

Nobody gave any reaction to this information.

Nandubhai asked, "Chamanbhai, have you seen Shri Vallabhbhai?"

"Yes, several times. I often go to Jitenbhai, Advocate for discussing business matters. He is a great admirer of Shri Vallabhbhai who is very active in the *Gujarat Sabha*. When Gandhiji came to Ahmedabad from Champaran, he studied the matter of tax assessment in detail and felt that the *Gujarat Sabha* should advise the people not to pay the revenue until their petition to government are replied. Shri Vallabhbhai called a meeting of the Executive Committee of the *Gujarat Sabha* at his residence. It was difficult to reach agreement because people were worried about the repercussions and victimisation. Gandhiji was not satisfied with a majority approval; he wanted nothing short of a unanimous support to his proposal. The Executive Committee met everyday for eight days at Shri Vallabhbhai's house. It was due to his efforts that finally a consensus was reached. Gandhiji wanted to have a full time companion for the campaign. He is lucky that Shri Vallabhbhai has offered his services to him."

Chamanbhai continued, "Jitenbhai had told me that a delegation of the *Gujarat Sabha* had met Mr. F.G. Pratt, the Commissioner, whose response was arrogant and unsympathetic. Mr. Pratt even gave a threat that he will recommend that the *Gujarat Sabha* should be declared illegal."

Nandubhai said, "This is a serious threat and is very unfair also. We should protest. Let us all go to Nadiad and listen to the advice of Gandhiji and Shri Vallabhbhai."

Jivanbhai said, "Gandhiji is fighting for our cause. Shri Vallabhbhai has decided to devote his time for this purpose, ignoring his practice. When these people, who do not have personal stake involved in the matter, are giving their time and energy for us, then how can we sit behind quietly? Is it not improper? We should give them full support. Let us attend the meeting at Nadiad."

Many persons agreed. Bhuvanbhai requested Madhavbhai to mobilise people from Ras and other villages. Some other persons also volunteered to help in the matter.

"Saara naseeb," Madhavbhai said. *"Sahjanand swami antaryami."**

"Where will Gandhiji stay at Nadiad?" asked Nandubhai.

"At the *Hindu Anath Ashram,"* Bhuvanbhai replied.

The Hindu Anath Ashram was a well-known place in the locality. It was a centre for social service for the orphans. Shri Gokaldas Talati and Shri Phulchand Bapuji Shah were the main leaders. Sufficient accommodation was available for the team which included Shri Vallabhbhai Patel, Shri Indulal Yagnik, Shrimati Anasuyaben, Shri Shankarlal Banker and others. Shri Ashabhai Patel was also associated with the Ashram.

In a mood full with enthusiasm and courage, Jivanbhai, his brothers and other people from Ras reached Nadiad on Thursday; March 21. A number of farmers from other areas had already arrived. Comfort was of no concern for them. They talked about Gandhiji, Shri Vitthalhbhai, Shri Vallabhbhai and their colleagues. Some of them were also aware of Mahatma Gandhi's brave leadership at Champaran. Nandubhai immediately got busy in finding more information about Gandhiji and about the next plan. He was full of excitement at narrating the events at Champaran.

Nandubhai proudly said, "What a brave person Gandhiji is! He stood like a rock against the might of the British Empire. He was served an order to leave Champaran by Mr. W.R. Heycock, the

* *See appendix for Hindi text*

District Magistrate of Champaran. Gandhiji refused to obey the order. He was produced before the court on 18 April, 1917. The court suggested that if Gandhiji leaves Champaran now then the case against him would be withdrawn. Gandhiji replied boldly that this cannot happen. He said, "*What to talk of now, after release from the jail, I will make Champaran my home!*"

"Gandhiji was asked to pledge a bond of rupees one hundred for his release, which he refused. Then the magistrate let him go without signing the bond! Finally Gandhiji and his colleagues were successful. Truth had triumphed."

He paused for a while and added, "Gandhiji is a great man."

Bhuvanbhai knew some account of the happenings at Champaran, but he listened with attention, he did not want to dampen Nandubhai's zeal. When Nandubhai enthusiastically transmitted his recently acquired information, Bhuvanbhai added, "In addition to Gandhiji's unique leadership, another important reason for the success was wholehearted support of the *ryots*."

A co-villager said, "We will also not lag behind."

3

Friday, March 22, 1918 was a significant day not only for Nadiad but for the entire Gujarat. Gandhiji addresses the historic meeting to start the Kheda Satyagrah. About 4,000 peasants were present to listen to their hero of Champaran who had courageously defied the arrogance of the government officers and had successfully led a non-violent agitation there.

Bihar had written history, what about Gujarat? Will Gandhiji, Shri Vallabhbhai and his colleagues lead the Gujarat farmers to victory? For them it is more a fight for self-respect than for survival.

All eyes were glued on Gandhiji when he rose to speak. He began his speech by praising the beauty of the district. He said that the district has delightful trees, the like of which he has not seen anywhere in the country except Bihar. While Bihar has natural beauty, the beauty of this district has been developed by the industrious and hardworking farmers. Although the farmers deserve to be proud of their achievements, it does not mean that they should pay the assessment even when the crops have failed.

Gandhijee reaffirmed, "The assessment should be paid on the basis of the sale value of the crop. The farmers are asking only for a postponement of the assessment. At the best, the government will lose only one years' interest on the assessment value. But the government is adamant on its own unfair stand."

Knowing the mood of the government, Gandhiji advised, "If the government does not accede to their request, people should not pay the land revenue and be prepared to face the consequences."

He warned that the government would resort to all kinds of repressive measures, including forfeiture of their cattle and other property, confiscation of *jagirs*, arresting people and insulting them.

The audience was prepared to follow his advice.

Inspired by Gandhiji's speech, the people signed a pledge that *since the crop has failed; it is less than four annas, they will not on their own accord, pay full or remaining part of the revenue. If the government agrees to suspend the second instalment of the revenue then those who can afford to pay whole or the balance of the revenue, will pay.*

About 200 people signed the pledge at *the Hindu Anath Ashram* the same day and the number increased every day.

Shri Vallabhbhai was full of enthusiasm and determination. In Kheda, the rude and arrogant government servants continued to abuse and insult the people. The people felt that it was necessary to fight for their self-respect.

Several volunteers were trying to convince the peasants in the villages to join the *satyagrah*. One such volunteer was Shri Bhulabhai Rupji Shah who was charged by the *tahsildar* of Kapadvanj to appear in his court on March 26. Bhulabhai was accused of inciting people to join no-revenue campaign. Shri Vallabhbhai defended his case forcefully. When the *tahsildar* saw Shri Vallabhbhai defending the case, he was so surprised that he said to Bhulabhai "You can say what you like!"

Soon Gandhiji left for Delhi and then for Indore to preside over the *Hindi Sahitya Sammelan*. There was a heavy demand on Gandhiji's time. During his absence, Shri Vallabhbhai took over the control of the *satyagrah*. He, Shri G.V. Mavlankar and several other persons worked from *the Hindu Anath Ashram* to promote the cause.

March 30 was a Saturday. Normally Chamanbhai used to go to his village on every Saturday, this time his company's advocate Jitenbhai had advised Chamanbhai to accompany him to Nadiad where Shri Vallabhbhai was going to address a meeting of farmers. Gandhiji was still at Indore but several important members of the Home Rule League from Bombay were attending the meeting. Chamanbhai thanked Jitenbhai for taking him along to Nadiad, else, he would have missed an excellent opportunity to listen to Shri Vallabhbhai's impressive speech.

Shri Vallabhbhai said that the spark of the Kheda Satyagrah will set the nation ablaze. He emphasised that in order to obtain lasting happiness, one has to be ready to undergo trials and tribulations. The government has granted postponement of rupees 1.75 lakhs out of the total revenue of rupees 23 lakhs, and the first instalment has already been paid. It is just a question of payment of about 10 lakhs rupees now. Some people may suggest that this amount of money can be collected as donation from well-wishers in Bombay, but that will be against the spirit of the self-respecting people of Kheda. Instead, if the people bravely face the hardships and continue their struggle then the government will be forced to change its policy.

In spite of the fact that Nadiad was his birthplace, Shri Vallabhbhai had not spoken in the earlier meeting which Gandhiji addressed on March 22. He had studied at the Nadiad High School and had passed out his matriculation examination in 1897 from there. But this time, Shri Vallabhbhai's nostalgic Nadiad brought the fire of *karmyogi* out of him in a familiar environment.

After the meeting, Chamanbhai went to Ras and told his family members and co-villagers about Shri Vallabhbhai's speech which was very inspiring . He also informed them that the *satyagrahis* are working very hard at *the Hindu Anath Ashram* and in the villages for the success of the *satyagrah*.

The government adopted several coercive measures such as confiscation of cattle and other household items of poor peasants. The government wanted to frighten the villagers by serving confiscation notices on their lands.

Gandhiji, Shri Vitthalbhai and other volunteers travelled to various villages in the district to boost the morale of the people and strengthen their determination to honour their pledge. They visited Kathlal, Kathana, Limbasi and other villages during the first week of April. Shri Rajendra Prasad and Acharya Kriplaniji-the fighters of Champaran came to give a hand. On April 4, Gandhiji addressed a meeting of farmers at Karamsad-Shri Vallabhbhai's own village. Rajendra Babu was also present. At the meeting, a villager said that if the government chooses to auction the confiscated land of the farmers then many people will be keen to buy the land. Gandhiji's observations were remarkable and precisely pointed towards his concept of *satyagrah* and its implementation. He frankly said, "This is a campaign to become beggars." At the same time, he confidently assured that if the government takes over the possession of any land, they would fight for the release of the land. If some people went on to buy the confiscated land in government auction, then the person will be unable to hold it. He asked, "Since it will be impossible to sell the confiscated land, why should we worry about its confiscation by the government?"

Shri Vallabhbhai had been watching Gandhiji's style of working, his involvement at the grass root, his sound knowledge of the situation and his precise advice in his encouraging speeches. When Gandhiji spoke, Shri Vallabhbhai quietly listened and carefully observed his mentor's approach.

Shri Vallabhbhai had cast off his western style coat and necktie and had almost said goodbye to his flourishing practice. At Karamsad, he was observing the changes, which had influenced the social behaviour in his own village. He frankly told that as a child he had seen the respect, which the elders of the village commanded from the revenue officials. The elders' advice was solicited, was respectfully acknowledged and mostly accepted. But now the situation was much different and the villagers were afraid of the revenue officials. He was pained at the lack of unity in his own village and asked the villagers to remain united.

This was the main task for Shri Vallabhbhai. Gandhiji was trying to infuse confidence among the people, exhorting them to remain steadfast in spite of the truculent behaviour of the officials. Shri Vallabhbhai had deep knowledge of the area. He encouraged people to be ready for sacrifices and assured them if they fight unitedly, victory will be theirs. They travelled a number of places such as -Vadthal, Uttarsanda, Navagam, Borsad, Sinhuj-Akiacha. The response was very encouraging. Even at small villages, about 2000 to 3000 people came to the meetings. As a result of their sincere efforts, the peasants felt assured that the struggle is for the right cause-for their self-respect and for a better future for them and for the whole country. Gandhiji advised them to ignore confiscation notices and to go on with their cultivation activities in the lands for which the government issues notices. The farmers took the advice to their heart. The government's threat backfired.

Though it was a hot April summer, Gandhiji, Shri Vallabhbhai and their colleagues mostly walked on foot. For two or three days Rajendra Babu also accompanied them. Some persons from Gujarat had been to Champaran and had participated in social activities there. The Champaran-Gujarat link established during the Indigo-struggle, was further strengthened. Shri Vallabbhai and Rajendra Babu developed an instant liking for each other. Both were comfortably settled in their profession, their legal practice was flourishing, yet both of them had left their practice for a greater cause. They adopted the difficult path of struggle, sacrifice and service to the nation.

Shri Vallabhbhai was closely observing Gandhiji's approach towards his opponents. Mahatma Gandhi was fighting with them on principles, he never harboured any ill-will against any individual, instead he talked to them with due curtsey and politeness. The Commissioner Frederick Greville Pratt, ICS, was known as a clever civil servant. He sought Gandhiji's help for addressing the peasants of the district. Mahatmaji obliged. He sent a note to the peasants advising them to attend the meeting. Gandhiji himself did not attend; he sent Shri Vallabhbhai and some other volunteers to participate. About 2000 agriculturists attended the meeting, which was convened in front of the Tahsildar's office.

Mr. Pratt, the Commissioner addressed the meeting with the mind and heart of a seasoned bureaucrat and with the aura of his authority. He said that Mahatma Gandhi and Vallabhbhai Saheb have been giving much advice, they have been visiting from village to village but today the audience should listen to him and convey to others; so that what he says will be known to the whole district. He said that the government determines the assessment through its officers, without the intervention of lawyers and barristers. The agriculturists have no legal rights to demand or to insist upon the postponement of the assessment.

Mr. Pratt stressed, "The orders are issued by the officers of the government and there can be no appeal against the final orders. This is not a matter for Gandhiji or Shri Vallabhbhai to decide."

He warned the agriculturists that their fight would not bring any results. He asked the farmers why they should suffer confiscation, fine, suspension of *Narva* rights and so on. *He insisted that the defaulters would not get back their land.*

The clever bureaucrat also spoke about the pledge. Mr. Pratt knew that Gandhiji's appeal to honour the pledge is going well with the people. In a bid to demolish their high moral ground he said that if somebody takes a pledge due to some misunderstanding or by mistake, he should not feel bound to it. It is not necessary to honour this kind of pledge.

In order to swing this point to his favour, Mr. Pratt said, "The millworkers in Ahmedabad had taken a pledge that they will not go to work unless they get an increase of 35% but when they realised that this was unreasonable, they accepted a rise of 27.5% and resumed their work."

It was a clever attempt by a shrewd government officer to win people in his favour by breaking their morale.

This backfired. The Commissioner had excellent knowledge of Gujarati and claimed to understand the people of the Kheda district very well. He even professed to be their guardian. But Mr. Pratt failed to gauge Shri Vallabhbhai's silent observations. Giving details of the agreement reached between mill owners and workers at Ahmedabad, Shri Vallabhbhai contradicted Mr. Pratt's statement threadbare. Then, quoting the Commissioner's own words, he reminded the audience that the Commissioner is right in saying that Gandhiji will give you the correct advice, and so has Mahatmaji done.

Shri Vallabhbhai said, "If the people follow Gandhiji's advice, then they would get justice from this very Commissioner. If the government agrees to appoint a fact-finding committee then matters will be easy."

After the speech, a farmer of Chikhodra village got up and argued, "The Commissioner Saheb says that 80% of the revenue has already been realised. Therefore, the postponement of the realisation of the remaining amount will only come to losing about nine months' of the interest for the balance amount. The government should be graceful in remitting this amount. This small gesture from the government will improve the relationship between the ruler and the ruled."

Several people in the audience nodded their heads in endorsing his argument.

A farmer drew attention to an instance of arbitrary and somewhat ridiculous action by the government officials. He said, "He has to pay an amount of Rs. 4 only. Let the government take land worth that amount. Is it fair for the government to confiscate land of much higher value for this petty amount?"

Again, the seasoned bureaucrat's reply was characteristic to the high-handed Commissioner. Mr. Pratt supported the action, "Yes, that decision depends upon the government!"

The meeting ended in a fiasco for Mr. Pratt.

After the conclusion of the meeting, Shri Vallabhbhai and several villagers went to see Gandhiji. Mahatmaji carefully listened to the details and he understood the cunning intention of raising the matter of honouring the pledge. For Gandhiji, the issue of moral stand was of paramount importance, without which, it was not possible to fight the injustice. Gandhiji and Shri Vallabhbhai were preparing the people for the high moral ground, which was essential for making sacrifices. Mr. Pratt wanted to dilute that position.

Gandhiji and Shri Vallabhbhai were satisfied that the audience was not influenced by the awe of the authority. People were developing the courage to tell the truth at the face of Mr. Pratt and his arrogant officials.

Gandhiji immediately circulated a pamphlet contradicting the points raised by Mr. Pratt and referred to the threats issued by him. He mentioned that deep-rooted anger in the heart is the main cause behind the threats of confiscation. For the agriculturists, there was land on the one hand and pledge on the other. Gandhiji emphasised that adherence to the pledge was a heritage to their children which was worth more than hundreds of thousands of rupees. He inspired and encouraged them to adhere to the pledge.

Volunteers were dispersed to various villages, they walked on foot, cooked their own food and slept in the open. They did not give any burden to the villagers. This was the spirit of *satyagrah* and Gandhiji depended much upon Shri Vallabhbhai for progressing and strengthening the movement. Thanks to their sincere efforts, an environment for sacrifice and patient struggle was already created. Fence-sitters were joining the *satyagrah* and were overcoming the fear of coercion. More and more peasants were coming forward to sign the pledge, including Jivanbhai and his brothers. Finally, the day came for which Jivanbhai and his fellow villagers were waiting. Gandhiji, Shri Vallabhbhai and their colleagues came to Ras on Thursday, 18 April. Bhuvanbhai, Chamanbhai, Nandubhai, Madhavbhai and others were full of enthusiasm. Ashabhai Patel, who had studied at the Borsad English School, had taken the lead in inviting Gandhiji to Ras. Gandhiji and Shri Vallabhbhai were given a hearty welcome. Gandhiji and his team members were very delighted at the scenic beauty of Ras. Shri Mahadevbhai Desai wrote in his

Diary, "The beautiful scenery and the big *maidan,* which looked like a natural open-air theatre, was a pleasant surprise to Bapu."

After Mr. Pratt's clever attempt to weaken the determination of the farmers about their pledge, this was an important opportunity for Gandhiji to uplift the morale of the peasants. About 2,500 people from Ras and neighbouring villages attended the meeting. Mahatma Gandhi gave a rousing speech in which he used the word *Loksangrah,* mentioned in Chapter 3 *shloka* 20 of the Geeta.*

The shloka reminds the example of King Janak who achieved perfection was performing his duties. "One should do likewise for the benefit of the common person." Gandhiji encouraged them to set an example.

Shri Vallabhbhai delivered an excellent speech. He said that Ras has become sanctified by the presence of Gandhiji. He requested the people to adhere to the pledge, maintain a high moral standard and remain steadfast to the principles of non-violence and truth.

Gandhiji, Shri Vallabhbhai and their colleagues were confident that the Kheda Satyagrah was a preparatory struggle for gaining *swaraj* for the country. Gandhiji had assured that the first act of the Swaraj Parliament would be to release the confiscated lands.

Jivanbhai, his brothers, their families and the villagers of Ras were happy that Ashabhai's efforts have been successful in inviting Gandhiji to Ras. They were feeling proud that Gandhiji had addressed a meeting in their village. Their morale was high and they were prepared for the struggle ahead under the guidance of Gandhiji and Shri Vallabhbhai.

In the next week, Gandhiji addressed meetings in several villages such as Kasor, Ajarapura, Samrakha, Pandoli, Sunav, Palaj etc.

Gandhiji was having regular correspondence with the high officials on the matter. On the 23rd April, a public meeting was organised under the auspices of the Home Rule League in Bombay, which was presided by Shri Vitthalbhai Patel. Lokmanya Tilak also participated in the meeting. Gandhiji gave the details of his observation. He said, "Not *only men, the women of Kheda district are also actively participating in the movement. The women are saying*

---

* कर्मणैवहिसंसिद्धिमास्थिताजनकादय:
लोकसंग्रहमेवापिसंपश्यन्कर्तुमर्हस *(Shrimadbhagvat Geeta Chapter 3 shloka 20)*

fearlessly, let the government take our cattle and ornaments, confiscate our lands but our men will not break their pledge."

In the meeting, Lokmanya Tilak moved a Resolution requesting the government to postpone the recovery of the revenue until the results of an independent enquiry commission are released.

On April 24, the Bombay Provincial Government issued a Press Release, which said that Gandhiji's enquiry was inadequate, and the assessment made by the Collector and his staff was the correct one. In addition, since the land revenue in most of the *talukas* has already been collected, there is no need for any further investigation.

The government was handling the movement in a non-transparent manner. Administratively it wanted to keep all options open. The government did not want to completely alienate Gandhiji who could be of great help in raising war resources from India. The Viceroy had invited Gandhiji to participate in the War Conference in Delhi on April 25. Gandhiji attended the preliminary meeting but refused to participate in the main Conference because Lokmany Tilak, Anne Besant and Ali Brothers were not invited. However, there were discussions between him and the Viceroy, subsequently, Gandhiji decided to participate on the 29th April. Later, on April 29, 2018, Gandhiji wrote a letter to the Viceroy mentioning, "*Champaran and Kheda are my direct, definite and special contributions to the war.*"

Perhaps Mahatmaji was drawing the attention of the Viceroy on using the powers of *satyagrah* and *ahinsa,* rather than resorting to wars in solving disputes.

Meanwhile, sensing that the Viceroy and Lord Chelmsford wanted to take help from Gandhiji in war efforts; Mr. Pratt ate his own words, and issued an order cancelling the confiscation orders and the *chothai* fine etc. Instructions were already given to *mamlatdars* not to recover the revenue from those who are unable to pay, not to confiscate land and not to seize any immovable property. This order, however, was not circulated among the people, it was kept confidential.

Whenever Gandhiji was not in Kheda, Shri Vallabhbhai led the movement. The support from the peasants was getting stronger and by early May, about 3500 people had taken the pledge. On the other hand, the officials were also showing over-enthusiasm in attaching the peasants' movable property. They used to break open the locks and take away whatever they could-grains, clothes, utensils, ornaments, cattle and anything they liked. The property thus snatched was brought at the *choro* and was auctioned.

On May 13, addressing the peasants at Dhunda Kuwa of Borsad on the topic "Soul Force vrs Coercion," Gandhiji said that partial victory has already been achieved. Mr. Pratt has been unable to implement his threat of confiscation although he had proudly boasted that the land will be confiscated and the names of the heirs will not be kept on government records. There will be no room for any future claims.

On May 17, Mahatma Gandhi left for Champaran and the responsibility of carrying out the *satyagrah* in this difficult situation fell upon Shri Vallabhbhai's shoulders. Shri Vallabhbhai and his colleagues worked tirelessly to keep the morale of the people high, assuring them that *if we keep our pledge, victory will be ours.* Shri Vallabhbhai used to issue pamphlets for communicating with the people. He mentioned about the atrocities committed by the government officials, the arrogant obstinacy of the Commissioner and the inhuman treatment to the peasants, which piqued their self –respect. He drew attention to the fact that *the government officials are no longer respected in the villages. They are unable to get services even for a price, which they previously used to get free of cost.*

The influence of Mahatma Gandhi on Shri Vallabhbhai was evident when he wrote, that *love can conquer even the hardest heart.* He emphasised that *we should try to win by pouring our love and affection on our opponents.*

At the same time, Shri Indulal Yagnik and others had developed a local system to warn the villagers about the arrival of government officials. Boys were asked to watch their arrival from the trees and sound a bugle to alert the villagers. On hearing the sound, the villagers set their cattle free in the village so that they could not be identified, and locked their houses. Nobody told them the correct addresses of the people they were looking for, no food or water was offered. This sort of unwelcome was quite unusual to them. They were used to have a much respectable reception in the villages. The steadfast approach of the people baffled the officials. They found that the *satyagrah* was progressing well even during Gandhiji's absence and the people were determined to honour their pledge. The fear of the local authority was considerably diluted among the villagers.

After his return from Bihar, Gandhiji addressed a meeting at Khandhli on the 27th May. He spoke about the importance and value of the *satyagrah*. On the 3rd June, Gandhiji addressed meetings at Uttarasanda and Navagam.

Shaken by the enthusiastic response of the people, the government was looking for a compromise. The *mamlatdar* of Nadiad taluka came to see Gandhiji and gave in writing that if those persons who are well to do, pay their dues, then the recovery will be postponed.

Gandhiji then wrote to the Collector that if such an order was issued for the entire district and the *chauthai* and other fines were waived then the satyagrah would be called off.

The government was looking for an opportunity of this type. The necessary orders were issued by the Collector. Gandhiji had a meeting with the Collector where he came to know that the orders on similar lines were already issued to *mamlatdars* on April 24, but the peasants were not aware of these orders . Repeat orders were issued on the 22nd May.

On June 6, a statement signed by Mahatma Gandhi and Shri Vallabhbhai was issued to the people of Kheda announcing the end of the *satyagrah*. The document said that *although the fight has ended, it lacks grace in its conclusion. The Commissioner had decided to say "No" to the genuine demands of the people, without understanding the real situation and once he had so decided, it was impossible to change this "No" to "Yes." Now the Collector was willing to admit that such relief can be granted. Although the dealing has not been graceful, it is a success for the peasants. The attention of the whole country has been drawn to Kheda. They have adhered to truth, self-respect, fearlessness and unity. This is a great contribution to the struggle for freedom.*

Gandhiji and Shri Vallabhbhai hoped that the people of Kheda will further cultivate these qualities, which will bring glory to the motherland. They expressed their firm belief in the people of Kheda who had truly served their own cause and had progressed the goals of *swaraj*.

The Kheda Satyagrah had an interesting climax involving Shri Mohanlal Pandya and his colleagues. In the Navgam village of Matar Taluka, a peasant had grown onions. The field was attached but the notice pronouncing the attachment did not specify the particular field. Gandhiji felt that this was a discrepancy and also the attachment of the standing crop was immoral. There was an apprehension that the monsoon will destroy the crops worth approximately Rs. 600. Gandhiji advised that it was the peoples' duty to take the onion away. Shri Mohanlal Pandya was looking for an opportunity for action like this. He, along with seven or eight friends, started removing the onions from the field. The *mamlatdar* of Matar Taluka arrived and arrested Shri Mohanlal Pandya and his four colleagues on the charge of theft. Both Gandhiji and Shri Vallabhbhai were present when the trial was going on, but they did not fight the case. Outside the court, Gandhiji said that any person can see that this not a case of theft.

Shri Mohanlal Pandya and two others were sentenced to 20 days in prison and the other two were jailed for shorter durations between 2 and 10 days.

They were the first *satyagrahis* from Gujarat.

When Shri Mohanlal Pandya and his colleagues were released from Jail, Gandhiji and Shri Vallabhbhai walked seven miles to meet them. After their release, Shri Mohanlal Pandya and his colleagues were given a grand reception. Shri Mohanlal Pandya earned the affectionate title of *Dungri Chor* (Onion Thief) which he liked very much.

After a series of celebrations, on June 29 a meeting was called at Nadiad to celebrate the successful end of Kheda Satyagrah. At the meeting, Gandhiji paid rich compliments to Shri Vallabhbhai. Gandhiji admitted that initially he was not sure whether the *stiff-looking* Shri Vallabhbhai was the person whom he wanted to have as his lieutenant. But the more he came to know about Shri Vallabhbhai, the more convinced he was that he must secure his services. Appreciating his contribution, Gandhiji said that the Kheda campaign would not have been carried out so successfully without the assistance of Shri Vallabhbhai.

Flowers were offered to Gandhiji as *guru dakshina.* Shri Vallabhbhai responded with humility, saying that *he has not done anything. The satyagrah has been successful due to the support, courage and forbearance of the people of Kheda. They owe the credit for the success.*

Kheda Satyagrah ended successfully, though not gracefully. It heralded the awakening of the ordinary farmers of Gujarat district; it removed the fear of authority from their mind and prepared them for making even greater sacrifices. The biggest gain to the people of Kheda and to the country was Shri Vallabhbhai who in Gandhiji's words 'found *himself*'. Gandhiji also acquired a trusted hardworking lieutenant in him. Earlier at Karamsad, Gandhiji had said, *Shri Vallabhbhai is going through the fire and he has to undergo further tests. I am sure that we shall find pure gold from the furnace.*

For Jivanbhai and his brothers, it was a huge moment for celebration. Although Gandhiji had addressed another meeting at Ras on the 26th June in connection with recruitment, people were not interested to support the government in its war efforts. They had become more mature. They were fully aware now that in Gandhiji they have a combination of a saint and a leader with foresight and a courageous enterprising lieutenant in Shri Vallabhbhai as his deputy. This was the first lesson for the peasants of Kheda in the *satyagrah* and they were very happy at its success. They were feeling proud to have actively participated in a unique struggle. They had found their soul and their strength, they had won their struggle for honour and were ready for the longer struggle that lay ahead.

The entire village celebrated the success. Madhavbhai again organised a *keertan*. He had always believed and said that God's blessing has brought the success.

Jai Jai Shambhukumar Shok sada Harta
*Dev Vishesh vichakshan, rakshanan karta**

---

* *See appendix for Hindi text*

4

The celebrations continued for a week. Although life had been difficult in the last six months or so, with the arrival of Gandhiji and Shri Vallabhbhai in the scene, the gloom of pessimism had vanished. People were prepared to lose their property and were losing it also, yet the feeling of self-respect and sacrifice was giving them the tonic of courage and enthusiasm. Everybody had realised that in handling the Kheda Satyagrah, the government was not graceful in its approach. After all, the government was only losing about one years' interest on the unrealised assessment. Had they postponed the collection for a year, they would have gained huge sympathy and goodwill from the people. The rules provided such concession; it was only the pride of the officials, their obstinacy and the desire to show their authority which had prolonged the *satyagrah*. The *satyagrah* brought far-reaching changes in the mind-set of the people. They were less scared of the officials; they had developed the courage to tell the truth at their face. The officials also realised that they can no longer command the same respect, they cannot avail *veth*, they cannot demand the services even on payment-facilities they had taken for granted free of charge.

The villagers knew that the Kheda Satyagrah is not an end in itself. It is the precursor of the more important fight against the British rule, which was not limited to Kheda or Gujarat alone. Before the start of Kheda Satyagrah, many people in Jivanbhai's village had not even gone beyond their neighbouring villages, they have now seen bigger places, have met people from other villages and have found a saint, a fighter and a guardian in Gandhiji whose deputy commander Shri Vallabhbhai was their own man from Karamsad. The satyagrah had provided them a goal and a leader. It has also prompted realisation of their self-respect and potential. An environment of sacrifice and enthusiasm was created.

It was a relaxed mood at the village *choro.* Jivanbhai's house had become a centre of discussion on such topics. The self-respect of the village was quite high. People from neighbouring villages visited to know about the latest details and to talk about the *satyagrah.*

It was a Saturday, a day for family celebration. Bhuvanbhai and Chamanbhai were scheduled to come home today. Jivanbhai was looking at the village pathway, his brothers could reach home any time.

He saw Nandubhai coming. Jivanbhai was in a mood to talk and was waiting for some like-minded company. Nandubhai was eager to release the information which he had collected from various sources enriched with his own brand of value addition. The newly acquired knowledge and experience was bubbling in his mind and he was looking for a receptive audience.

Jivanbhai said, "Welcome, Nandubhai. We have not seen you for about a week."

"Yes, Jivanbhai, I had been to Nadiad. People are talking about Gandhiji and Shri Vallabhbhai. They say that earlier Shri Vallabhbhai used to dress like a saheb with coat, trousers and necktie. He has now given up the formal dress of a barrister, he wears *dhoti-kurta.* Although Shri Vallabhbhai has resumed his practice in Ahmedabad, people say that he can quit it anytime. His house at Bhadra is more a place for thinking and discussing about *swaraj* than a place for attending his clients."

Jivanbhai asked, "Gandhiji is full of praise for the people of Kheda. He is very pleased that we have not let him down. There was doubt in the minds of the leaders that we may yield to threat or pressure; we may not honour our pledge due to the fear of confiscation and other troubles. At some stage, even I was thinking of paying the assessment."

This was an opportunity for Nandubhai to show his wisdom. He said, "Land is very dear to a farmer. He protects it with all his strength. Even the leaders were having doubts, but Jivanbhai, the people of Kheda have shown to the world that they are brave and a self-respecting people."

Jivanbhai said, "Sometimes, during the *satyagrah*, we were apprehensive whether the *satyagrah* will succeed? What can we gain from this struggle? Why should we take so much of trouble and risk? Why should we annoy *talatis, mukhis* and *mamlatdars*? After all, we have to live with them."

"This was the feeling in other villages also. But see what these two great leaders have done!" Nandubhai said.

Some more co-villagers joined them. One of them looked around and said, "Where is Madhavbhai?"

"He must be visiting some other village!" a person replied.

Another person remarked, "Now we should concentrate upon our work in the fields. We have to recover the losses."

"Yes," another fellow commented. "See our cattle. Although our women have been taking their care, our cattle are not in the best of health. We have to pay more attention to them."

Bhuvanbhai arrived first. He looked happy. He touched the feet of his brother, conveyed his greetings to others and went inside home.

Nandubhai said, "Bhuvanbhai is quite relaxed. He is smiling. Perhaps his *ghee* business is picking up!"

Jivanbhai said, "No, Bhuvanbhai always remains happy. Even when the situation was difficult, he was smiling. During the *satyagrah,* he was busy in touring the villages for promoting the cause of *satyagrah*, he did not bother much about business. The ladies in our home had taken good care of the cattle. We could have exploited the opportunity to supply *ghee* and other products in the market at higher prices, but Bhuvanbhai did not like the idea. He said that this is the time for making sacrifices, not for making unethical profit."

Nandubhai remarked "This is a great transformation, Jivanbhai. Cash income is always scarce in a farmer's family. It was more so during the *satyagrah,* but you and your brothers did not hanker after money. This is remarkable."

Jivanbhai was modest, "Not only *our* family, Nandubhai, many people in the village and neighbouring villages have done the same. The main objective was to honour our pledge, to preserve our self-respect and to strengthen the hands of Gandhiji and Shri Vallabhbhai."

Nandubhai commented, *Jaagya tyan thi savaar*.*

They saw Madhavbhai coming. Nandubhai smiled, "We were talking about you. We did not see you for quite some time."

---

* *It is never very late to start doing a good deed.*
See Appendix for Hindi text

Madhavbhai greeted them and said "Yes, I had been to Vadtal. There the people are very happy at the success of the *satyagrah*. They are relieved and life is returning to normal."

Madhavbhai had special attachment for Vadtal. Unfortunately, his parents and other family members had died of bubonic plague. He was a small child-the lone survivor of his family. Some charitable persons took care of such people affected by the disastrous plague. A kind man had brought young Madhav to Vadtal which was well known in the area for the Swaminarayan temple.

The Swaminarayan temple was constructed in November 1824 by Shri Swaminarayanji whom his followers revere as God. Madhavbhai lived there. The agriculturists of the neighbouring area were devotees of Lord Swaminarayanji.

Madhavbhai had seen Mahatma Gandhi and his followers there when Mahatmaji went to assess the crop in the area. Vadtal was the place where the government had to confess that the previous assessment made by the government officials was not correct.

Bhuvanbhai came out of his home and touched the feet of Madhavbhai.

Madhavbhai asked, "Very nice to see you, Bhuvanbhai. In the villages, people are very happy. They feel that they have fought for justice and respect. They are united. There is moral uplift also. Many people have left drinking. Some of them have become vegetarian. You know that Bhagwan Swaminarayanji had asked the people to become vegetarian and abstain from drinking. It is His blessings that people are becoming more pious. They are taking care of their cattle and do not beat them unnecessarily."

He started singing praise to the Lord, *Jaagya tyan thi savaar*.

Madhavbhai said, "It appears that the world does not want peace! People are fighting, we are also sending our people to fight for the same government, which is oppressive. In this way, we are encouraging fighting. We love peace, why should we support war?"

Nandubhai said, "The government does not think about us! They want to rule us forever. They oppress us at every opportunity, yet they want our people to fight for them and die for them! I am unable to understand why should Gandhiji support them in their war efforts?"

Jivanbhai commented, "The war is being fought somewhere else, not here. We have offered some support only due to Gandhiji and

Shri Vallabhbhai. Madhavbhai, it is very difficult to say 'No' to Gandhiji and Shri Vallabhbhai."

Nandubhai argued, "The war is not being fought in our soil. Why should we be asked to help? We are not rich like them, we are very poor people and they have exploited us for years. We are in fact supporting our enemy!"

Madhavbhai said, "Gandhiji does not think this way. He is a very pious man; In fact, he is a saint. He thinks differently."

Bhuvanbhai was listening patiently. He was not convinced, "That is true. We are very lucky to have a person of eminent goodness like Gandhiji and a brave leader like Shri Vallabhbhai. Both of them have personally volunteered to fight for the British! But what is our situation? We received inhuman treatment from them, they never lose any opportunity to hurt our pride and self-respect. And see the prices of commodities which are jumping every day! This is all due to the war!"

Nandubhai said, "You are right. Gandhiji has said that our fight has not ended at Kheda. We have to fight for *Swaraj*. We have to prepare ourselves for the a much greater fight."

"For that, we must have our self-respect high and we should be prepared to make sacrifices as told by Gandhiji and Shri Vallabhbhai."

Nandubhai was hopeful, "Recently, Champaran has given us the team of Gandhiji, Rajendra Babu, Brajkishore Babu and others. Kheda has given us the excellent combination of Gandhiji and Shri Vallabhbhai. We are lucky, Jivanbhai!"

Jivanbhai said, "But we must offer all help and cooperation to them. What can the leaders do if we do not follow them wholeheartedly? We should be proud that we did not compromise our self-respect."

Nandubhai agreed, "This is just the beginning of a long struggle for a greater cause, Jivanbhai. Gandhiji has removed fear from our heart: He has infused the feeling of sacrifice and simple living in us. Shri Vallabhbhai has always said that our self-respect is more important than our property. We must learn how to live and die for self-respect."

A fellow villager asked, "But how can this help in winning *swaraj*?"

Bhuvanbhai said, "A strong feeling of self-respect will remove the fear of the British Government. Gandhiji and Shri Vallabhbhai have said that our self-respect will inspire us to fight. Champaran and Kheda are good examples of non-violent satyagrah which is based on self-respect. Such kind of movements can be started in every part of the country."

Jivanbhai interrupted, "And now our leaders will tell us what to do and when."

Another fellow villager remarked, "But will the British leave India? Why should they? They are very powerful and they rule many countries of the world."

Nandubhai said, "But they are busy in war. Our struggle will force them to leave. If all Indians get united and start the struggle, then they will not be able to rule us."

The co-villager was not convinced, "But can we be united? We became slave because we were not united. See here, even two neighbouring villages are not united; there is competition, jealousy and bitterness among the people of the same village. Then, in our neighbourhood and elsewhere in the States, many citizens are under their rulers. They have their own way of looking at the things!"

Bhuvanbhai said, "Our internal conflicts, jealousy and ill-will were the root cause of our slavery. History is full of accounts of a handful of invaders who took advantage of the internal conflicts and chaotic situation and plundered the country. We must learn from the past and must stand united. We need a national leader who should unite us and lead us against the foreign rule."

He lamented, "Will that ever happen?"

Nandubhai said, "People who do not stand against oppression and misrule quickly lose their freedom. We must have courage to fight unitedly then only we can win freedom. We need good leaders and we also need devoted followers."

Madhavbhai remarked, "Have some patience. We have our leaders now, there is a greater awakening among the people. The success of Kheda will further inspire us. God will help. He is kind and merciful. Let us pray for His blessings."

*"Jai Ganpati pyara, Jai Ganpati pyara, vighn vinayak murti, sukhdayak sara."**

---

* *Hindi text in the appendix*

5

The *satyagrah* had kept Chamanbhai thoroughly occupied. Successful completion of the *satyagrah* had brought a surge of enthusiasm among the people. Chamanbhai realised that the success of the satyagrah had wiped out tiredness and had infused new energy in the heart and mind of the workers. Chamanbhai and his friends were in excellent fettle. Chamanbhai soon became quite busy. Now he had some time of his own-a carte blanche and he devoted this opportunity for completing the pending works of procurement, storage and distribution of food grains. Occasionally eagerly awaited clouds were lurching on the sky but were also evading any promise. This was a gentle reminder to Chamanbhai. He must finish most of his travels to rural interiors before the start of rains.

His job demanded frequent travels from Ahmedabad to Nadiad and to the concerned villages which quite often involved walking long distances on foot. His business associates were aware of his involvement in the *satyagrah*. Wherever he went, people asked him several questions about the struggle for swaraj and the situation in other villages. Knowing that Chamanbhai lives in Ahmedabad, they also raised several queries about the leading luminaries-Gandhiji and Shri Vallabhbhai.

Chamanbhai used to visit the Bhadra residence of Shri Vallabhbhai along with his *vakil* sahab, Jitenbhai. Shri Vallabhbhai would sometimes ask, Jitenbhai to join him for visiting Sabarmati Ashram. Gandhiji was still recovering from his illness but he was always thinking about the reforms and *swaraj*. Chamanbhai used to sit with other workers and carefully listen to the conversation among his advocate Jitenbhai, Shri Vallabhbhai and others. They were talking of reforms and bills about which he did not know much, but his common sense told him that they are talking about *swaraj*, self-respect and *satyagrah*.

One evening, Jitenbhai asked him to come to the Sabarmati Ashram where Gandhiji and Shri Vallabhbhai were going to discuss some important matters with other leaders and workers. Jitenbhai was also invited. Many people were waiting in the Ashram and they were talking about Gandhiji.

Although everybody was showering encomiums upon him, they were affectionately concerned about the inexorable demand on Gandhiji's time and his apparent neglect of his own health.

One person said "Gandhiji has overworked at Kheda and Nadiad which has badly affected his health. On one occasion, while planning for the recruitment and training for war support, he fainted. Seth Ambalal Sarabhai brought him to his home. Gandhiji was suffering from fever and dysentery. He was still running high fever when he came to the Ashram from Sethji's home. People at Seth Sarabhai's house wanted Gandhiji to stay there but you know sometimes Gandhiji does not listen to anybody!"

He continued, "Even during his serious illness, he did not take proper rest."

Another person added, "Some days ago, Babu Rajendra Prasad came to see him. He saw Gandhiji crying."

Chamanbhai was surprised, "Why? Gandhiji is a very pious and courageous person, he is like a saint. Why did he cry? Does his illness bother him?"

"No, no, he is not bothered about himself. When Gandhiji came from Seth Ambalal's house, his temperature was very high. He knew that many people did not like his abrupt return to the Ashram. They felt that Gandhiji was much more comfortable and well looked after in Sethji's house. He should have waited for the fever to go down."

"Yes, that's right. His health is very important for all of us," Chamanbhai said.

The person at the Ashram continued, "Gandhiji was lying on his cot and Rajendra Babu was sitting on a mat. Suddenly, Gandhiji called Chaganbhai and said, 'My sudden arrival at the Ashram has not been liked by you and other well-wishers. Although my body was suffering from fever, my heart was burning with the feeling that my place is not in the mansion, it is in the Ashram. Lot of work remains to be done at Champaran, Kheda and at other places. I have not been able to complete these works. I have established the Sabarmati Ashram with much hope and aspirations. But I do not know whether I will be cured of the sickness or not!'

He continued, "Rajendra Babu and Chaganbhai watched him crying. In presence of his two trusted colleagues, Gandhiji's aching heart found an outlet in his tears. His both lieutenants just watched thinking how lucky they are to come in close contact with such a great soul."

Chamanbhai enquired, "How is his health now?"

"Not good. But Gandhiji never thinks of his own health. He is now having discussions with Shri Vallabhbhai, Sarojini Naiduji, Shankarlalji and others."

Another person commented, "Gandhiji always thinks about our country and the people, personal care and comfort does not matter for him. During the Kheda Satyagrah he walked barefoot in the villages under the hot sun. Once Rajendra Babu wanted to spread a bed sheet so that Gandhiji could walk comfortably but Mahatmaji did not permit him to do so. His frail body was stressed during the *satyagrah* and his mind never got rest. Now even during his sickness, he is taking so much strain for us."

Somebody queried, "What are they discussing now?"

"Gandhiji is worried about the Rowlatt Bill," the person replied. "While on one hand the government is talking about Montague - Chelmsford reforms, on the other hand it is pushing the enactment of the Rowlatt Bill which proposes to give tyrannical powers to arrest on petty matters without trial. It is aimed at suppressing any opposition to the British rule."

After the meeting, the invited persons came out discussing the matters among themselves. Chamanbhai could see a sense of satisfaction on Shri Vallabhbhai's face. He was resolute and some what prepared to face a new challenge.

Chamanbhai asked Jitenbhai, "*Vakil Sahab*, What is happening now? All of you are serious. It appears that Shri Vallabhbhai has again found some worthy cause to fight for."

"You are right Chamanbhai," Jitenbhai said, "We have just signed a pledge to defy the Rowlatt Bill if it becomes an Act."

"What does it mean?" Chamanbhai asked.

"It means that we will oppose the Act and in opposing it we will adhere to truth and non-violence. This is a major decision, because Champaran and Kheda *satyagrahas* were launched to address local grievances mostly generated by the arrogant and insensitive bureaucracy. This opposition will be by the whole country."

"Is it possible to organise a country-wide *satyagrah*? The meeting had a participation of only some twenty people," Chamanbhai doubted.

Jitenbhai replied, "Don't go by numbers. Even one determined person can bring about a visible change. Altough Gandhiji is not well, his frail body has a tremendous fighting spirit. He has a dedicated leader like Shri Vallabhbhai with him. I am confident, Chamanbhai, that this will have a big impact in the country. Just wait and see."

Chamanbhai could not sleep that night. He had seen how a pious and determined person is working in the interest of the nation and the people. He weeps like an innocent child and fights like a brave lion. His charismatic leadership has drawn thousands of people from different parts of the country who follow him sincerely. He inspires tremendous confidence and infuses a deep sense of sacrifice among the masses. How a brilliant person like Rajendra Babu has become his follower without caring for his career, how a distinguished barrister like Shri Vallabhbhai is following his footsteps, how prominent person from different walks of life-poetess Sarojini Naidu, industrialist Umar Subhani, editor Mr. B.G. Horniman and several others are willing to follow him! They are all motivated with the feeling of truth, justice, sacrifice and national interest.

Chamanbhai was quite busy with his job. His brother-in-law, Mukundbhai depended heavily upon him for his business. Chamanbhai liked his work which gave him a good opportunity to know the country side as well as the big city-Ahmedabad. The success of the Kheda Satyagrah and peaceful settlement between mill owners and workers in Ahmedabad had changed the mood of the people in both rural and urban areas. In both cases, the success was not perfect, yet it was a victory for the moral values. A subtle change in the thought process of the people was quite visible which also prompted more graceful business dealings. Senior people were advising their colleagues, business is done for earning profit, but greed ruins the character. A business partner quoted a proverb *Loabh siva sobh na hoye, pan jaje loabhe lakshan bhaye.* *

Jitenbhai had suggested that this is the right time to settle pending cases through negotiations. Mukundbhai had agreed to this idea and had asked Chamanbhai to proceed accordingly. Chamanbhai used to visit Jitenbhai almost every day and sometimes more than once to discuss disputes, which mostly concerned with payment of outstanding dues and return of material on flimsy or inadequate grounds.

When Chamanbhai reached Jitenbhai's chamber, he found some other people talking to him. They were businessmen and lawyers. Chamanbhai understood that they were also trying to have negotiated settlement of their disputes. When Chamanbhai went in, Jitenbhai greeted him with a smile.

Jitenbhai was a medium built, fair complexioned man in his early forties. He looked at Chamanbhai and remarked, "You look tired, Chamanbhai."

"Yes, Vakil Sahab, I was busy with work. Business is picking up. We want to finish as much work as possible before the onset of the rainy season. People are cooperating. Wherever I go, they enquire about Gandhiji and Shri Vallabhbhai. People have found their leader in them."

"Yes. This is a very good combination. Shri Vallabhbhai keenly observes Gandhiji's way of working. Even when he does not agree fully with Mahatmaji, he follows his advice or decision," Jitenbhai said, "He believes that Gandhiji's decision will finally prove to be correct."

Chamanbhai asked "What about the pledge taken at the Sabarmati Ashram the other day? The Viceroy has not responded to Gandhiji's request and the Rowlatt Bill has already become an Act. What will happen now?"

Looking into his eyes, Jitenbhai said, "This is most unfortunate. The government has a ruthless disregard for the public sentiments. It is trundling and bulldozing all protests. Gandhiji and Shri Vallabhbhai are very upset. Gandhiji has decided that the entire country should

---

* *Although without saving there cannot be any luxury but more greed will spoil your character.*
Hindi text in the Appendix

observe protest day on April 6. We have to prepare for a long struggle, Chamanbhai. It is good that you are trying to finish as much business as possible now. Things are going to be tough in the coming days, we will have more work to do. The people have to be informed, encouraged and requested to be prepared to face the situation."

Chamanbhai's eyes sparkled with hope and enthusiasm. He said, "Vakil Sahab, this will be a memorable day. We will participate actively in the protest and will request others to do so. Let us finish our work, I want to go to Ras today, so that I can share this information with my family and co-villagers."

"Volunteers have already been sent to the villages, but your contribution will be useful. I will finish the work soon so that you can leave for Ras comfortably."

When Chamanbhai arrived at his village, he found the message about the protest on April 6 has already reached there. People were talking enthusiastically about observing fast and following their leaders' advice on the matter. On his return to Ahmedabad, he found that the city is well prepared for the eventful day. The strike was complete. Chamanbhai fasted on April 6, so did many people in Gujarat and in the entire country. The Satyagrah Day was observed in a dedicated and united manner throughout India. In Ahmedabad, a big procession was taken out under the leadership of Shri Vallabhbhai, which started from the railway station and culminated into a huge public meeting at the Sabarmati. Chamanbhai joined the procession and the meeting. Shri Vallabhbhai sold copies of banned *Hind Swaraj* and *Sarvoday.* People enthusiastically bought the books at prices higher than the printed one.

After the successful meeting, Jitenbhai asked Chamanbhai to come to Shri Vallabhbhai's house at Bhadra the next day. There he found the *Satyagrah Patrika* was being cyclostyled. It was published without registration and was priced at one paisa per copy. Selling of Gandhiji's books *Hind Swaraj* and *Sarvoday* and the printing of the *Sarvoday Patrika* were acts in defiance of the law but the government did not take cognisance.

Gandhiji himself was in Bombay. A huge meeting attended by about 200,000 people was organised at the Chawpaty Beach. A Prayer Meeting was held at the Madhav Bagh which was attended by people of all communities. It was decided that a pledge will be taken on the forthcoming *Ramnavmi day*. Public opinion was being quickly mobilised.

In an unusual notice to its subscribers, *The Satyagrah Patrika*, edited by Gandhiji, made it clear that the journal has not been registered under the law and there is no guarantee that its publication will continue. It was mentioned that the paper would continue to be published as long as the Rowlatt Act remains effective, meaning thereby that its publication will cease after the withdrawal of the Rowlatt Act.

Political situation in the country was becoming more uneasy and unpredictable. Jitenbhai was mostly busy with Shri Vallabhbhai, but he tried to find time for his professional work.

It was the Ramnavmi day on April 9. Chamanbhai came out of his home for offering prayers at the local temple. He found that people were all agog with the news that Gandhiji has been arrested at Palwal on his way to Delhi. He was being sent to Bombay and for part of his journey, he was put in goods' train. Chamanbhai was shocked, he offered his prayers and quickly returned his home. By the evening, the situation became tense, he came out of his home and found that everywhere people were talking about the arrest of their leader. Later, some disturbances broke out.

Next morning it was announced that strike will be observed throughout the country in protest against Gandhiji's arrest. Chamanbhai came out to see the situation.

Mobs had gathered at different places. The people were getting restive and violent. They burnt police stations, telegraph offices and other office buildings in Bhadra area. As the day progressed, violence increased and more people came out on the road. Police was ineffective. He heard that riots have broken out at Viramgam also.

Chamanbhai was anxious to know about Jitenbhai and Shri Vallabhbhai. He walked towards Jitenbhai's house. On the way, he saw angry mobs being chased away by the police. The mob was agitated. Police opened fire. Chamanbhai and several others ran towards a safe shelter and waited for the situation to calm down. After sometime, Chamanbhai saw Shri Vallabhbhai and his friend Shri Kanuga making appeals to the people to remain peaceful. Jitenbhai and other volunteers were following them. Chamanbhai joined the volunteers. They were arranging to send the injured to the hospital. Jitenbhai was distributing some food to the houses of the people who were killed or injured in the police firing.

Chamanbhai did not think of himself. Like Jitenbhai and several others, he followed the instructions of Shri Vallabhbhai who was working tirelessly to restore peace. Ahmedabad was placed under martial law.

News of violence kept on coming. There were disturbances at Nadiad also where people removed a part of the railway track for stopping a train which was transporting solders from Bombay to Ahmedabad.

Jitenbhai told him that Gandhiji has been released in Bombay and Shri Vallabhbhai has briefed Gandhiji about the situation in Ahmedabad. Gandhiji was expected to reach Ahmedabad soon. He informed Chamanbhai that about fifty people have been killed in the police firing. News about disturbances in Lahore, other parts of Punjab and Calcutta had reached Ahmedabad.

Gandhiji came to Ahmedabad with Anasuya Sarabhai and others. He went to meet the Commissioner Mr. Pratt directly from the railway station. Mr. Pratt was very angry. The officials were blaming Gandhiji for the disturbances in Ahmedabad, Viramgam and other places. But knowing fully well that peace can be brought only with the help of Gandhiji and Shri Vallabhbhai, he allowed Gandhiji to hold a public meeting at the Sabarmati on the next day, April 14th. Mr. Pratt said that he will have the necessary arrangements made for the people to reach there.

On hearing this, Jitenbhai said, "This is strange! The government itself creates difficult situations and when it is unable to control, it seeks help from Gandhiji and Shri Vallabhbhai."

Chamnbhai agreed, "Yes. I am surprised, why did they not allow Gandhiji to visit Punjab? Gandhiji's visit to the affected areas would have helped in maintaining peace there."

"The government officers are peculiar persons. On many occasions, they go by their whims and they do not want to come down from their stated positions. Here also, the officers know it fully well that Gandhiji and Shri Vallabhbhai are of immense help in bringing peace, they want to show that they are in control of the situation."

Granting the permission for holding a meeting at Sabarmati was a fair and frank recognition of Mahatma Gandhi's influence and Shri Vallabhbhai's contribution. Chamanbhai had also played a small supporting role in the process. He was happy that at least sometimes, the government admits the pacifying influence of these great people.

Chamanbhai and his friends tried to inform as many persons as possible about the forthcoming meeting at Sabarmati. They explained that although Martial Law was enforced in Ahmedabad, a relaxation has been made for the people to facilitate their participation in the meeting. At Gandhiji's request, the authorities had agreed that the people coming to attend the meeting would not be harassed by the soldiers.

Chamanbhai and his friends were satisfied about the response to the call. Despite the Martial Law and disturbances, about two thousand persons attended the meeting at the Sabarmati Satyagrah Ashram. Gandhiji was still weak, his address was read by Shri Vallabhbhai.

In an environment filled with sorrow and grief but not devoid of excitement, Shri Vallabhbhai read Gandhiji's speech in which Mahatmaji addressed the audience as *brothers*. He said that the events of last few days, which happened in his name, were most disgraceful to Ahmedabad. He emphasised that *satyagrah* does not allow any violence, yet in the name of *satyagrah* buildings were burned, telegraph lines were cut, money was extorted, innocent people were killed and weapons were stocked. These deeds have not benefited anyone.

He condemned violence against the British and emphasised that those joining the *satyagrah* movement should totally abstain from violence. He said, *"In addition, we should also do penance for the sins committed by us."*

He asked for voluntary contribution of not less than eight *annas* for helping the riot-hit families. Gandhiji announced that he will fast for 72 hours. He called upon the people to observe fast for 24 hours if possible.

Gandhiji's speech had a great impact upon the audience. People were feeling remorseful. Chamanbhai felt that now peace will soon return to the city.

But the officers were thinking in a different manner. An officer asked Gandhiji whether Shri Vallabhbhai and Shri Mohanlal Pandya did not have a hand in Ahmedabad violence. Gandhiji said that the charge was absolutely false. They are the people who tried their best to bring peace to the city in the shortest possible time.

Chamanbhai had himself seen the situation. Shri Vallabhbhai was exposing himself to great personal risk in moving from one part of the city to the other, providing relief, requesting people to shun violence and helping the administration in restoring peace.

But rumour mongers were busy. Jitenbhai told him about an incident involving a Municipal Counsellor who was a known sycophant. The Counsellor had informed the police that he has seen Shri Vallabhbhai burning the Telegraph Office. A CID officer from Poona was deputed to investigate the charge. When the Collector came to know about it, he said that Shri Vallabhbhai was having a meeting with him at that time! Not only this, the Superintendent of Police of Ahmedabad Mr. Heeley had remarked, *"It will not be possible to maintain law and order without the help of Shri Vallabhbhai."*

The people of Ahmedabad were yet to recover from the shock when the news of the terrible massacre at Jallianwala Bagh, Amritsar reached them. The heinous crime shook the whole nation. It showed the brutal face of the concerned British authorities and their biassed hatred for Indians. The massacre was a cruel exposure of the mind-set of the arrogant racism of the concerned authorities. People were forced to crawl, were brutally whipped and all sort of humiliation was inflicted upon them. Their self-respect and pride was demolished. The whole country was livid with anger at the inhuman act showing the insensate rage of the authorities. Chamanbhai and many others felt that no amount of penance or *satyagrah* can melt the stone heart of the British authorities. His own belief in *satyagrah* was shaken. In a dejected mood he wanted to go to his village with the hope that the soothing family environment will bring some peace to his turbulent mind. When his brother-in-law Mukundbhai came to Ahmedabad on a business visit, he asked for a week's leave so that he can have peace of mind in his village.

Mukundbhai said, "Don't go alone. Come to Nadiad. Bhuvanbhai has also requested Janki to visit Ras. We will all go together."

6

Ras and surrounding areas were recovering from the combined economic impact of last season's almost dry monsoon, epidemic and *satyagrah*. Jivanbhai's family was slightly better off because they had taken good care of their cattle and agricultural produce.

When Chamanbhai arrived his village with his sister and brother-in-law, he found that the enthusiasm generated by the Kheda Satyagrah had waned. Passengers coming by train from Bombay and other places had brought shocking news. A mixed feeling of anger and some kind of pessimistic helplessness had enveloped the people.

Janki's arrival at the time of gloom and despair changed the mood in the family. Women came out of the house and warmly embraced her. Singing some sweet folk songs, they took her inside. Although Bhuvanbhai and Chamanbhai were frequently meeting Janki, Jivanbhai had not seen her for quite some time. The news of Janki's arrival was quickly circulated in the village and the womenfolk in small groups started coming to meet her.

Finding Janki in a happy mood, a lady remarked, *"Sona jeyun sasarun, pan peerjeyun nahi."**

Mukundbhai found himself in a relaxed environment. The pace of life was comfortable in Ras. For a while, he did not have to bother much about his business. Nadiad had observed strike on the 10th April, people had participated actively in the strike and had attended the meetings in large numbers. Although a part of the rail track was removed at Nadiad, it did not result in any casualty. People used to ask him and Chamanbhai more details of the *satyagrah* and the disturbances in Nadiad and Ahmedabad.

* *Although in-laws house may be of gold, there is nothing like parents' home. See appendix for Hindi text*

Chamanbhai was trying to quieten his sad mind. Jivanbhai and Bhuvanbhai had more trust on human goodness and they were still feeling that Gandhiji's approach of *satyagrah,* fast and penance conveyed the right message to the people. After all, the method had been successful in Champaran and Kheda.

One afternoon, Jivanbhai told Chamanbhai, "Now it is time for you to marry. I want to solemnise your marriage this winter."

Janki supported him, "Yes, Bhaia. Now Nanabhai is also 14. If Chamanbhai does not marry now, how can you settle Nanabhai's marriage?"

Nanabhai, Jivanbhai's eldest son was studying at Nadiad, Nanubhai-four years younger to him was a student of the local school.

Chamanbhai hesitated, but he could not say no to his brother. He just kept quiet. Bhuvanbhai saved him from further embarrassment, "Think and let us know in a day or two."

This was an interesting topic for the women of the house. They started teasing Chamanbhai. "Tamne *to gameej hashe*"*, Damyanti quipped.

Chamanbhai liked the changed environment. He had not thought of his marriage. But he liked the idea. He was around 19. If he does not marry soon, he will not get a good wife. Mukundbhai had a frank talk with him. He convinced Chamanbhai that if he delays his marriage, he will not be able to mould his wife in his family tradition. Jivanbhai repeated his question after two days. Chamanbhai kept quiet. Mukundbhai asked, "Bhaia, have you received some proposals?"

"Yes, several. But I am waiting for Chamanbhai's consent. There is a proposal from Anand. But the family is quite rich and I do not want to marry him in a wealthy family. I prefer a family of similar status, not much higher, not much lower."

"You are right. It is important that the bride quickly adjust herself to the traditions and customs of her new family."

Bhuvanbhai suggested, "Let us look for a good family. Mukundbhai, you know many people. You can find a good match for him."

---

* *You are very happy. "Tamne to gameej hashe"*
For Hindi text see Appendix

"I will keep in mind, Janki will also be quite helpful," Mukundbhai said.

The brief stay at Ras gave the much-needed relaxation to Chamanbhai as well as to Mukundbhai and his family. When Chamanbhai came to resume his work at Ahmedabad, he found Jitenbhai in a sad and dejected mood. Jitenbhai said that although the entire nation has protested against the Jallianwalla Bagh massacre, the government is still behaving in a rude authoritative manner and is trying to justify the cruel massacre. The main problem lies in their attitude towards the Indian people whom they regard as slaves and treat them in a very disgusting manner. Some of them say that we are primitive and barbaric people. Let the world decide–who is barbaric-the one who attacks innocent people and relishes the attack in a sadistic manner or the innocent one who helplessly suffers from the attack!

Chamanbhai shared his views.

It took some time to bring them back to their normal routine. Jitenbhai had done some homework for settling pending matters. By now, Chamanbhai had developed a good business sense and he understood the pros and cons of the settlement proposals. Mukundbhai had given some guidelines to him. Based upon his advice, Chamanbhai discussed the matters with Jitenbhai, suggested some changes and after satisfying himself, came to Nadiad for taking Mukundbhai's final instructions.

Mukundbhai looked worried. He said, "Chamanbhai, now the government has slapped a fine of about fifteen thousand rupees to us for maintaining extra armed police force of 45 personnel."

"But Nadiad was not much disturbed. The only problem was removal of the rail track which did not cause any damage and cutting of some telegraph lines. The protest was all along peaceful," Chamanbhai said.

Mukundbhai brought his right hand on his forehead, "Chamanbhai, there is no reason for imposing the fine. Even during the disturbances, in a communication to the President of the Nadiad Municipality, the Collector had praised the conduct of the people of Nadiad and that of its leaders for maintaining peace in the area. The same Collector has now promulgated the order imposing fines. How ridiculous!"

Chamanbhai said, "They are working in a strange manner!"

Mukundbhai further added, "The officers want to settle the scores of Kheda Satyagrah. The government has asked the *patidars* and *vaniyas* to cough up the money. They felt that the railway track was removed by *patidars*. *Vaniyas* were slapped the fine because the key leaders Shri Phulchand Bapujee Shah and Shri Gokaldas Talati are *vaniyas*! They are not even ashamed of mentioning the caste of Mahatmaji also!"

These and other unfair actions were troublesome and painful. Discontent was brewing in the mind and heart of the people.

Jitenbhai told him that a special tribunal has been set up for hearing the Kheda cases. Fine was imposed on the two violence-affected places-Ahmedabad and Viramgam. Ahmedabad was fined Rs. 9,00,000 and Viramgam Rs. 42,000.

The tribunal for Kheda disturbances began on 22 July, 1919. Jitenbhai informed that Shri Vallabhbhai would be the main defence lawyer for the accused.

Jitenbhai and Chamanbhai closely followed the proceedings.

Shri Vallabhbhai was at his brilliant best. He secured acquittal for the accused in most of the cases. In the interesting case of removal of rails at Nadiad, he argued that the two main witnesses for the police were well-known criminals whom the people of Nadiad disliked. In another interesting turn, he showed that the spanner recovered from one of the accused and produced by the police as a proof for dismantling the rails was of the wrong size, which could not unscrew the bolts. This spanner was meant for tightening and loosening the nuts of his well pump!

The entire case fizzled out. Shri Vallabhbhai's reputation soared. For the people, he was not only a brilliant lawyer; he was also their leader on whom they could always depend upon.

The government imposed the fines. The Collector was given discretionary powers to exempt people. The Collector asked Shri Vallabhbhai and Dr. Kanuga to *contribute* towards fine. This was done despite the fact that these two leaders had cooperated closely with the authorities in restoring law and order. The officials attached Dr. Kanuga's cash box and Shri Vallabhbhai's sofa. The sofa was sold and the proceeds were accounted for as a part of the contribution towards the fine of nine lakhs! At the same time, the District Judge of

Ahmedabad tried to disqualify Shri Vallabhbhai and some other barristers from practicing on the plea that they had participated in the *satyagrah* against the Rowlatt Act! However, the High Court did not disqualify them, it issued a warning which just remained on the paper!

Chamanbhai was busy travelling between Ahmedabad and Nadiad. He was trying to settle as many cases and disputes as possible, and was quite successful in his efforts. Both he and Mukundbhai knew that the political situation will be different now and the business will be affected by *satyagrah*, strikes, meetings and other activities. Chamanbhai was in Nadiad, when a meeting of the Executive Committee of the Gujarat Political Conference was held there. A friend of Mukundbhai had told him that in the meeting Shri Vallabhbhai had proposed a resolution in support of non-cooperation. He had also informed that the Gujarat Political Conference will be organised in Ahmedabad from August 27 to 29. Mr. Abbas Tayyabjee would be the President and Shri Vallabhbhai the Chairman of the Reception Committee. Chamanbhai noted the dates in his diary and also realised that Jitenbhai will become quite busy now. He should quickly finish Mukundbhai's business works with him.

Jitenbhai always tried to maintain a balance between his professional and public work. He was not alone. Many established lawyers like him were doing likewise.

Shri Vallabhbhai made a very effective speech in the conference in which he mentioned about the Rowlatt Act, the wash out report of the Hunter Committee, the tacit and explicit support in the House of Lords of the Jallianwala Bagh massacre, the Martial Law in the Punjab and other related issues.

He denounced the tyrannical and brute actions such as asking people to crawl, whipping publicly for petty reasons, stopping water, being a moot spectator to molestation and ill treatment of women, the betrayal of Khilafat and other important issues. He asked–*could these attempts to humiliate Indians be forgotten? He warned that if we put up with these insults we would be looked down by the civilized nations.*

Chamanbhai felt that this was a voice from his own heart. After all, for a nation nothing is more important than honour. How can we protect our honour if do not have self-respect? Determined attempts are made to demolish India's pride, to humiliate Indians and to treat them as trash. Why Indian people should take it lying low? We must protest and oppose these acts.

Shri Vallabhbhai called for a radical change in the administration. He said that we will not gain anything by falling in the trap of reforms. *The government of India must be run for the people of India.*

The Conference also decided to establish the *Rashtriya (Gujarat) Vidyapith* as an institution for imparting value-based education. The objective was to establish an institute which grooms its students in such a manner that they become persons of noble character, more patriotic and fully self-reliant.

Jitenbhai was very impressed. He said, "What an excellent speech Shri Vallabhbhai made yesterday! He touched upon many important things and called for action. His mind is very clear. His speech has made a very good impression on the people and they are full of enthusiasm."

Chamanbhai readily agreed, "Yes, it was a memorable speech. Shri Vallabhbhai always speaks from his heart and speaks frankly. We are lucky to have a bold and courageous leader like him."

He continued, "And he is very practical. However, I have a question, Jitenbhai. The government is proposing reforms and many people are in favour of accepting them. Is it not good for us?"

Jitenbhai replied, "As Shri Vallabhbhai said in the meeting, sometimes reforms are clever traps. Reforms are proposed by the bureaucrats and approved by their bosses. Many of the proposed and implemented reforms are just perfunctory and some of these are even aimed at strengthening the bureaucracy rather than making it more responsive to the public."

Chamanbhai asked, "The public does not know much about these matters. They are mostly concerned with their day-to-day business in courts, police stations, revenue and other offices. They are fed up with difficulties created by the officials. They believe that only *swaraj* can bring solution to their problems..."

He queried, "Vakil Sahab, what will happen now?"

Jitenbhai replied, "Next month the resolution will be presented in a special session of the Congress in Calcutta. We are very hopeful that it will be accepted there."

"What will it mean to us?" Chamanbhai asked.

"This will be a call for a major public action. People will be asked to stop dealing with the courts, withdraw their children from the government schools, not to cooperate with the government etc. Those who have received titles from the British Government will be requested to return those honours. In a way this will be a major public protest against the government."

Chamanbhai liked this step very much. This was a change from talking about pledges and sacrifices. So far, there has been a heavy dependence upon the goodwill of the authorities. The Jallianwala Bagh massacre had changed the perception of the people.

Jitenbhai attended the Calcutta session of the Congress. Chamanbhai was eagerly waiting for him. Jitenbhai looked satisfied. He was tired but a feeling of enthusiasm and boldness appeared on his face. He asked Chamanbhai to wait for a while, went inside his house and came back with a small bowl containing *Rasgulla*.

"Eat it Chamanbhai, Rasgulla-the special Bangali sweet."

"Very tasty. What about you Vakil Sahab?"

"I have already taken five. Anyway, I will take another one with you. They prepare it so well!" Jitenbhai continued, "I will tell you what happened at Calcutta. The session was very well attended. When the resolution was proposed in the meeting, several persons like Malviyaji, Jinnah Sahab, Chittaranjan Das Babu, Anne Besantji and others opposed it. Finally, it was put to vote. The resolution was adopted with a huge majority with 1852 delegates supporting and 908 opposing it."

"There was enthusiasm for action. It was also decided to boycott foreign clothes; people have been asked to wear *Khadi*."

Chamanbhai went out of the room to wash his hands; the *rasgulla* was very tasty. Chamanbhai's feelings were being echoed in the room. Jitenbhai had brought some good news from Calcutta along with the famous *rasgulla!*

"Now the political activities will be brisk and focussed, Chamanbhai."

"What will happen to our business? Will it not be disturbed?" Chamanbhai asked.

"Support for Gandhiji and Shri Vallabhbhai will increase. People have full confidence in them. Our leaders want the welfare of the people. I am certain that the normal agricultural, industrial and commercial activities will continue and grow. At times people will be requested to participate in various actions, which will be aimed at achieving *swaraj*. After all, our final objective is *swaraj*. What we lose now will be redeemed manifolds after getting swaraj."

Jitenbhai said, "At the Calcutta session, the resolution for non-cooperation was adopted by a good majority. The moderates opposed it, some of them even left the meeting, and some have left the Congress itself. But it was clear that the leadership of the Congress will be in the hands of Gandhiji. Gandhiji has excellent followers in Shri Vallabhbhai, Rajendra Babu, Shri Rajgopalachari, Pandit Jawaharlal Nehru, Maulana Azad Sahab and others. More and more young people will join him."

Jitenbhai looked into his eyes, "What about you, Chamanbhai? Will you not join them?"

"I will," said a determined Chamanbhai.

Chamanbhai could not sleep that night. He was at an important stage of his life. His heart was asking him to join Gandhiji's movement on a full time basis. It meant not only losing his job, but also plunging into an unknown river. He may not gain anything. How will he live without having any source of income? Is this struggle worthwhile? Will Mahatmaji with all his spiritual power, moral force and large following will be able to compel the British to leave India? What is the guarantee that *swaraj* can be achieved by non-violent means especially from a colonial power which has just shown its barbaric ruthlessness in the Jallianwala Bagh massacre of innocent people? Will the people rise to the occasion? Moreover, what about his own contribution? Does that matter? There are millions who are already responding to Gandhiji's call. Who bothers about his support or aloofness? Should he forget about all this and continue with his present position? On the other hand, should he heed to the clarion call of his conscience?

Sleep and peace eluded him. Now, he must consult Jitenbhai, Jivanbhai, Bhuvanbhai and Mukundbhai more seriously on this matter.

The thought of consulting Jitenbhai and his family members gave him some solace. Practical wisdom lied in the situation in which he could ensure some regular income so that he can devote his time for the national cause.

He had seen several young volunteers at the Sabarmati Ashram, at Nadiad and elsewhere. Many of them were full timers. They looked happy and satisfied. Why can't he also be like them?

Will God guide him at this critical juncture?

Jitenbhai belonged to a middle class business family of cloth merchants. Ahmedabad was the centre of textile business. His family used to buy *seconds* material from the mills on the wholesale basis and sell it to the retailers. As the business grew, it was felt that at least one person in the family should become a lawyer for safeguarding the business interests of the family. Jitenbhai, who was good at studies; was the obvious choice. During his student days, Jitenbhai came in contact with persons from various areas of Gujarat and Bombay. His travels, contacts and interaction with different people shaped his views. He felt quite satisfied at his family's decision for him.

Like his many young friends, Jitenbhai was attracted to the ideas of *swaraj* and was influenced by the views of nationalist leaders. In his professional work, he handled the cases concerned with his family business and that of some selected clients like Mukundbhai. He was finding more satisfaction in the works involving *swaraj*.

He was quite clear in his advice to Chamanbhai. "Yes," Jitenbhai said, "People like you must join the movement more actively. You will not be alone, Chamanbhai. You will see that thousands will leave their jobs and studies soon for the national cause."

"What should I do?" asked Chamanbhai.

"When you make up your mind, let me know. I will introduce you to Shri Vallabhbhai. There will be many persons like you, they are all needed and there is work for everybody."

"Thanks, Vakil Sahab. However, I also have to think about my expenses. I must earn enough to meet my needs," Chamanbhai said.

"Talk to Mukundbhai. After you leave your job, you can still help him on a part-time basis. It will not disturb your main work for *swaraj*."

Chamanbhai did not want to make any commitments at this stage. He said, "Let me consult my family."

Chamanbhai was coming to Ras after a long gap of two months. He used to come home almost every week either in connection with his work or for relaxation. This time the visit was delayed due to disturbances and subsequent pressure of work.

It was a nice evening at Ras. The pleasant breeze was wafting across the fragrance from the flowers and the trees. Some children were waddling around. Older people, agog with curiosity, were gradually gathering at the *choro*. When they saw Chamanbhai, they felt that their thirst for getting the latest update would soon be quenched by their reliable representative Chamanbhai who has just come from Ahmedabad.

Chamanbhai touched the feet of his elders and went inside. His sister-in-laws started teasing him.

"Where were you all these days? Busy finding a wife?"

Chamanbhai smiled, "No, Bhabhi, I was very busy with my work, there was no time to think about these matters."

They did not believe, *"Chor pakaday, chattu pakadaye, khota bolu na pakdaye."**

"If he does not think of his wife now, when will he dream about a sweet young girl?" Bhuvanbhai's wife commented, *"Didi*, he must have been thinking of the beautiful girl in his neighbourhood!"

"Why not? He is a clever young man from Ras. That is why he was not coming for several days."

"He is a handsome youngman. The girls in the neighbourhood must be talking about him!"

At the *choro*, Nandubhai was discussing about the tussle between the municipality and the government at Nadiad where the people were responding to the boycott of government schools. The Nadiad Municipality had decided not to accept the grant of Rs. 21,000 for the schools. The schools were to function as *Rashtriya* schools. They had planned to raise funds from the public.

Nandubhai said, "The government wants to stop the salary and pension of the teachers. But we, the teachers, cannot be cowed down by such threats. Everywhere, people want to strengthen the hands of Gandhiji and Shri Vallabhbhai."

Chamanbhai joined them, "What are you talking, Nandubhai?"

Jivanbhai said, "He is talking about the non-cooperation in Nadiad Municipal schools."

Nandubhai clarified, "The protest is not limited to the schools. It is spreading to business, courts and to several other activities."

Bhuvanbhai added, "After the Calcutta session, the Congress is more active, confident and determined."

Chamanbhai said, "Jitenbhai was telling that the next session as Nagpur will be very important. Preparations are already afoot. Many

* *A thief can be caught, fish can be captured but a liar cannot be caught. Hindi text in rhe Appendix.*

persons are expected to attend. Even those who had opposed the non-cooperation at Calcutta will support it now."

He then asked, "And what is happening here?"

"Here, people are adopting Khadi, they are trying to avoid courts. In business disputes, many compromises are being made and negotiated settlements are being reached. People are quitting the habits of drinking." Bhuvanbhai said, "Next time when you come, bring two spinning wheels and other material. Your Bhabhis want to do spinning."

Nandubhai was happy, "This is very nice. Let other women of the village also do that."

"And why not men also?" a co-villager asked.

"We do not have much free time," Jivanbhai said, "But we should also join them whenever possible."

Chamanbhai found the situation conducive to his plan. After dinner, he opened up his mind to Jivanbhai and Bhuvanbhai.

Jivanbhai was not averse to the idea, but he did not want to make a comment at this stage. He knew that his would be the last word on the matter. He wanted to get views of other members of the house.

Bhuvanbhai was more practical, "This is a major decision in your life. I have come to know that some people at Nadiad, Borsad, Bardoli and Anand have also devoted themselves for the work. But this life is full of struggle and it requires sacrifice at every step."

He asked him directly, "Are you prepared for that?"

Chamanbhai had never looked directly at the face of his elder brothers in response to any question. However, this time he did. He raised his head and replied in a firm voice, "Yes *Bhaia*, I am prepared for this life. I have thought over it deeply. Perhaps I cannot live any other type of life now."

Bhuvanbhai said, "Why do you say so? You are young. Your views are prompted by your enthusiasm. Once you have your family and enter the *grihasth jivan* you may like to lead a different type of life. Why don't you wait for some more time?"

"*Bhaia,* I have waited. I wanted to join the movement on the day Shri Vallabhbhai read Mahatmaji's speech at the Sabarmati Ashram. Whenever I went to the Ashram, I met a number of dedicated workers who have devoted their life for the nation. I think this is my life-this will be my life."

"Then go ahead," Jivanbhai broke his silence, "Don't worry about your livelihood. Whatever God has given to us will be shared among all family members. There will be enough to support you. But before that, discuss your plan with Janki and Mukundbhai."

This was the last word. Chamanbhai felt immensely happy and touched the feet of his two elder brothers. Tears rolled down from his eyes when he said, "*Bhaia*, this is a big sacrifice from both of you. You know that I will not be able to bring money to the house any more. Even then, you have gladly allowed me to join the *swaraj* movement. I will always remember your kindness."

Bhuvanbhai's eyes were moistened. He embraced Chamanbhai and said, "You are the youngest member of our family but you are doing what we elders have not done. God bless you."

Damyanti was listening the conversation with interest. She asked Jivanbhai, "What was the hurry to allow him to join the *satyagrah*? He is a young boy, he has not seen the world. We are planning to marry him, but you have permitted him to lead a life of sacrifice and struggle! Do not allow him to join the movement now. Let him wait for some time."

"Damyanti, I have looked into his eyes. He cannot wait. Give your blessings and best wishes. May God guide him."

Chamanbhai went to consult Mukundbhai and Janki. For Mukundbhai, this did not come as a surprise. He has been observing that although Chamanbhai was very sincere and devoted to his work, his heart was with the national cause.

Chamanbhai has been frequently visiting the Sabarmati Ashram. He used to see that more people were joining the Ashram as full time worker. They are devoted to the national cause. Jitenbhai had also praised his patriotism and appreciated his intention to join the satyagrah movement. Mukundbhai did not want to lose him, yet he did not like to put any obstruction in Chamanbhai's plans. He worked out a solution.

"Chamanbhai, I will shift Kailashbhai from Nadiad to Ahmedabad. He will work under you. Since he is an old hand, he will pick up the work very soon. However, he may not be able to handle the legal matters. I want you to manage those with the help of Jitenbhai."

Kailashbhai was a trusted manager, who had worked with Mukundbhai's father. He was sincere and practical. Chamanbhai knew that with his sharp common sense, Kailashbhai would manage the grain business very well. Chamanbhai did not want to disappoint his brother-in-law. He agreed to Mukundbhai's proposal.

Janki supported this arrangement. She had seen several activities concerned with the *satyagrah* and social service at Nadiad. Many-women were desirous of supporting the movement as much as possible. She also felt that the arrangement would ensure continuity of some cash income for Chamanbhai. Chamanbhai's eyes were full of tears when he touched his sister's feet.

Janki handed over a packet to Chamanbhai and pushed some money in his pocket, "You will need it."

7

Janki has been very affectionate to Chamanbhai. Although married to an affluent family, she lived a simple life. She always tried to carry the entire family along with her and took care of the sentiments of the family members from both sides. Mukundbhai's parents appreciated her affectionate and loving nature and her vital contribution in strengthening the family bondage. Mukundbhai's own brothers, sisters and cousins were enjoying the warm family environment at home.

Mukundbhai and Kailashbhai came to Ahmedabad with Chamanbhai. Mukundbhai felt it necessary to introduce Kailashbhai to his business associates. Many of them already knew Kailashbhai who had worked for a long time with Mukundbhai's putative father. Chamanbhai felt confident that the transition will be smooth and he will not have any difficulties in pursuing his aim now.

This was also a very convenient adjustment for Jitenbhai. He thanked Mukundbhai for his understanding. Mukundbhai left Ahmedabad satisfied with the arrangements.

Wishing good luck to Chamanbhai, he said, "You are doing something for all of us. Don't think that you are alone, we are with you and you are representing all of us."

Chamanbhai's heart was full of love, admiration and gratitude for his brothers, sister and brother-in-law. They had supported him not only in implementing his decision to devote more time for the national cause, they had also given financial support to him for the purpose. The arrangement was practical and very helpful for him. The family came forward to support him wholeheartedly; he did not have to plead much. Chamanbhai asked himself, *Is it not due to the influence of Gandhiji and Shri Vallabhbhai? Perhaps his family members and relatives would also have joined, they find their representation and participation in him.*

"I want to introduce you to Shri Vallabhbhai," Jitenbhai said, "Come tomorrow at nine in the morning."

This was a very welcome gesture from Jitenbhai. Chamanbhai's heart leapt with joy. He was going to have an opportunity to meet his idol. What will he talk to Shri Vallabhbhai who is known as a man of few words? What will he ask? How should he conduct himself before the respected leader ? What should he wear?

He remembered the packet given by Janki. It contained a set of Khadi *kurta-dhoti* Chamanbhai thanked his sister from the core of his heart-*thank you Didi for your good wishes and your very nice gift. This is going to be my dress now.*

That night, several pleasant thoughts occupied his mind. He did not have a clear vision of *swaraj,* he did not want to think much. He was just concentrating on his first determined step. He may not get anything, no name, no fame, no pecuniary benefits, yet he was getting everything he wanted and could think of. One meeting with Shri Vallabhbhai was all that he wanted to cherish.

A golden sun ray from a slit in the window warmed him. He opened the window and looked at a sparrow chirping on the adjacent roof.

The bird is sharing my joy-Chamanbhai thought. He was in a very pleasant mood that lovely morning. Several thoughts came to his mind but he did not want to get flustered. He felt that he should not get awed in the presence of the great personality, he had heard of Shri Vallabhbhai's penetrating eyes, which could read the person in front of him, in a flash. He should not be flummoxed by any searching questions, which Shri Vallabhbhai may ask him.

When he met Jitenbhai, Chamanbhai's mind was busy with the same thoughts. He asked Jitenbhai, "Vakil Sahab, what will Shri Vallabhbhai ask? What I should say to him?"

"He may not ask anything. He will understand you with one glance. He has a special knack of judging people. He will know whether you are firm and sincere in your approach or not. He may ask you about your village and the people in that area. I cannot say Chamanbhai. But I can tell you from my own experience that although he may look tough and stern outwardly, he is very soft in his heart. He may even cut jokes with you."

Jitenbhai added with a smile, "But now onwards don't address me as Vakil Sahab. Call me Jitenbhai."

When they reached Bhadra, Shri Vallabhbhai was busy talking to some people. After sometime, Jitenbhai went inside and a few minutes later he called Chamanbhai in. For Chamanbhai, it was rare fortune to see his idol so closely. Shri Vallabhbhai was wearing a Khadi dhoti kurta. He was in a relaxed mood.

After accepting his greetings, he asked, "What is your name? You belong to which village?"

"Chamanbhai from Ras."

"O, I see. Ras is important for our work. What are you doing here in Ahmedabad?"

Chamanbhai briefly explained his work.

Shri Vallabhbhai said, "I know Mukundbhai's family. They are nice people. Jitenbhai has told me about your desire to serve the nation. This is very good. But your life will be full of struggle. You will have to forget the comforts of the life you are currently enjoying. Your life will be much different as a *satygrahi*."

Meeting his source of inspiration was a golden opportunity for Chamanbhai. He was delighted at the auspicious initiation in the path of *satyagrah*. He felt pride in being addressed as a *satyagrahi* by his idol. He imagined himself moving from one village to the other in the white khadi dress. His only desire was to follow his leader for bringing *swaraj*.

Shri Vallabhbhai said, "Jitenbhai will advise you what to do."

This was a signal to end the meeting. Some more people were waiting to see Shri Vallabhbhai.

Chamanbhai's fears were misconceived. He did not find himself in the spell of the awe of his leader; in fact, he felt that he is talking to a guardian. The pleasant feeling that now onwards his life will be directly or indirectly under the influence of Shri Vallabhbhai, filled his heart with joy.

He thanked Jitenbhai for this great help. "Vakil Sahab"...

Jitenbhai interrupted, "No, Jitenbhai."

Chamanbhai smiled, "Sorry, will try but it may take a few days."

Jitenbhai agreed, "Yes, old habits die hard. I know you are very happy with the meeting and I must say you are lucky to have the blessings of Shri Vallabhbhai so early in your life."

"Yes, Jitenbhai. I do not know how to express my gratitude to you."

"No, no," Jitenbhai protested. "You are making a sacrifice for serving the country. That is the reason that your family members are supporting you wholeheartedly. Shri Vallabhbhai is currently busy with several matters concerning the Municipality, the Rashtriya Vidyapith, the Nagpur Congress session etc. We will soon know what plans he has for us."

Jitenbhai continued, "Try to finish your pending work as soon as possible. You are going to be closely involved in the work for swaraj very soon."

Kailashbhai just took a week to fully assume his responsibilities. He possessed a sharp business acumen. The legal matters were dealt by Chamanbhai. Most of the disputes were in the last stages of settlement. The situation helped Chamanbhai in preparing for the new life. His meeting with Shri Vallabhbhai had filled him with more enthusiasm. Jitenbhai was also quite busy, Chamanbhai was able to meet him only after two days.

"Where were you? I came to meet you, but you were away." Chamanbhai asked him.

Jitenbhai told him, "I was working with Shri Vallabhbhai. He is involved in many important matters. Establishment of national institutions is an essential feature of the non-cooperation movement. The July meeting of the Gujarat Provincial Committee at Nadiad had decided to establish the Rashtriya Vidyapith. Gandhiji is very keen to open such national institutions of learning which will focus on patriotism, self-reliance and moral values. We need to inform the people about the plan and seek their support for the institution. People should be encouraged to send students to the Vidyapith."

He added, "The establishment of the Vidyapith is a favourite project of Shri Vallabhbhai. We need to propagate his ideas. Gandhiji will be its Chancellor and Shri Vallabhbhai will manage the affairs of the Vidyapith."

This was a task, which Chamanbhai liked. Many people in Ahmedabad were aware of it but people in the villages needed to be informed and convinced. Jitenbhai drew a plan for visiting a few places and assigned some additional works to Chamanbhai like raising awareness among the people about non-cooperation and Khadi.

Chamanbhai remembered the request from his family for buying *Charkhas*. This was the right time for the purchase.

Jivanbhai was quite pleased to see Chamanbhai in his new role. He had seen the spark of determination in his eyes and was satisfied to observe that Chamanbhai was happy with his new way of life. The family members were delighted to hear about his face-to-face meeting with Shri Vallabhbhai.

His sister-in-law Damyanti said, "You are lucky that you could meet Shri Vallabhbhai personally. Nandubhai says that he is a tough man and does not speak much. What did he talk with you?"

"He has sent me to you." It was Chamanbhai's turn to tease her, "On his advice I have come to seek your blessings. Now spin yarn for your own clothes, do not wear printed saris. You are already very beautiful and will appear very elegant in the Khadi sari."

Yashoda, Bhuvanbhai's wife said, "And what about your marriage? Are you not looking for a nice girl?"

Damyanti said, "He is a clever young man. He will not tell us about that. You will see Yashoda, one day he will bring a very beautiful girl to this house."

Chamanbhai said, "Nobody can be more beautiful than both of you. Why don't you tell one of your sisters to marry me?"

"Go, get your hair cut first!" Damyanti said.

The two women started looking at the *Charkha* with curiosity.

The Rashtriya Vidyapith was founded in October. People came forward to support the institution. How dear was the project to Gandhiji was obvious from his speech which he made to the first batch of students on the 15th November 1920. Mahatmaji said that although he has completed many tasks of great responsibility, but no work done so far could be compared with the establishment of the Vidyapith.

Shri Vallabhbhai was managing the Vidyapith. He was keen that the people should send their wards to the Vidyapith, not to the government schools. Many families in the town had responded to his appeal, but it was necessary to attract students from smaller cities and villages.

The Rashtriya Vidyapith was later re-named as the Gujarat Vidyapith.

When the government stopped the payment of salaries and pension for the municipal schoolteachers in Nadiad, the Vidyapith even contributed some money for the purpose. Jitenbhai would ask Chamanbhai to do some miscellaneous work concerning the Vidyapith.

There was a huge demand on Gandhiji's time. He was travelling to many places in the country, motivating people to join the non-cooperation movement, urging them to promote Hindu-Muslim unity, encouraging opening of national schools, strengthening the Congress, pressing the government for *swaraj* and doing several other works. Shri Vallabhbhai was managing the socio-political activities in Gujarat.

Jitenbhai advised Chamanbhai to attend the Nagpur Congress which was scheduled to be held from December 26-31, 1920." You will get a good idea of how the various matters of national interest are discussed."

About 15,000 delegates attended the 35th session of the Congress, which was presided by Shri Vijayaraghavachariar. Gandhiji's stamp was evident throughout the session. A new Constitution drafted by Gandhiji was adopted. Mr. Jinnah opposed the non-cooperation resolution but only one person supported him.

It was a learning experience for Chamanbhai. His vision was broadened and he, for the first time, saw the matters being discussed in the national perspective by great leaders at such a largely attended meeting.

Later, in a meeting of All India Congress Committee it was decided to institute a Fund named after Lokmanya Tilak with a target to collect ten million rupees, to enrol 10 million *four-anna* members and to ensure that at least 2 million spinning wheels are operational in the country. These nation-wide targets were divided into smaller ones for the provinces. The target for Gujarat and Kathiawad for the Tilak Swaraj Fund was rupees one million, 300,000 *four-anna* members and 100,000 spinning wheels. Though these targets were rather disproportionate for Gujarat, Shri Vallabhbhai assured the meeting that Gujarat will not be lacking in response.

Jitenbhai said, "Chamanbhai, just few months ago you were asking me what will you have to do when you join the *satyagrah*. Now you can easily see that there is more than enough work for you. Just go ahead."

This was what Chamanbhai liked-action oriented agenda. He has to show his mettle. This was the right opportunity to prove that Jitenbhai and Shri Vallabhbhai can trust him.

Chamanbhai put his heart and soul in the campaign, travelling from one village to the other mostly on foot, sleeping on the floor or in the open space, eating whatever was available, sometimes cooking his own food without asking for any hospitality. This was the real test of a *satyagrahi*. It required the spirit of sacrifice and devotion. His work kept him engaged all the day, Chamanbhai did not realise how quickly the day finished.

It was an immensely satisfying experience for him. He enjoyed doing hard work, liked meeting people, talking about their welfare, convincing them to become a *four-anna* member, promoting the use of spinning wheel etc. He himself was essentially a village lad who could easily understand their problem. He used to get warm welcome in most of the places. In some places, people knew his family and relatives. This was an added advantage.

Chamanbhai closely watched the life of the people in different villages. He also noted the impact of the recent movements and the peoples' preparedness to join the struggle.

Chamanbhai did not realise how fast the time passed. Gujarat exceeded the target of collection for the Tilak Swaraj Fund. Gujarat and Kathiawad contributed 1.5 million rupees against the target of rupees one million. It also achieved the target for enrolment of *four-anna* members and that of promoting the spinning wheel. At the end of June, the provincial targets were achieved.

Jitenbhai congratulated Chamanbhai for his dedicated work. Chamanbhai had proved his worth and has given the hope that he can be depended upon. A new task awaited him and other workers. Jitenbhai told him that it has been decided to boycott the foreign clothes by the end of September. On August 1, which happened to be the first anniversary of Tilak Maharaj's death, a bonfire of foreign clothes was to be organised.

Chamanbhai was finding more interest in the work. He loved this action.

Jitenbhai had told him that once the British administration is weakened due to peoples' non-cooperation, then the government was as good as gone, freedom was imminent.

People whole-heartedly participated in the bonfire. Shri Vallabhbhai emptied his wardrobe and threw all clothes in the fire. So did Jitenbhai and thousands of people. One afternoon Jitenbhai took him in front of a liquor shop. Several women-old and young were picketing. He was very impressed with their determination. The shop owners and their supporters were trying to prevent them from obstructing their business. Sometimes the backdoor was used for delivery of bottles.

At one place, Jitenbhai saw a commotion. Some people were in an agitated mood near a liquor shop. The front door was closed but here was confusion all around. Somebody said that the goons hired by the shopkeeper were trying to abuse the women. Suddenly a young girl came running from the back side of the shop and shouted, "They are trying to misbehave with us. Help, help."

She looked at the people around, came to Jitenbhai and said, "Please come with me."

Jitenbhai, Chamanbhai and some other people rushed towards the backdoor. When the goons saw the crowd coming, they fled away. Jitenbhai and Chamanbhai went near the back door. Some women were hurt and bruised. Some had their clothes torn.

Jitenbhai requested the people to maintain peace and order. Chamanbhai rushed to a nearby pharmacy and quickly brought bandage and dressing material. He asked the girl to provide first aid. Woman volunteers came forward and took charge of the situation. Jitenbhai knew some of them.

A middle aged woman came to thank him, "Jitenbhai, you and your friends arrived just on time and saved us from the goons."

She was Jitenbhai's neighbour Lakshmiben.

Jitenbhai said, "This is very bad and shameful, Lakshmiben. How can the shopkeeper do it? It was good that the girl ran to the front side and informed us."

"She is my niece, Uma. She has come for Nadiad for spending some time with us. She is a very nice girl and takes active part in the picketing. We have been facing resistance from the shopkeepers, but this had never happened to us. We are *satyagrahi* and we cannot indulge in violence; but look at the shameless shopkeeper, see what he has done!"

"Come, let us see the shopkeeper," Jitenbhai said.

They went to the front side, the shop was closed and the shopkeeper absent!

"The coward has escaped. Let us come here tomorrow," Lakshmiben said.

"Ok, we will come tomorrow evening."

The next day, the shopkeeper had arranged police protection. When Jitenbhai and Chamanbhai reached the place, they found that the picket were not allowed to go in the vicinity, they were stopped a few yards before the shop. When the woman pickets reached there, they attempted to go near the shop and to the backdoor. This was not allowed. The shopkeeper wanted to continue his business from the backdoor. When the women insisted, they were pushed back.

The satyagrahis wanted to go forward. The policemen were stopping them but some young people defied the police and moved forward. Chamanbhai was also among them. Seeing that the youngsters are moving ahead, Jitenbhai came from behind and took the lead. Others followed him. The police tried to stop them but the picketers did not stop. Then the police resorted to *lathi charge*. Several policemen came brandishing their *lathis* and beat the protesters. A policeman tried to hit Jitenbhai on his head. Chamanbhai, showing a great presence of mind, quickly came forward to protect him, took the blow on his shoulders and shielded Jitenbhai from direct blow on his head. Chamanbhai was badly hurt on the shoulders and chest and fell down. His prompt action had saved Jitenbhai from a very serious head injury. The police was in no mood to relent. Several protesters were injured and carried away for first aid by volunteers. Another group of *satyagrahis* replaced them.

This continued for some time and the number of injured increased. The women rushed to provide first aid.

By that time, a motley crowd had collected at the scene and some persons wanted to pelt stones at the policemen but the women stopped them. A lady said, "No brothers, we are *satyagrahis*. Please do not respond violence with violence. Let them hurt us, we will take all such injuries smilingly."

The crowd was pacified. People concentrated on giving the first aid and moving the injured to the hospital. When Chamanbhai was able to open his eyes, he found himself in a hospital. He saw that a number of injured persons were lying on the floor, Jitenbhai was next to him. Chamanbhai tried to lift his hand but could only move it slightly. His body was aching with pain, he could only convey his greetings to Jitenbhai with his eyes.

The next morning Shri Vallabhbhai and some other leaders came to see them. Chamanbhai tried to offer his greetings but was unable to fold his hands. Shri Vallabhbhai patted him and said, "Brave man. This is the true spirit of a *satyagrahi*."

Jitenbhai was able to convey his *namaskar* to Shri Vallabhbhai. He said, "Chamanbhai saved my life yesterday. He took the blow on his body."

Shri Vallabhbhai again looked to Chamanbhai and patted his shoulders. Chamanbhai's eyes were moist with gratitude and satisfaction. This was a very satisfying reward for him; the gentle affectionate pat from his idol was worth having several injuries. He felt all his pain vanished for the moment.

Visitors kept on coming. In the afternoon, a group of woman picket arrived. Lakshmiben and Uma came to Jitenbhai.

"Thanks God, the blow did not hurt your head. It was a brutal act," Lakshmiben said.

"I was saved by Chamanbhai. He took the serious blow on his body," Jitenbhai pointed towards Chamanbhai's adjacent bed.

Lakshmiben and Uma came to Chamanbhai. Lakshmiben softly touched his forehead and gently said, "Chamanbhai, you have saved Jitenbhai's life, we are grateful to you."

Chamanbhai conveyed his greetings to them. Uma looked at Chamanbhai from the corner of her eyes and responded with a silent greeting. She was a simply dressed young girl in her mid teens. Her black eyes were shining and her face showed a healthy glow. She looked at Chamanbhai with admiration. Chamanbhai simply smiled.

Lakshmi and Uma proceeded to see the other injured *satyagrahis*. They returned after sometime. Lakshmi asked, "Do you need anything Jitenbhai? I will bring some food for you in the afternoon."

Jitenbhai said, "No, no. Do not do that. There are several persons like me. I will eat the food provided by the hospital."

However, in the afternoon Lakshmi, Uma and some other volunteers brought lunch for them. Lakshmi said, "There is enough for everybody."

Jitenbhai, Chamanbhai and some others were unable to eat with their own hands. Woman volunteers helped them with support from the hospital staff. Uma brought rice and *kadhi* for Jitenbhai and Chamanbhai. Lakshmi and Uma helped them in eating with spoon.

Chamanbhai's body was aching with pain and eyes were heavy. He soon fell asleep.

Jitenbhai was discharged after five days, Chamanbhai a week

later. His family members had reached from Ras, Mukundbhai and Janki had also arrived from Nadiad.

Damyanti was in tears. She had seen Chamanbhai as a child and had given the love and affection of an elder sister to him. She pointed to Jivanbhai, "I told him not to allow Chamanbhai to join the *satyagrah.* But he did not listen to me. Now see what had happened to the young boy!"

Bhuvanbhai tried to defend, "Bhabhi, Chamanbhai is mature now. He knows what he has to do. He has chosen the path himself, no body had persuaded him to do so. It is his decision and he is happy at it. It was not correct to stop him against his wishes. Bhaia was right in allowing him to become a *satyagrahi.*"

Mukundbhai added, "He is not alone. Many young persons like him have joined the movement."

Janki added, "And a number of girls have joined also. In Nadiad, we everyday see woman and girl pickets."

Mukundbhai said, "They picket foreign cloth shops also. The shopkeepers are resisting and are using all means to stop them. Their business is at stake."

Suddenly there was a knock at the door. Lakshmi arrived with Uma. Mukundbhai looked at her and exclaimed, "Lakshmiben, do you recognise me? I am Mukund."

"Oh, Mukundbhai, yes, yes, you are the brother of my close friend Rukmini. How do you know Chamanbhai?"

Mukundbhai said, "He is my brother-in-law."

Lakshmi introduced Uma to him. "She is my niece. Uma is a volunteer like me and takes active part in the *satyagrah.* We were there when the rude police lathi charged the picket."

She asked Uma to touch the feet of all elders.

"We came to see Chamanbhai. He is much better now. He took the blow on himself and saved Jitenbhai. Brave man!"

She told, "I was there. It is all due to the connivance of the police with the shopkeeper."

Lakshmi gave full details of the incidence and praised Chamanbhai's courage and presence of mind. Janki was talking to Uma. She asked about her family and her Nadiad connection. Janki knew her relatives.

"I am going to see Jitenbhai," Mukundbhai said.

"I will also join," Janki and Lakshmi accompanied him. Uma followed.

The recovery was slow but Chamanbhai was eager to move out. Jivanbhai and other family members had returned to Ras. Bhuvanbhai used to come frequently to see him.

When Chamanbhai was able to walk, he went to see Jitenbhai. Jitenbhai reprimanded him, "Why did you come? I was thinking of coming to you. You need rest."

Chamanbhai said that he wanted to see him.

"I am fine, do not stress yourself. When are you going to see the doctor?"

"Tomorrow."

"OK, let me know what the doctor says. Do not disturb yourself for me. I will come to you when I find time. If you have something urgent, ask Kailashbhai to send a messenger. Take enough rest. You have received severe blows."

Next day, Bhuvanbhai took him to the hospital. The doctor said that although Chamanbhai is progressing well, he needs to take rest for about a month. Bhuvanbhai brought him to Ras.

8

The soothing family environment at Ras and the affectionate care of Damyanti and Yashoda accelerated Chamanbhai's recovery. Bhuvanbhai used to bring the news about Shri Vallabhbhai. He said that Shri Vallabhbhai was actively involved in the Ahmedabad, Surat and Nadiad Municipalities, the latter two were taken over by the government.

Shri Vallabhbhai was also very busy with the work in the Gujarat Provincial Congress Committee. Chamanbhai was eager to go to Ahmedabad for attending the Congress session. Bhuvanbhai took him there a few days before, got him examined by the doctor and stayed with him for some time.

There was lot of talk in the air that *swaraj* will be achieved by 1921. This hope had created much interest among the public for the Session. Elaborate arrangements were made for the Session under the able guidance of Shri Vallabhbhai who was the Chairman of the Reception Committee. Khadi was used for decorations, for shoe-bags and for other applications. A *swadeshi* exhibition was also organised for promoting homespun yarn and hand woven clothes. Shri Vallabhbhai said that about 200,000 pounds of yarn had been spun and woven for this purpose. Most of the Khadi used for the session was produced in Gujarat.

It was decided that a mass civil disobedience movement would be inaugurated in Bardoli Taluka in January. Anand was also a friendly contender for the honour.

Government servants were asked to resign and the *patels* were requested to send their letters of resignation for use at a later date. Chamanbhai was quite enthusiast about the campaign and he visited Bardoli several times for promoting the civil disobedience.

Bardoli was very active in the movement. People had refused to deal with government agencies, there was a strong support for national schools, which had been started in about 50 villages out of the 80 in total. Almost every house had a spinning wheel and people were spinning in a joyous mood. Women were playing a very active role. An environment was being created to prepare people for non-payment of revenue. Some songs requested women to discard foreign clothes and wear beautiful khadi.

This was a major success. Chamanbhai saw enthusiasm in every village he visited, people were more convinced that the struggle for *swaraj* is in the full swing. The tempo was very encouraging and satisfying. However, his happiness was short-lived. On February 4, 1922, a violent incident took place at Chauri Chaura in the U.P. in which 21 police personnel were killed. Gandhiji was terribly shocked and at a meeting in Bardoli on February 10, he decided to suspend the Civil Disobedience movement.

Like many other persons, Chamanbhai was surprised and severely disappointed at the abrupt decision to postpone the *satyagrah*. The movement was going strong and people were enthusiastically supporting that. People were unable to understand the rationale behind the decision to stop the movement at a time when it was getting mass support.

"Why the movement has been suspended? Why a freak incident in one part of the country has influenced Gandhiji to suspend the movement when it was getting good public support?" He asked Jitenbhai.

"Gandhiji feels that the people are not fully prepared for a non-violent *satyagrah*. Non-violence is very dear to Gandhiji's heart. He cannot make a compromise on that. In his opinion, it was necessary to concentrate on the constructive programme for some time. This will prepare the people for the civil disobedience movement," Jitenbhai tried to convince him.

Chamanbhai was not enthused. In his spell of disappointment, he went to Ras. People in the village were also surprised and dejected at the abrupt suspension of the civil disobedience movement. His co-villagers were asking, "Why Mahatmaji has thrown ice water on the bubbling enthusiasm of the people?"

Chamanbhai also had the same questions in his mind. He knew that it will be extremely difficult to regenerate the same enthusiasm among the people. He could not find any convincing answer for the postponement.

He decided to utilise his time to help his brothers in the agricultural work. People used to come to the *choro*. They talked mostly about Gandhiji and Shri Vallabhbhai. Nandubhai never felt tired of repeating in the village that Chamanbhai is very lucky to have met Shri Vallabhbhai personally. Chamanbhai's friends and other young persons from Ras and neighbouring villages frequently came to meet him. They were feeling proud that a young man from their area has played an active role in the *satyagrah*. Inspired by him, some young men showed willingness to join the movement.

Gradually Chamanbhai forgot about the injury and started lifting heavy loads in the field or at home. This caused some pain in his shoulders. Jivanbhai advised him to see the doctor at Ahmedabad. The doctor diagnosed that Chamanbhai needed to undergo further treatment and exercise for about a week. He also advised Chamanbhai to take sufficient rest. After completing the treatment, Chamanbhai went to see Jitenbhai.

Jitenbhai was talking to Lakshmi, Uma and some other persons. He heartily welcomed Chamanbhai, "Come in Chamanbhai, we were thinking of you!"

Chamanbhai looked around. About fifteen people were sitting in the room, Chamanbhai joined them.

"We are going to enrol volunteers for the picketing foreign cloth shops. We need your help," Jitenbhai said.

Lakshmi looked at him with a smile, "Now some people know you for your courage. You join us tomorrow. We will start our campaign to enrol volunteers. Shri Vallabhbhai has given us a target of enlisting 2500 volunteers."

They discussed their plan.

Although the response for enrolment of volunteers was lukewarm, the old hands were at work and they could re-start the picketing. The owners of foreign clothes shops responded. People were not buying foreign clothes. The shop owners were pleading that they should be allowed to sale clothes made in India. The picketing was successful.

By this time, people have started using Khadi. There was a healthy competition within and among the families-who is able to spin more yarn? Even the young children started singing Khadi songs. In one popular song, a child asked his mother to buy a khadi cap and other khadi dresses for him. He wanted to look handsome in Khadi dress.

It was a scorching mid-June summer, Chamanbhai was negotiating with a business partner for closing an old case involving demand for a few hundred rupees. Suddenly Jitenbhai arrived with some people. Looking at the business partner, he said, "This is a trifle matter, sort it out now. We have much more important things to do."

Chamanbhai stopped his work. Both partners were interested in knowing what is in Jitenbhai's mind! He appeared to be full of enthusiasm.

Jitenbhai sat on the only empty chair, others made themselves comfortable sitting on the floor.

Jitenbhai said, "The disappointment of abrupt end of the civil disobedience is over. Now we have a golden opportunity to serve our country. Shri Vallabhbhai has asked us to mobilise support for the Flag Satyagrah. We need to enrol volunteers for joining the *satyagrah* at Nagpur."

Chamanbhai's business partner was not aware of the *satyagrah*. He asked, "What is going to happen at Nagpur?"

Jitenbhai said, "Two months' ago, the Nagpur police had beaten and thrown the *satyagrahis* who were carrying the national flag in the Civil Lines area. The Commissioner of Nagpur Mr. Charles Clark thundered that he would teach a lesson to *satyagrahis*. He has ordered that the flag carrying *satyagrahis* should not pass through his residence in the Civil Lines area. If they do so, he will shoot them. *Satyagrahis* are disobeying the order and are carrying flag in the Civil Lines area. They are beaten, stopped and arrested."

Chamanbhai's heart leapt with joy. He was looking for such an opportunity.

He asked, "What we have to do?"

"Enrol volunteers for offering the *satyagrah*."

Chamanbhai said, "I am ready."

"So am I," his business partner said.

"Very good," Jitenbhai said. "Shri Vallabhbhai has exhorted the people to jump upon this opportunity of demonstrating our non-cooperation. Now go to the villages and request people to enrol."

The momentum which was slackened earlier by the sudden postponement of the civil disobedience movement, picked up. Chamanbhai went to Ras and visited some neighbouring villages with a group of co-workers. People were coming forward to join. Leaders like Shri Mohanlal Pandya, Darbar Shri Gopaldas, Shri Phulchand Shah, Mr. Abbas Tyabjee and several others were quite active. District authorities and other government officials were trying their best to stop the movement. Mr. Charles was a very influential civil servant; he was the president of the ICS officers' association, and was having a powerful clout in the government.

Chamanbhai and his friends left for Nagpur. The situation was quite tense, it was a standoff between the *satyagrahis* and the government. Shri Jamnalal Bajaj and Shri Vinoba Bhave were arrested and Shri Vallabhbhai was leading the *satyagrah* now. People from various walks of life, from town and villages were offering *satyagrah* and were being arrested.

Chamanbhai and his friends were dressed in white *Khadi dhoti - kurta* or *kurta-pajamah.* They were carrying flags in their hand and were shouting slogans. Suddenly the train was stopped at a local station and they were asked to get down.

"You cannot go to the Civil Lines," said a police officer in a stern voice.

Chamanbhai asked, "Why?"

"Because the government has ordered that."

"We have orders from Shri Vallabhbhai to go to the Civil Lines area in Nagpur and offer *satyagrah,*" Chamanbhai argued.

By that time, several *satygrahis* tried to push forward and they started raising slogans. One of them asked the policeman also to join him!

Soon other *satyagrahis* got down from the train, some people waiting at the platform also joined them. The crowd was becoming strong.

A senior police officer arrived and shouted, "They are very truculent. Arrest them."

For Chamanbhai, it was the first experience for being arrested. He felt huge satisfaction at the opportunity to join the distinguished *satyagrahis* who were in the jail. He had heard that Shri Ravishankar Maharaj was also in the jail. Chamanbhai and his colleagues were full of enthusiasm and satisfaction. Chamanbhai was asked to grind 25 *seers** *of* grain. Some *satyagrahis* were asked to crush stone.

The condition in the jail was deplorable. The toilets were open, a time limit of 3 to 5 minutes was fixed for each individual's use.

They were given two meals –one time *jwarchapati* and *daal* and the other time *jwar* bread and vegetable. The food was tasteless. The *chapati*s were half cooked, the *daal* was like warm water on which some turmeric powder was dissolved and the vegetables were tasteless.

The behaviour of the jail officials and wardens was humiliating. Chamanbhai's heart protested with anger. He could not comprehend how these people can be so harsh on *satyagrahis*-patriots who were fighting for the cause of the country. They were treated as criminals and were subjected to all sorts of humiliation. He was wondering how the system can treat people so mercilessly!

The only solace was the company of like-minded *satyagrahis* in the jail which was soon full to capacity. New prisoners coming to the jail were source of eagerly awaited news. They brought the news that there is a tremendous enthusiasm among the people and many persons are coming from various provinces to join the *satyagrah*. Many *satyagrahis* were arrested on the way itself.

Amidst the feelings of humiliation, Chamanbhai and his friends had the consolation that the jail was full. They were told that *satyagrahis* were also being sent to some other jails. This was indicative of a welcome change in the mood of the people.

News arrived that the government is alarmed at the increasing number of *satyagrahis* who were coming from various parts of country. The government, finding it difficult to manage the large number of prisoners was now looking for a settlement.

Shri Vitthalbhai and some other members of the provincial legislature were making efforts to solve the problem. A resolution was moved in the legislature, which wanted the withdrawal of the cases against *satyagrahis*, their release from jail and withdrawal of the order prohibiting the taking out of flag procession. Hope for negotiated settlement rose.

This resolution was passed by an overwhelming majority but was rejected by the Governor. Shri Vallabhbhai then wrote to the

* *Seer—unit of measure. One Seer =0.93310 kg*

police authorities asking for permission to lead a procession through the Civil Lines on the 18th August. The planned route for the procession was attached with the application.

The procession started at 12.00 noon. Police personnel were posted throughout the route and the Superintendent of Police along with mounted police moved with the procession. About 100 *satyagrahis* carrying the national flag and shouting slogans marched along the pre-decided route. The procession was allowed to pass as planned and dispersed at the Sadar Bazaar.

Shri Vallabhbhai regarded it as the success of truth and non-violence. He said, "The *honour of the National Flag stands vindicated and the right to take out peaceful procession on the public roads has been restored.*"

The police however could not digest it. The ICS officers took it as an affront and raised the matter with the Government of India. They tried to derail the settlement and put all sort of hurdles delaying the release of the prisoners. Shri Vallabhbhai patiently waited for the release of *satyagrahis*. People in the country were becoming restive and were feeling that the government has gone back on the settlement. Finally Shri Vallabhbhai's patience worn out and he gave an ultimatum that if the prisoners are not released within 24 hours, then he will publish the entire correspondence between him and the government on the subject. He would also resume the *satyagrah*.

The government acted swiftly on this ultimatum. All *satyagrahis* were released on September 3. After their release, the *satyagrahis* marched with national flag through the Civil Lines. In the evening, a public meeting was organised in which Shri Vallabhbhai explained the facts and contradicted the mischievous propaganda against him. Thanking the *satyagrahis* for the success of the struggle, he said that they deserve the honour for the success. He was also graceful in thanking the provincial and the central governments.

Chamanbhai was very satisfied with his direct involvement in a successful *satyagrah*. When he came to Ahmedabad, Jitenbhai congratulated him and thanked him for enduring the hardships in the jail. Jitenbhai told him that like him, many *satyagrahis* are having a sense of satisfaction at their participation. The sufferings in the jail are of no matter to them and they are full of enthusiasm. Some of them want Shri Vallabhbhai to find another appropriate task for them for serving the motherland.

Chamanbhai was tired but happy. He found that he is capable of adapting to the new life and will not find it difficult to undergo even a more severe test than this.

One afternoon Jitenbhai invited some *satyagrahis* to his residence.

Chamanbhai was walking leisurely to Jitenbhai's house when he met Uma and some other girls who were also going there. Uma came forward offered *namaskar* to him and with a smile said, "Congratulations. You have done your duty in a very significant manner. We are very happy."

Chamanbhai felt a smile in his heart. He said in a modest manner, "My going to jail for a short period is a very small matter compared to the sacrifices made by many *satyagrahis*. It is not my success, it is success for all."

"But enduring the hardships of the jail is no easy matter," Uma said. "Some *satyagrahis* could not bear it, apologised and asked for release from the prison."

"Yes, the conditions are really bad and the treatment of the officials even worse. However, we know what we have to do. Once we have chosen the life of a satyagrahi, we have to put up with these difficulties," Chamanbhai said.

On the way, Uma asked a few questions about the life in Jail. On reaching Jitenbhai's house, she looked into Chamanbhai's eyes and greeted him with a smile. A thousand roses blossomed in his heart.

Jitenbhai was in a very happy mood. He came forward to welcome Chamanbhai and others. He embraced Chamanbhai and said, "You have passed the examination. Congratulations. More such visits may be in store for you. "He then thanked all satyagrahis and said, "Now, relax a while and meet your family. They were anxious about your welfare. Meanwhile, I will discuss with Shri Vallabhbhai and other leaders about our next course of action."

This was a very pleasant evening for all *satyagrahis*. Appreciation of their work gave them much satisfaction and encouragement. Jitenbhai offered some snacks and sweets to all.

After washing his hands, Chamanbhai was looking for a handkerchief, which was not with him. He took a piece of an old newspaper and wiped his hands.

The next day, he was preparing to go to Ras. There was a knock at the door. Chamanbhai was delighted to see Uma with a packet.

"I am going to Nadiad. This is a packet of Khadi handkerchiefs woven from the yarn spun by me."

"Thanks very much. I need them."

"I saw that yesterday." Then looking at him from the corner of her eyes, "Come to Nadiad sometime."

The sweet look in her eyes sent a melody in Chamanbhai's heart.

9

The sky was frequently changing its colour from light blue to various shades of black. The vast expand of sky was magnanimous enough to accommodate all their changing patterns. Some rays of sun penetrating their passage through the layers of cloud offered a soothing greeting to the earth. Light drizzles, even in the presence of a mild sun, and, occasional intermittent rains made the weather a very pleasant one. It had not rained much this season, people were waiting for the mercy from the above. Whenever the clouds appeared on the sky people looked up with prayer and hope.

Chamanbhai was delighted for several reasons-he was coming to his sweet home after proving his worth as a *satyagrahi*, he had received admiration from Jitenbhai, and his fellow *satyagrahis* liked him. As a very special gesture, which was a precious treasure for Chamanbhai, Uma was showing a feeling of care and concern about him. It was a relaxed and pleasant time, which he liked to enjoy.

Chamanbhai's family members and friends were delighted to see him. There was a larger gathering at the *choro*. People asked details of the Flag Satyagrah and his experiences in the Jail. Chamanbhai felt pleasure in describing his experiences. Quite often, it was a repetition for frequent visitors but they enjoyed it, nevertheless.

When Chamanbhai reached home, Bhuvanbhai had been to Borsad in connection with his business. On his return to Ras, Bhuvanbhai brought the bad news that punitive tax has been imposed on the people of the Borsad Taluka. The government was of the view that this was necessary for maintaining additional police force in order to check the sharp rise in robberies in the area.

In the late afternoon, many people from the village gathered at the *choro*. They were all concerned about the indiscriminate imposition of the tax on the people for no fault of theirs. It was the failure of the police and their deliberate connivance with the criminals, which had resulted into sharp rise of crime in the area.

Chamanbhai had heard about some activities concerned with the matter in Nagpur Jail and in Ahmedabad. Even before that, the police had been accusing the *patidars* of the Borsad Taluka for supporting the criminals and giving them shelters in their homes.

Chamanbhai had heard several tales about Babar Deva who was a *Patanvadia* from Golel village. A notorious act known as The Criminal Tribes Act was enforced which required some people to mark their attendance every morning and evening to the *Police Patel.* Even for visiting another village, people were required to take permission from the police. It was said that Babar Deva was falsely implicated in a theft case and jailed. When his mother went to see him she said, "I have four well-built sons. You are here in the jail and the Village *Patel* always coerces and abuses me."

Babar Deva assured his mother that soon her troubles would be over. He escaped jail, came home, killed the Patel and fled. He remained a vagabond and became a ruthless murderer. He did not hesitate to kill even his close relatives. He organised a gang and soon became a terror in Borsad and Anand. The police was unable to protect the people. It tried to hide its inefficiency and connivance by blaming the people for giving shelter to the criminals.

The police had tried to use a dacoit Alia to catch Babar Deva. Alia was a friend of the *mukhi* of Uttarsanda and with his influence; he was provided with a gun by the police on the promise to help the arrest of Babar Deva. This careless action by the police gave a free hand to Alia who liberally used his newly acquired weapon for committing crime. The government failed to control crime in the area. The people believed that the increase in crime is due to the connivance of the police, which was despised for its corruption, rudeness and inefficiency.

Chamanbhai knew that some discussions were going on in this matter and Shri Vallabhbhai had been informed about it. Bhuvanbhai brought more details. He informed that about 400 extra policemen were deployed in Borsad and Anand Talulkas for checking crime. The cost of the deployment had to be borne by the public. A punitive tax of about 2,40,000 was imposed on the people, which amounted to a fine of about Rs. 2.5 on every adult head.

"The first collection will be made in December," He said, "The businessmen of Borsad have already called *hartal.* I could not do much work there. The people of Anand have requested Shri Darbar Gopaldas to do something in the matter."

He saw Ashabhai coming. Ashabhai was looking tired. He had just returned from Borsad and repeated what Bhuvanbhai had said. "Shri Bhogilal Choksi, the President of the Borsad Municipality has offered to resign. We must also do something. Let us write to the government protesting this imposition of fine."

Everybody agreed. Chamanbhai saw an opportunity to help. The people of Ras were eager to sign. The petition was sent with overwhelming support from the villagers.

In the evening Damyanti asked Jivanbhai, "Navratri is coming. Invite Janki to celebrate the festival here."

"Make arrangements. Chamanbhai will go to bring her."

Damyanti and Yashoda lovingly arranged a basket of *khajli*, other homemade sweets, *khakra*, fruits, clothes and other materials for Janki.

Mukundbhai had gone out in connection with his work. An inadequate monsoon had affected his business. The farmers were requesting for advance payments, collection of food grains was also slow and inadequate.

One evening Janki asked Chamanbhai to accompany her to the local temple. It was a festival season and people were busy making preparations for celebrations. A number of devotees were coming for prayers.

Chamanbhai offered his obeisance and waited outside for Janki to return. Suddenly he saw Lakshmiben, Uma and another woman coming. He came forward and greeted them.

"O, Chamabhai! How nice to see you here. When did you come?"

"Yesterday," Chamanbhai replied.

"I also came yesterday. Meet Uma's mother, Gangaben. She knows Janki's family well. Where is Janki?"

"She is offering pooja in the temple."

The ladies went ahead. Chamanbhai watched them going. Suddenly Uma turned her face, looked at him, smiled and proceeded. Chamanbhai responded with a pleasant smile. He waited patiently for another opportunity for exchanging smile with Uma. His patience paid. After sometime, he saw Janki coming with them.

"How long will you be here?" Lakshmiben asked.

"I am waiting for Mukundbhai. I have to take them to Ras," Chamanbhai said.

"Very nice. That's the reason Janki looks so happy," Gangaben commented.

"Come sometime to our home," Janki invited them.

"Will come in a day or two. I also have to return to Ahmedabad soon," Lakshmiben said.

This was all sweet fragrance to Chamanbhai. He was eagerly looking for an opportunity to talk to Uma.

One afternoon the ladies arrived. Janki took them inside. Chamanbhai waited in the gents section of the house. His patience was rewarded. After some time, Uma came and asked for a pen and paper.

"Jankiben needs that." She said with a smile. "They want to note down your home address."

Chamanbhai tried to delay the delivery of these materials which were kept in the drawer. He was sometimes looking at a pen sometimes at a pencil, then pretending to find these again! Uma was watching him closely, containing her smile with much difficulty. She was also in no hurry!

This was a very brief meeting worth several hours. The smile on Uma's lips and the soft gleam on her eyes lit Chamanbhai's heart up.

He asked, "When are you coming to Ahmedabad?"

"Don't know yet. When are you going?" She asked.

Chamanbhai smiled and imitated her "Don't know yet."

Mukundbhai came the next day. He said, "I have some urgent work to finish. I need to go to Ahmedabad for business work. Perhaps it may not be possible for me to come to Ras now."

Chamanbhai was disappointed. He said, "Everybody is waiting for you there. If I return without taking you and Jankiben then they will not allow me to enter home."

Mukundbhai smiled. He thought for a moment and said, "Let me see. Can you go to Borsad and handle some matters there? That will save some time for me, In that case, I can try to reach Ras before Navratri."

He gave a list of works, which included collection of some pending amount from business partners and looking for some new agents in the grain market.

"OK, I will proceed to Borsad. We will meet at Ras," Chamanbhai said.

Chamanbhai tried to finish his work quickly, but Borsad was agog with excitement. People were talking about the punitive tax and about Shri Vallabhbhai's efforts to convince people for not paying it.

The traders were busy in finishing the ongoing transactions because they wanted to prepare themselves for any sudden call for strike. Chamanbhai tried to complete the works assigned by Mukundbhai and informed the progress through a messenger who was going to Ahmedabad.

Shri Vallabhbhai was invited to address a conference in which people from various affected villages were expected to participate. Preparations were afoot and appropriate messages were conveyed to the concerned villages.

This was a God -sent opportunity for him. Senior leaders and Jitenbhai had already arrived. Jitenbhai told him that Shri Vallabhbhai has already studied the entire matter and has cross-checked all the facts. He has also obtained some classified information from the government files.

The Taluka Conference was well attended. Chamanbhai was delighted to listen to a magnificent speech by Shri Vallabhbhai, which was full of facts. Shri Vallabhbhai vividly exposed the callous attitude, misdeeds and connivance of the police and asked why should the innocent people pay for the inefficiency of the police? He emphasised that it was not a question of paying a fine of just Rs. two and a half, it was the false implication of complicity in crime. He then asked whether the people are willing to fight like Mahatmaji's men.

Everybody present raised his hands in affirmation.

Shri Vallabhbhai had also obtained copy of a confidential circular from the police department, which had advised the sub inspectors and head constables to ignore the crimes committed by Alia. It was well known that the *mukhi* of Uttarsanda was not only his friend, he also had a share in the loot! But the police was shamelessly accusing innocent people of giving shelter to the dacoits!

Shri Vallabhbhai asked the people to establish their own volunteer crop for which they were advised to give their names to Shri Durbar Sahab Gopaldas.

People were full of enthusiasm. Chamanbhai returned home preparing to help Jitenbhai and other leaders in launching the *satyagrah*. Now he was himself an experienced *satyagrahi!*

The people of Ras had cast their gloom off. The *choro* was crowded. Everybody was interested in knowing about the details of Shri Vallabhbhai's speech. Ashabhai had not returned, he was busy helping the leaders in their future planning.

Nandubhai said, "Shri Vallabhbhai is always well prepared. He does lot of homework before deciding what to say."

Bhuvanbhai agreed, "Certainly. That is why he is so effective."

This was a right time for Chamanbhai to add something. He said, "Jitenbhai had told me that Shri Vallabhbhai analyses the facts very critically, he does not spare even his trusted colleagues in this matter. He wants the truth to come out. Once convinced, he puts his heart and soul in his task."

Nandubhai commented, "After all, he is an accomplished Barrister. He examines the facts carefully and argues forcefully."

He looked at Chamanbhai and said, "More work awaits you, Chamanbhai."

"But now it is time to celebrate *navratri*," Jeevanbhai said.

Mukundbhai, Janki and their children arrived the next day. Damyanti, Yashoda and other persons in the house took her inside singing sweet songs. They and other ladies in the neighbourhood were very happy to see Janki. Like her, some childhood friends of Janki had also come to Ras to celebrate *navratri*. The village was drenched into the festive mood.

Damyanti and Yashoda had already made preparations for a joyful celebration. Colourful dresses were stitched or purchased for all members of the family and dependents. Special *garba* earthen pots were painted artistically and betel nuts, some coins and coconut were placed inside. Every evening a lamp was lit inside the *garba*.

The *choro* and its surrounding areas were well decorated. The entire village was in *navratri* mood. Every evening, the women danced *garba and* the men *ras* which had martial overtones. Sometimes they mixed it with *dandia*. The dancing circles expanded and contracted in a delightfully smooth manner.

Chapti bhari chaukha ne ghee no che divdo
He srifal nee jod laee ne halo halo Pavaagadh
Same nee pol thee malido aave
Aye, gajra nee jod laee ne halo halo Pavagadh
Same nee pol thee dosido aave
Aye, chundri nee jod laee ne halo halo Pavagadh
Same nee pol thee kumhree aave
*Aye, maata ne garbo laee ne halo halo Pavagadh**

The beating of musical instruments and the singing of traditional songs created a highly enjoyable environment of devotion, family love and entertainment.

The women sang sweet devotional songs in praise of *amba or matajee.* As the festival progressed, more items were added. Some songs depicted the plight of woman, some described the rudeness of a difficult mother-in-law in a light manne. Humour was also mixed in some songs. Young unmarried girls of ages not more than 10 or 12 moved from house to house in a group carrying a *garba* on their head. They were respected and well treated.

The ten days were tiring but thoroughly enjoyable. The woman, though fasting for most of the days, were full of enthusiasm and were imbued with devotion.

During these days, Chamanbhai forgot about his work, he just enjoyed the festival –its message of love, joy and devotion.

One afternoon Janki told Jeevanbhai that Uma's parents are interested in marrying her to Chamanbhai. She briefed him about their family.

"How is the girl?" asked Damyanti.

Janki said, "She is good looking, not very fair, but quite attractive. Her eyes are shining and she has an innocent look. She takes care of her parents and helps her mother in household chores."

---

* *Take a spoonful of rice, an earthen lamp of ghee and a coconut and come to Pavagadh. From the neighbourhood, the gardener comes and brings a pair of garlands. Take all these and come to Pavagadh. From the neighbourhood, the cloth merchant comes and brings a chunri for the mother. Take it and come to Pavagadh. From the neighbourhood, the potter's wife comes and brings a pair of garbos. Take that and come to Pavagadh.*
(See Appendix for the Hindi text).

Damyanti and Yashoda showed interest in the proposal.

Janki added, "And she is very good at spinning. Her friends are members of the *satyagrahi* group which does picketing at liquor shops, and foreign clothes shop. Recently she had been to Ahmedabad with her relatives and friends for picketing."

Damyanti smiled, "She can teach us spinning."

"But Chamanbhai had said that he does not want to marry!" Yashoda remarked.

"Go on listening such falsehood! Once he sees the bride, he will be eager to marry the same day," Damyanti smiled.

"Chamanbhai has already seen Uma and I feel he likes her," Janki said.

"The boys from Ras are very smart!" Yashoda commented.

"Then ask her parents to come with proposal," Damyanti suggested.

Uma's parents acted quickly. The *Gol Dhana* ceremony was performed in a simple manner. Both families felt satisfied at the new relationship.

Chamanbhai was initially not in favour of marrying at this time. He was apprehensive that the marriage will distract him from being a *satyagrahi*, but when he met Uma, he felt that she is the girl for him. Uma followed the same ideals. She would be a very suitable life partner in fighting for the freedom of the country. Sentiments and reasoning both favoured the alliance.

Uma thanked God for His blessing in arranging a good match for her. She had no choice in choosing or rejecting a proposal-her opinion did not matter. It was the decision of her parents. She might have got a businessperson from Nadiad or any other place as her husband. Her desire to serve as a *satyagrahi* might have been crushed in its infancy. But in Chamanbhai, she is going to have an ideal husband-wedded to the same life which she wants to pursue. He has got blessings and support from his family. This is an ideal environment for her.

She thanked the shopkeeper at Ahmedabad who was selling liquor from the back door. Had he not arranged the police to use force, she would not have been able to meet Chamanbhai. Now she was assured of getting full support from her would-be husband and his family. They all admire her ideal-Shri Vallabhbhai. Life was worth living, working and enjoying. Providence had also given her an opportunity to join the struggle for self-respect which will ultimately bring freedom for the country.

10

Jitenbhai was very pleased at the engagement of his two energetic lieutenants, "There could not have been a better match for both of you. I am delighted. My hands are further strengthened. You and Uma will feel more joy and enthusiasm in actively participating in the struggle for self-respect and freedom."

He continued, "There is work at hand. Shri Vallabhbhai is going to address the Provincial Committee at Borsad on the 1st December. He is expected to guide us for our future action."

The Taluka Conference was well attended. The *pandal* was full and many people were waiting outside to listen to their respected leader. Shri Vallabhbhai spoke from his heart. He knew the people, their patois, their colloquial style and their favourite proverbs. He was able to resonate their inner cords. He asked them to fight for self-respect and honour. He also excelled as a competent barrister who knew the twist and camouflage of legal strategies. He analysed the situation threadbare, tore apart the bureaucratic steel frame and led the people as a courageous fighter. Shri Vallabhbhai was there at his brilliant best. He held the government responsible for the atrocities committed by Alia. He said that the opposition to the punitive fine is not for the sake of the paltry amount of Rs. 2 and 8 *annas*, it is against the government view of branding the innocent people as criminals or accomplice.

Shri Vallabhbhai exposed the dubious role of the police. He cautioned the people that police may retort with vengeance and may provoke them to become violent. He said that the government is unable to capture an outlaw and a notorious criminal Babar Deva, but it will not have any difficulty in arresting innocent peasants. He kept on reminding them to always remember Gandhiji's principles of non-violence.

The people decided to respond to Shri Vallabhbhai's call and resolved that they will not pay the tax. The no-tax campaign was very efficiently organised under Shri Vallabhbhai's guidance. The police had set up special stations for tax realisation and confiscation. They were resorting to all sorts of means to recover the fine.

The headquarter for the *satyagrah* campaign was set up at Borsad under the leadership of Shri Darbar Gopaldas, publicity work was assigned to Shri Mohanlal Pandya. Volunteers were deputed for each group of villages who used to caution the people when they saw the police arriving to recover tax. The people had decided that anyone buying any attached property will be fined Rs. 50. Every day, two bulletins were issued which gave the details of the campaign. It named the villages where the authorities attempted to collect tax, mentioned whether any timid person tried to pay and whether the police have been able to take away any utensils, cattle or other movable property. The bulletin also described how the brave woman had responded when the police wanted to confiscate their goods.

Chamanbhai was assigned the task of distribution of the bulletin, which was read to the people at *choro* and was distributed to several houses. The police tried to trouble the peasants who came to sell their items at the Borsad bazar. The people decided to close the bazar during the day, it was opened at night.

Shri Vallabhbhai addressed several meetings, boosting the morale of the people and asking them to remain steadfast. The people responded well. They were united. When some weak heart paid the tax out of fear, the person was asked to pay fine. Even junior government functionaries refused to take out utensils and other items from the homes of the poor peasants. The government's plans to confiscate property failed. Although the *satyagrah* was launched soon after the Flag Struggle, the response was overwhelming.

The Government of Bombay, which had kept itself aloof, now came to defend the imposition of the punitive tax through a statement, which was torn apart threadbare by Shri Vallabhbhai. The anger of the people against the government mounted. Shri Vallabhbhai also made a very effective speech in Bombay in which he mentioned that he has copies of official documents in his possession, which prove the charge of police-criminal nexus beyond doubt. His speech was well published in the newspapers. On reading the report, the new

Governor of Bombay, Sir Leslie Wilson asked the Home Member, Sir Maurice Hayward to visit Borsad and get a first-hand impression of the situation there. One hundred fifty people were chosen to meet Sir Hayward. Among them was Rambhai Fakirbhai Patel–a colleague of Shri Vallabhbhai from Karamsad.

More than 2000 people gathered near the Home Member's camp. The 150 leaders went in a procession to the Vinay Mandir and then joined the meeting. Rambhai strongly and bravely narrated the inefficiency and arrogance of the police. He said that their complaints to the authorities have not been even replied.

Rambhai quoted several instances of harassment by the police. Pointing the finger at the Deputy Superintendent of Police, he said that two days ago, he had visited a village called Nisraya and had threatened the people that if they do not pay, he will send the goons, who have come from Jhalund, to their village. The police officer tried to save his face by telling that he had said that if the villagers do not pay, the additional police force will be removed and then the outlaws will be free to rob them.

On hearing this, a peasant from Nisraya got up and said that this was a false statement. There was no police force in his village, which the officer threatened to remove!

Rambhai also said that if the police continue to act and behave in this manner, not only the outlaws would have a free time, new criminals will also be created. He referred to the government announcement that Alia was arrested from the jungle of Uttarsanda. But there was no such jungle near Uttarsanda. In fact, Alia was arrested from the house of his friend. Inspector Maganlal who was a personal friend of the goons.

The Home member asked the police what steps they have taken to arrest the outlaws? In response, the Superintendent of Police read the names of 30 to 40 people whom they had arrested. On hearing the names, Rambhai said that none of them was known to be a criminal.

After narrating these instances, Rambhai said that the people can afford to pay the amount, they are not paying because this is a matter of principle.

Chamanbhai felt very satisfied at the proceedings. People were no longer afraid of telling the truth even at the face of the police officers. They made it clear that they are fighting for a cause, against the misdeeds of the police. Chamanbhai and other workers were very happy that Shri Vallabhbhai had organised the no-tax campaign efficiently. His colleague Rambhai had argued their case very convincingly.

Thanks to the brave resistance from the people, on 8 January, the government declared the withdrawal of the punitive tax and decided to pay the cost of the police deployment from the government revenue.

After this decision, Shri Vallabhbhai announced the successful end of the Borsad Struggle. He held it as a victory for truth and non-violence in which both parties have come out victorious.

A huge meeting was held on 12 January at Borsad to celebrate the victory. The organisers had anticipated a gathering of about 5000 to 6000 people, but the crowd swelled to more than 25,000. Women were also present in a large number.

In his speech, Shri Vallabhbhai showed his magnanimity. He congratulated the people for their courage, unity and adherence to non-violence. He said that this struggle has been successfully concluded, but the greater struggle for freedom lies ahead. The people are welcome to celebrate the victory, but they should also invite police and other government officials to their celebrations. They should forget all bitterness and maintain friendly terms with them.

Shri Vallabhbhai also emphasised upon the need to create an atmosphere in the villages in which no outlaw can survive. He called upon the outlaws to leave the evil career and advised them to become peace-loving citizen.

Shri Vallabhbhai and other leaders went to various villages, they thanked the people for their support and congratulated them for the success of the struggle.

The Borsad Struggle continued for two months and eight days. During this period, Chamanbhai visited several villages and found that the people were adopting a simple, pious life. They were becoming conscious of the need to fight for their self-respect and were prepared to make sacrifices for the struggle of independence.

During the Borsad Satyagrah, Mahatmaji was in Jail. Shri Vallabhbhai's competent handling of the *satyagrah* proved that Gandhiji's principles of non-violence have reached the masses and they can remain non-violent even when he is not personally present to lead them.

When Gandhiji was released from jail, he was operated upon for appendicitis at the Sasson Hospital, Poona by Surgeon General Col Maddock. After Gandhiji's release on the 1st February, Shri Vallabhbhai went to meet him. Welcoming him, Gandhiji said, *"Welcome, the King of Borsad."*

Chamanbhai understood that now Borsad is ready for adopting and promoting Gandhiji's message of truth and non-violence. Many outlaws in the area had responded to Shri Vallabhbhai's call, had shun criminal acts and were now leading a normal life. Occasionally there was a welcome change in the behaviour of police and administrative personnel. Gandhiji and Shri Vallabhbhai were very satisfied with the development.

In a message, Gandhiji hailed the success of the Borsad Satyagrah. He said that by its sacrifices and by its successful *satyagrah,* Borsad has rendered magnificent service both to itself and to the country. He then called upon the people of the Borsad Taluka to use only home spun *Khadi* for their clothing. He also urged the people of Borsad to quit all kinds of intoxication-alcohol, opium, tobacco or drugs. He exhorted them to shun untouchability and to create a situation in which there is no theft and there are no disputes.

Later, Jitenbhai showed him an article written by Gandhiji in *the Young India* in which he had paid rich tributes to Shri Vallabhbhai and had admired his administrative and organisational skills. He had also praised him for preparing a band of devoted and capable workers.

Gandhiji had written, *"The Borsad Satyagrah is a magnificent example of public activity governed wholly by public considerations. The Borsad Satyagrah was in many ways superior to that at Kheda. In Borsad, there was a complete victory for the Satyagraha; honour was vindicated and the object was achieved after a straight struggle."*

"Be ready Chamanbhai, Borsad is going to be an important centre of constructive work," Jitenbhai commented.

11

Chamanbhai and Uma were married in a simple ceremony. There was no pomp and show. Most of the decorations at Ras and Nadiad were done by their satyagrahi colleagues. Grace and decency was evident everywhere. But the womenfolk were full of enthusiasm –they were singing delightful songs expressing their emotions during various ceremonies. Damyanti, Yashoda and other relatives created and maintained a very happy environment in their house. Songs and laughters drew everybody in a very pleasant mood.

The mood was different at Nadiad. The joy of a decent family union was also mixed with the sorrow of separation. Jitenbhai and some other workers came from Ahmedabad to participate in the function. Jitenbhai brought a message of blessings from Shri Vallabh-bhai who asked them to come to Ahmedabad when convenient.

Relatives of both sides were very happy and were enjoying the rituals. The signature of simplicity was evident during the functions. The food was simple and delicious. No drinks were served. Uma's friends affectionately presented khadi dresses made by the yarns spun by them. In the same manner, Jitenbhai and Chamanbhai's fellow satyagrahis also presented khadi dresses to Chamanbhai.

Mukundbhai knew many persons from both sides. Though Uma's mother and her other relatives were finding it difficult to control their tears, they came to thank him and Janki for their help in the negotiations.

Mukundbhai said, "Thank Jitenbhai. He is the main person who deserves our thanks! Now he is going to be a marriage negotiator for his colleagues."

A woman said, "We need such negotiators everywhere. Request Vallabhbhai to train some more disciples like Jitenbhai for this purpose."

Jitenbhai said, "Look around, you will find that everybody is very happy at the marriage of two of my favourite workers."

He glanced at the persons present and found Uma's mother and some other ladies weeping! He drew the attention of Mukundbhai and asked, "Jitenbhai, do you know how many types of tears are shed ?"

Mukundbhai said, "I know about two kinds of tears-tears of joy and tears of sorrow."

Jitenbhai asked, "Any other type?"

"I think we can classify all kinds of tears in these two categories," Mukundbhai answered.

"There is one more type Mukundbhai. See the tears in the eyes of Uma. We cannot say whether these are tears of joy or sorrow! When a young bride leaves her paternal house, she weeps her heart out, at the same time, if she is married to a person whom she likes she feels happy at her good fortune. Then the fear of the unknown-the response to her arrival in her new home and the burden of new responsibilities makes her heart heavy. The tears coming out at that time are caused by a combination of these emotions."

Mukundbhai said, "Advocates can find argument for every occasion Jitenbhai!"

Uma's relatives and friends gave her an affectionate send-off. Elders had given her several advices, married friends-practical tips. Amidst the load of these do's and donts there was an undercurrent of confidence in Chamanbhai. He is a nice person-the family must be like him. By God's grace all will go well.

And so it happened. Uma was very pleased with the warm and affectionate welcome she received in her new home at Ras. Relatives and other women from the village used to come quite frequently. Uma had heard some good compliments about her. When a relative congratulated Chamanbhai on acquiring such a good wife, Chamanbhai asked him, "How do you say that she is going to be a good wife?"

The woman smiled, *"Dikra na lakshan paarana ma, ane vav na lakshan ma."**

Uma saw that there is harmony in her home. She attributed it to Damyanti. The eldest daughter-in-law has to show the way by making

* *Child's nature can be seen in his cradle, daughter-in-laws nature can be understood when she steps in the house.*

sacrifices for maintaining love and understanding in the family. Damyanti and Yashoda were treating each other like sisters. She has to quickly make herself as the third member of the team in a completely harmoneous manner.

Chamanbhai felt that there was no need to advise her on these matters. Uma is aware of her responsibilities. All family members were quite happy at her charming manners and her sweet nature. Uma and Chamanbhai did not realise how quickly the affectionate rays of a new morning sun greeted them.

Now it was the time to go to Ahmedabad. Another phase of meetings and greetings kept them occupied. Jitenbhai gave them some practical advice. He suggested that both of them should promote spinning and use of *Khadi* in Ras and nearby villages. They could take *Khadi* and village products from Ahmedabad and sell these items to the villagers. This will bring some money to them and broaden the base of *satyagrahis* and well-wishers.

Upon their request, Jitenbhai took them to Shri Vallabhbhai who expressed his happiness at their marriage. He said, "Now both of you can work together and promote Gandhiji's message of the Constructive Programme among the people. We have to prepare them for the bigger struggle."

He gave them some *Khadi* clothes and local sweets. He asked them to follow the advice of Jitenbhai. "We will call you here when required," He said.

This was a memorable day for the young couple. At the beginning of their conjugal life, they were blessed by their idol whom they adored. Chamanbhai said, "From the outside, Shri Vallabhbhai appears a very strict person but he is like a coconut-under the hard and strong shell, there is a tender white fruit and pure juice of love."

Jitenbhai introduced them to the suppliers of the spinning wheel and other related products.

"You are entering a new phase of your life. At the beginning of your conjugal life, you have been affectionately blessed by our leader. This is very special. You are lucky!"

Jitenbhai informed that in order to become a member of the congress, 2000 yards of handspun yarn should be sent every month to the Congress Committee.

"Uma is very good at spinning. Both of you can easily meet this requirement," Jitenbhai said.

This was a new interesting life for Uma and Chamanbhai. They had not imagined that the conjugal life is imbued with so much of sweetness and joy. They had enjoyed love and affection in their respective families, but this was an entirely different kind of experience. A strong feeling for taking care of each other filled their lives with love. At the same time, Uma was always conscious about her duties towards the family members who warmly responded to her affectionate gestures. Jivanbhai's and Bhuvanbhai's children quickly became closely attached to her.

Chamanbhai brought some literature about Gandhiji's Constructive Programme and started discussing his views with Uma. This was also a current topic of discussion at the *choro.* His ideas of rural development raised hopes of a better life for the farmers. People were getting interested in revival of village industries and in enhancing agriculture production. They were also realising the importance of education and were more inclined to send their children to national schools. *Khadi* promotion was a key element of the programme.

As a newly married *bahu*, Uma was not allowed to move out for a few days. Chamanbhai started visiting some villages.

The people of Borsad Taluka gave an enthusiastic response to the Constructive Programme. Uma and Chamanbhai taught spinning, sold the required materials and encouraged them to live a simple life.

One day Chamanbhai received a message from Jitenbhai. He was coming to Borsad and wanted Chamanbhai and Uma to meet him there.

Borsad was vibrant with activities. People were wearing *Khadi* and a variety of rural products were on sale. A happy Jitenbhai welcomed them. "You see, Borsad is very active. People are coming here from many places for education or business. *Khadi* and village industries' products have lot of potential."

He continued, "Shri Vallabhbhai is very interested in launching a programme in Borsad for *gram sevaks*. He desires that every village should have *gram sevaks* who should promote the constructive programme vigorously. I want both of you to join the programme."

Chamanbhai asked, "Will it be similar to the programme run by the Gujarat Rashtriya Sevak Mandal?"

He was referring to a training programme which was launched in Ahmedabad under the guidance of Shri Indulal Yajnik. After a good start, the programme could not be continued. People had lost interest in the programme after the postponement of the non-cooperation movement. Chamanbhai was apprehensive-whether this programme will also meet the same fate!

Jitenbhai understood the motive of the question. He replied, "This is a special programme for the Borsad Taluka and Shri Vallabhbhai is very keen to launch it. Persons trained under this programme will live in villages and promote the Constructive Programme. The programme is also aimed at generating rural income. It will give a much needed boost to the rural economy and will enhance the self-esteem of the villagers."

Since Shri Vallabhbhai had launched the programme of *gram sevak* and *gram sevika*, there was no need to ask any further question.

Chamanbhai and Uma enrolled themselves for a one-year term. They became devoted *gram sevak and sevika.* Uma concentrated on spinning and rural handicraft work for woman. She trained young girls and women and helped them to improve the quality of their work.

Chamanbhai used to take the collected yarns and other products to Borsad and other places. He also brought raw materials and accessories for distribution in the village. Life was busy and interesting.

Interest in the Constructive Programme was growing. Side by side, there was a focus on promoting moral values. Chamanbhai was frequently travelling to several villages. He found that the people were becoming more sober, there were fewer quarrels and the crime level was coming down.

Uma's dedicated work and her affectionate personality won her many admirers. Young girls were eager to acquire new skills. They were designing and preparing attractive handicrafts. The number of woman and girls in spinning sessions also increased. The work was strenuous and demanding. This was in addition to Uma's daily household chores. She was always eager to give a hand to Damyanti and Yashoda. Quite often she felt exhausted. One afternoon she fainted in the spinning class. Yashoda was also spinning there. She and other women rushed and lied her down. After some time they brought her home.

Later in the evening they asked Chamanbhai, "She had fainted today. Don't ask her to work hard, she is going to become a mother."

When the joyous occasion came, Chamanbhai's happiness was boundless. He had become a father of a lovely son! The joy of becoming a mother was glowing on Uma's lovely face. For several days, the family enjoyed sweet songs, music and fun. Most of their kindred lived in the nearby places-they came, stayed for two-three day and enjoyed the functions.

It was Saturday, July 23, 1927. It had been raining cats and dogs almost continuously for several days. By evening, the heavens poured with abundant generosity and the intensity of the rains increased in the entire Kheda district. The unprecedented and uninterrupted rainfall for about a week created havoc in many places. Several villages were flooded with knee-deep water. Many mud houses were washed away, several trees were uprooted and a number of cattle were lost. Scores of people climbed to the trees and spent days and nights in emergent co-existence with snakes and other animals.

Many other parts of Gujarat were also affected but Kheda was the hardest hit. Shri Vallabhbhai was mobilising food, clothes and other items of daily needs and was sending the items by train. Volunteers were deputed to collect and distribute them. Chamanbhai and his friends worked hard. Often wading into knee-deep water, they brought food and essential supplies to the affected people. Relief materials were even sent to the Collector of Kheda who was marooned at his bungalow!

Shri Vallabhbhai called a meeting of Volunteers at Anand on August 11 with a view to organise relief to the people who had become homeless, had lost cattle and property and did not have clothes to wear. A programme for providing relief and rehabilitation was finalised.

Soon relief material was organised. Special grain and cloth shops were opened to counter hoarding and price rise. Chamanbhai and his team worked tirelessly to implement the programme. They were successful in training a number of people-young and old, men and women in various *Khadi* and village industry related works. Inspired by Shri Vallabhbhai, the band of trained workers was ready and willing to fight for *self-respect which will ultimately lead to swaraj.*

One day, Bhuvanbhai returned from a short business trip to Surat. He said that people in the area are adopting *Khadi* in a big way.

Opportunities are available for opening a Khadi shop in Bardoli. One of his business contacts had offered him a newly constructed shop for this purpose at a reasonable rent. Opening a khadi and village industries shop will also serve the cause of the nation.

Bardoli was quite active in the Civil Disobedience Movement. Shri Kalyanji and his brother Shri Kunvarji had invited Gandhiji to Bardoli in 1921. Gandhiji had selected it as the first place for launching the movement. Local centres were set up at Bardoli, Vankaner, Valad and Sarbhon for progressing the work.

Bhuvanbhai sought Jivanbhai's permission. He argued that the shop would open new avenues for the next generation. Soon, agriculture alone will not be able to fully meet the needs of the family and additional sources of income will have to be explored. Though Bardoli Taluka was quite far from Borsad, it was a good place for doing business. Jivanbhai agreed with the proposal. The brothers decided that initially Jivanbhai and Chamanbhai would go to Bardoli to set up the business.

Chamanbhai made a quick visit to Ahmedabad and consulted Jitenbhai on the matter. Jitenbhai readily gave his consent and said that Bardoli will also be a good place for Chamanbhai and Uma for progressing the constructive programme.

"Both of you are devoted workers. You will like the work of promoting *Khadi* and village industry there. I have also heard that the government has conducted a revenue assessment for the Bardoli Taluka and has fixed a highly unreasonable assessment. Some complaint in the matter has already been made to Shri Vallabhbhai. Who knows-you and Uma may have to do more work there. Go ahead."

Jitenbhai also helped Bhuvanbhai in establishing business contacts in Ahmedabad.

"I hope to come Bardoli soon. Good luck." He said.

Setting up a small *Khadi* business was no problem-the supplies were streamlined and local retail chain was being established. People were gradually adopting the Constructive Programme. Almost the entire Taluka had shunned mill-made clothes, many woman were wearing saris prepared from the yarn spun by them and family members. Uma found it very convenient to get involved with the women's group. She met some previous acquaintances also. Her spinning class was quickly organised.

Bhuvanbhai took care of the shop, Chamanbhai helped with sourcing and marketing. He soon established useful contacts in Bardoli and neighbouring areas.

The business was progressing. Little did they realise that Jitenbhai was almost prophetic when he said that perhaps more work awaits them in Bardoli area!

12

Jitenbhai arrived Bardoli with a couple of workers from Ahmedabad. He called a meeting of local workers, which Chamanbhai attended. Jitenbhai explained that the settlement of the land in Bardoli Taluka, which is done every 30 years, was due in 1926. The settlement work was done by an officer of the state civil service, Mr. Jaykar, who recommended an increase of 25% in the existing rates and also reclassified 23 villages from a lower tax category to a higher one. The total increase for the Taluka was about 30%. Mr. Jaykar had cited several reasons in support of the enhancement, which included improved communication due to opening of the broad gauge of the Tapti Valley Railway, increase of population by about 4,000, increase in the number of milch cattle, rise in prices of food grains, rise in wages, rise in land prices etc.

In an act typical of the then, *"I know it all, obey me without questioning"* attitude of the bureaucracy, the report was not disseminated to the public, instead, a copy of report was kept at the *kachehri* which the farmers could refer. When congress leaders offered to pay for a copy, they were not allowed to have one, they were, however, permitted to take notes in the *kachehri*.

Some peasants represented their case to the Revenue Member who did not pay any attention to their petition. Several other representations and a threadbare analysis of Mr. Jaykar's report bringing out its fallacies and contradictions also failed to solicit any positive response from the government. The farmers' argument that Mr. Jaykar had not visited the villages, he had prepared the report based on the *talati's* recommendations, also failed on deaf ears.

Jitenbhai explained, "Now the people of Bardoli know that the government will not listen to their representations. Khushalbhai, the

Secretary of the Taluka Congress Committee and the two devoted local representatives Kalyanji and Kunvarji had met Shri Vallabhbhai and had requested him to lead a *satyagrah* in Bardoli for bringing the attention of the government to the farmers' plight. Shri Vallabhbhai asked them to go back to the farmers and explain to them the risk and hardships involved and the consequences of launching and continuing a *satyagrah*. The government was unlikely to yield easily. He warned, *'The government will resort to oppressive measures of all sorts, will take away their cattle, utensils and other immovable property and threaten them with attachment notices for their land.'*

Jitenbhai informed that accordingly, the representatives had visited several villages and conveyed Shri Vallabhbhai's message to them. Most of the people were determined to bear the consequences, very few of them wanted to pay the assessment at the old rate.

After assessing the mood of the people and their readiness to offer the *satyagrah,* the representatives again met Shri Vallabhbhai along with his trusted and respected colleagues Shri Darbar Sahib Gopaldas, Shri Ravishankarji Maharaj and Shri Mohanlal Pandya. He listened carefully, asked several cross-questions and then sought Gandhiji's advice on the matter.

Gandhiji listened to the details, discussed the matter with Shri Vallbhbhai and said, *"There is nothing more to consider. Go ahead, Victory to Gujarat."*

Jitenbhai explained the mind of Shri Vallabhbhai." He wants to be convinced that the peasants are fully prepared to wage a long campaign, which will call for immense forbearance and enormous sacrifices. He is coming here to address a meeting of farmers."

Before presiding over the meeting, Shri Vallabhbhai met the workers and sought their opinion on the matter. Chamanbhai was also present in the meeting. Some workers requested him to directly talk to the representatives of the villages before taking any final decision. Agreeing to their advice, Shri Vallabhbhai discussed the matter with the representatives of 79 villages. He cross-examined them thoroughly.

Addressing the Conference, Shri Vallabhbhai explained the details of the assessment order. He said that the settlement decided by the government was unfair and was based on wrong assumptions. However, this sound logic alone was not sufficient to ensure the success. The farmers had to be convinced of their strength. He asked, *"Are the people prepared to take part in along non-violent struggle against a mighty government which can deploy huge government machinery to crush the movement ?The matter will not be confined to just Bardoli Taluka alone, it will also involve other talukas and perhaps the entire nation."*

Shri Vallabhbhai asked the people to think over the matter for about a week and then decide whether they are really prepared to launch the *satyagrah* or not. Meanwhile, he will try to persuade the government to reconsider their request of conducting an impartial inquiry. Three members of the legislative council, who were present in the Conference, said that they have already exhausted all constitutional means available but have failed to convince the government.

Chamanbhai knew the mood of the people. The young workers were full of enthusiasm and wanted to take the plunge. He himself was very keen to join the *satyagrah.*

On his return to Ahmedabad, Shri Vallabhbhai wrote a letter to the Governor, which explained the situation. Shri Vallabhbhai requested appointment of an independent tribunal. He showed his anxiety for avoiding a conflict with the government. He clarified that if this was not done, he will be left with no other alternative but to advise the people not to pay the revised assessment and peacefully face the consequence of their refusal. Shri Vallabhbhai said that he will wait upon him for discussing the matter, if the Governor so desired.

The letter was replied in a typical bureaucratic fashion. The Private Secretary to the Governor replied Shri Vallabhbhai that his letter has been sent to the Revenue Department for consideration and disposal.

Chamanbhai visited several villages. Everywhere he found people discussing the *satyagrah*. Their trust in Shri Vallabhbhai's leadership was enormous and they were eager to prove it to him.

Came 11th February, Shri Vallabhbhai did not receive any reply. The due date for the realisation of payment, 15th February was approaching fast. Shri Vallabhbhai met the representatives of the villagers on the 12th February in an interactive session. Many farmers had sent their signed pledge through their representatives. The people of Chorasai Talukawere also subjected to unfair assessment done by the same officer. They requested Shri Vallabhbhai to allow them join their Bardoli brethren for *satyagrah*. Shri Vallabhbhai declined. He said that it was difficult for him to handle *satyagrah* in two talukas but he felt that if the struggle in Bardoli succeeds, Chorasai would get the same relief.

Chamanbhai listened to his speech with interest and admiration. Shri Vallabhbhai inspired the audience in brave words. He said that the only asset the people have with them for fighting an insensitive and authoritative government is their own determination and their capacity to face the suffering inflicted by the government.

Chamanbhai's heart became full of admiration for Shri Vallabhbhai when he said, *"It is not a question of some money, it is a matter of self-respect."*

A resolution was adopted to refuse payment of the revised assessment; until *the government is ready to accept the old rates towards full settlement, or until the government appoints an impartial tribunal, to settle the issues on the basis of an on the spot investigation and inquiry.*

Recitations from the holy Koran and the Ramayan followed. The resolution was adopted in a solemn environment.

A huge task lied ahead for Shri Vallabhbhai. He and his colleagues were well aware that the government would try to drive a wedge among different communities by adopting various means. In addition, funds were needed to run the struggle.

Shri Vallabhbhai showed great organisational skills and a down-to-earth practical approach in organising the campaign. Initially four centres were set up-at Bardoli, Madhi, Vedchchi and Sarbhon. Each centre was placed in charge of competent people and well known leaders like Shri Ravishankarji Maharaj, Shri Mohanlal Pandya, Dr. Tribhuvandas, Shri Chunilal Mehta, Shrimati Mehta and others. Shri Jugatram Dave was made in charge of the publicity unit. In the bulletin, important news of the day and Shri Vallabhbhai's speeches were published. For about a week, the bulletin was cyclostyled but arrangements were soon made to get the bulletin printed at Surat.

Later, additional centres were opened at several places. Although Shri Vallabhbhai did not give a call for volunteers, people were coming forward on their own to offer their services. Swami Anand came to help Shri Vallabhbhai and worked in a very devoted manner as his private secretary during the entire period of *satyagrah.*

Chamanbhai was anxious to get actively involved in the *satyagrah.* He helped in distribution of the bulletin and explained the contents to the people in the villages. He got an excellent opportunity to listen to the inspiring and sometimes fiery speeches by Shri Vallabhbhai and other leaders.

Although the people had signed the pledge and had given assurance for remaining steadfast, it was essential to forge unity among the various groups. The marriage season was in the offing and people were preparing for celebrations in an unperturbed manner. Perhaps they thought that since difficult days of struggle lie ahead, they should enjoy *this* marriage season to their satisfaction.

Shri Mohanlal Pandya who had visited many villages to raise awakening among the people was disappointed. He wanted the people to avoid show and pomp which may dilute the *satyagrah* mood.

Shri Vallabhbhai advised the people to quickly solemnise the marriage ceremonies in a simple manner and prepare themselves for the *satyagrah*. He cautioned the people that in order to avoid attachment, they might have to lock their doors, go out during the day and return only in the evening. They will have to show solidarity. They should ensure that when the government officials come for confiscating their properties, they receive no co-operation from the people. They should not be able to get any manual labour even for taking away the confiscated property such as their cattle, utensils and other household goods. He called upon the *mukhis, patels, talatis* and other government officials to be bravely tell the government that the honour of their village is their honour. He said that their face should show the glow of determination and the fragrance of independence should pervade in the environment.

These inspiring thoughts were close to Chamanbhai's heart. He found a resonance of his feelings in many other young and old men and women in the villages. True, they wanted to celebrate the marriage functions with gaiety, yet they were always conscious of their responsibilities and the pledge. Shri Vallabhbhai had been consistently advising them to fight for self-respect and honour.

Shri Vallabhbhai reminded them of the fact that Gandhiji had chosen Bardoli as the first taluka for commencing the Civil Disobedience Movement. They were prepared to fight a battle for the freedom of the country. Now here is a smaller local challenge, which gives them an opportunity to show that they are capable of fighting the bigger battle for India's independence.

Shri Vallabhbhai asked them to forget their petty differences and stand united in the struggle. He insisted that the government will try its best to crush the movement by hook or crook, only the strong rock of their unity will stand out stoutly against all such attempts.

On February 17, Shri Vallabhbhai received the response to his letter which was sent to the Revenue Department for consideration and disposal. It was bluntly replied that *the government is not prepared either to postpone the collection or to reconsider the revised rates or to give any kind of relief.* The curt reply even thundered-*although this is well-known, if the people of Bardoli whether on their own initiative; or on the advice of "outsiders," fail to pay up the land revenue, the Governor-in-Council will not have the slightest hesitation in taking whatever steps they are entitled to take under the Land Revenue Code ...*"

The rude reply from the Revenue Secretary, Mr. Smyth, who referred Shri Vallabhbhai and his colleagues as *outsiders,* deserved a befitting answer. Shri Vallabhbhai was however more polite in responding than the letter deserved. He clearly said, "You regard me and my colleagues as outsiders, I am helping my own people and am bringing to light *your* misdeeds. *You are forgetting that you speak on behalf of a government which is composed mainly of outsiders.*"

Shri Vallabhbhai reminded him– "Though *I claim to belong as much to Bardoli as to any other part of India, I have come to Bardoli at the request of the distressed people of the Taluka* and *it is open to them to tell me to clear out at any moment.*"

This was a reply similar to the one which Mahatma Gandhi had given to the District Magistrate of Champaran Mr. W. B. Heycock when he had ordered Gandhiji to leave the district.

Shri Vallabhbhai further added candidly, *"How much nicer had it been if they had it in their power equally easily to dispense with the administration of foreigners which has been sapping their vitality and which is maintained in power by force of arms."*

Not unexpectedly, Mr. Smyth was livid with rage and he wrote another arrogant reply. Later, after taking permission from the government, Shri Vallabhbhai sent the entire correspondence for publication.

Chamanbhai came to know that the government has issued notices to some people at Valod. He went there and found out that notices were served on 15 prominent people for making payment of the full assessment. They were also warned that the defaulters would have to pay a fine of 25%.

Valod was a soft target. The local government officials also intimidated and even physically assaulted poor farmers. Some middle-level functionaries tried to persuade them for making even a token payment. Attempts were made to hoodwink the co-villagers by clandestinely giving them own money and taking back from them in presence of a number of people to demonstrate that the amount has been collected.

However, such tactics failed to demoralise the people. Two persons had paid the assessment out of fear, but public sentiment became very strong against them. The people wanted to boycott them. Shri Vallabhbhai tried to pacify the angry villagers reminding them that violence has no place in *satyagrah*. But the people were in no mood to treat them with warmth. They despised their action.

The two persons, who had paid out of fear, tendered a public apology and promised that they will not pay the balance amount. One of them even made a contribution of Rs. 800 towards the Satyagrah Fund on his own volition. Later, the other person also contributed an amount of Rs. 651. These contributions were made as an act of penance. This was a clear sign of following Gandhiji's advice on *satyagrah*.

Chamanbhai and his colleagues were trying to influence the people of Kadod which had remained indifferent to join the *satyagrah*. Some villagers had even paid part of the tax although no notice was served upon them!

The people decided to boycott them. They refused to cultivate their lands even on lease, labourers declined to work in their fields and the entire village was ostracized. These action prompted Gandhiji to chasten the people on judicious use of boycott, which can be violent as well as non-violent.

The government was alarmed at the growing strength of the *satyagrah* and strengthening of unity among the farmers. Local officials were cold-shouldered. They were unable to receive any courtesy or help from the villagers. They were looking for soft targets for breaking the unity. In an act of retaliation, they again chose Valod and on March 25, served notices on a businessperson and seven big landowners to pay the revised assessment by 12th April. They warned that failure to do so would result in confiscation of their land. Such a notice signed by the *mahalkari* of Valod was pasted on the house of Sheth Shri Virchand Chenaji of village Bajipura.

Shri Virchand retorted back and gave a bold reply to the *mahalkari.* He wrote *"You must have regarded me as the weakest landholder in the whole Mahal. But like all others, I am determined not to pay land revenue until justice is done."*

He even advised the *mahalkari* to honourably resign from his job rather than carrying out the cruel task of attaching the land of peasants.

The seven landowners did not lag behind. They wrote to Shri Vallabhbhai, *"The government will not succeed in their efforts to frighten us with the notices of confiscation."*

Local people were very happy with their response and they facilitated these persons in a meeting, which was addressed by Shri Vallabhbhai. Shri Vallabhbhai said that the government exploits the weakness of the people. The farmers have nothing to worry-they should firmly believe that the land will remain theirs, the government cannot confiscate that. The government has failed to attach even one *bigha* of land in Kheda, how can they hope to succeed in attaching lands of the farmers in Bardoli? He praised the people for their courage and said that they need not be afraid of the government officials. If things continue in the present manner, the *mahalkari* may not be able to get the services of even a peon!"

Throughout the taluka, the people were very eager to know on a daily basis, what Shri Vallabhbhai had said on that particular day. He was inspiring the humble peasant to become brave. He said that the *government* has reasons to worry, the peasants should not fear. At the same time, he was also reminding them that they are going to fight a longer battle for India's freedom.

The local government personnel were finding themselves in a difficult position. Most of them were sympathetic towards their fellow villagers and did not want to do the unfair act of confiscations and attachments. Some of them assured Shri Vallabhbhai that they would desist from doing such work.

Every day, Shri Vallabhbhai and his lieutenants addressed several meetings in the villages. The number of people present in these meetings was sharply increasing. Chamanbhai attended some meetings and he was delighted to find that women in large numbers were coming forward to attend. They were encouraging their husbands to participate actively in the struggle and were assuring them that they should not worry about going to the jail. The women will take care of the children, cattle and the house. Woman used to put *tilak* on their forehead and pray for the success of the struggle. Even poor women were offering their savings for the cause.

Shri Vallabhbhai was a great source of inspiration. He was a representative of the peasants and a peasant himself. He said, *"If any one deserves to walk on the earth with his head erect, it is the farmer for he is the producers, the rest are parasites. Although the world depends upon the farmer and the labourer but they are the most neglected lot."*

Jivanbhai agreed. "He is very practical and sincere in saying that. Our entire life is devoted for agriculture but the farmers are never in a comfortable position."

Nandubhai said, "Shri Vallabhbhai always advises us that we should have courage and should never compromise our self-respect. The farmers should not be fear–stricken. He wants them to throw a challenge to the government to take our land to England!"

Asha Bhai added, "He has said that *we should challenge the government to surround the entire taluka with machine guns and aeroplanes. We do not have an army of weapons but we have the higher force of truth to face that."*

Chamanbhai observed that an important change has taken place in the attitude of the people. They were not afraid of the government officers or their orders, they were prepared to face the worst. Even the Collector was unable to get a taxi, his arrival was greeted with doors shut and no body coming forward to meet him. The deserted village streets were a blow to his arrogant authority.

The repercussion was repressive. More *japti* notices were served but no labourer was coming forward to help the officials in carrying the confiscated cattle or property. The government then deployed the services of rogue musclemen for this purpose.

Many people told several funny instances of attachment to Chamanbhai. In one case, buffaloes were attached in the name of a defaulter who did not own any land, in another one; buffaloes belonging to somebody else were attached! In yet another case, a large number of buffaloes were attached without any proper description, in another instance, the attached buffaloes were left back because no labourer was available to carry them! No respect was paid to the attachment rules.

Chamanbhai was finding a change in the approach also. More women were joining the struggle. They eagerly awaited their leaders' arrival and while waiting for him cheerfully sang *bhajans,* some specially prepared for the *Satyagrah*.

Shri Vallabhbhai was a great source of strength and, in fact, the only hope for the farmers. His inspiring oratory appealed to their heart. He asked the people to say, *even if you cut me to pieces, I will not pay.*

He was never tired of reminding the farmers that their grim determination to fight was the strength, which can compel the mightiest tyrant to agree to their demands.

It was at Bardoli that the women decided to call Shri Vallabhbhai *Sardar*– a title which got affectionately attached with his name.

13

Jitenbhai arrived one afternoon, he was full of excitement. He said, "I want to thank the women of Bardoli. They have given a very appropriate title to Shri Vallabhbhai. Many people have started calling him *Sardar*. Who knows, this name may become as popular as his original name."

Appreciating the wisdom of the women of Bardoli he said, "Shri Vallabhbhai does lot of homework, meticulously studies every aspect of any matter brought before him and then decides his course of action. He is a fighter, not a fence-sitter. He likes to plunge himself in works of national interest which ask for courage, sacrifice and dedication. These qualities make him an ideal leader-*the Sardar.*"

Jitenbhai said, "He has been spending three days a week at Bardoli, now he wants to spend more time here. The number of *japti* notices has increased and he feels it necessary to remain with the people of Bardoli when they need more moral support."

Chamanbhai liked the decision very much, "That will be very helpful. Although the people are earnestly responding to Shri Vallabhbhai's call, his continued presence amidst them will make a huge difference. "

Chamanbhai added, "Recently, the government issued notice to Ibrahim Patel of Bardoli and to some people of Valod. They remained unperturbed, the people of Valod even celebrated the event by hosting a party to the *satyagrahis* and other friends."

"There are several cases of high-handed handling of the situation by government officials. They have been troubling innocent people on petty matters and sometimes without any reason. Even people who do not own land have not been spared. We came across many funny instances of such actions."

"Jitenbhai, in spite of all this provocation and injustice, the people are determined and they are prepared for a long fight."

However, the arrogance of senior government officers continued to disturb the people. The commissioner, Mr. W.W. Smart labelled the *satyagrahis* as a "*swarm of agitators.*" His comments drew the attention of Gandhiji who wrote in the Young India, *"Those whom the Commissioner in his anger and intoxication of power calls as the "Swarm of agitators" are honourable servants of the nation who are giving free services to Bardoli at considerable sacrifice."*

Gandhiji also praised the sacrifices being made by Shri Vallabhbhai, Abbas Tyebji Sahab, Imamsaheb Bavzir, Dr. Sumant Mehta and Mrs. Mehta, Shri DarbarSaheb and his wife Bhaktiba and others.

Bardoli drew the attention of the entire nation. People offered their services and expressed their desire to contribute for the success of the struggle. Naming dedicated workers as *swarm of agitators* by the Commissioner had hurt the national pride. People's reaction was sharp. The struggle was getting more support and strength.

There was a great awakening among the people-they eagerly waited for the bulletin and addresses by Sardar Patel and other leaders. Sardar's speeches were read aloud at the *choro*, in bazars, bus stops, trains and in public places. As days passed by, his speeches became more inspiring - always reminding the people that they are fighting for self-respect which will finally bring *swaraj.* Sardar Shri always stressed that the struggle must remain non-violent. At the same time, he inspired the people to remain fearless and united.

Many patriotic songs were written by rural people as well as by celebrated poets praising the valour of the people of Bardoli. Famous Urdu poet Ravish Siddique wrote :

Julm-o-bedad ki shiddat ha, magar fir khush hain
Joshe-toofane-shakavat hai magar fir khush hain
Han, musibat pe musibat hai, magar khush hain
Jante hain ki bhalai se bhala hota hai
Sabr valon ka madadgar Khuda hota hai. *

* *The intensity of tyranny is severe, yet they are happy. The tempest of cruelty is vigorous, yet they are happy. There is trouble-after –trouble, yet they are happy. They know that if one does good, he will receive good. God helps those who are patient.*

The government continued to issue threats of attachment. However, the more they tried, the more they strengthened the will of the people and Sardar's resolve to fight.

At the same time, many well-wishers were trying to find a solution of the problem. However, Sardar Patel knew that the solution will come from struggle and not by constitutional debates. Several meetings were held in Bombay and people tried to work on an agreeable formula to solve the problem.

The government was anxious and shaky, though it outwardly showed a strong posture. The senior officers knew and admitted that Shri Vallabhbhai has paralysed the administration at Bardoli. Hectic activities began to reach a solution. The Governor went to Shimla to consult the Viceroy. Consequently, on the 18th July, an invitation was sent to Shri Vallabhbhai to have a meeting with the Governor along with a dozen Bardoli *satyagrahis.*

Shri Vallabhbhai and his selected colleagues Abbas Tyabji Sahab, Ms Mithuben Petit, Mrs Sharda Mehta, Shrimati Bhakti Lakshmi Desai and Shri Kalyanji Mehta had a meeting with the Governor. Though the meeting was held in a cordial atmosphere, it did not produce any result. The government insisted that the full assessment or the difference between the new and the old assessment should be paid and that the movement should be called off. These frustrating one-sided conditions were in no way going to help the settlement. It was also apprehended that Shri Vallabhbhai might be arrested any moment. Anticipating such an eventuality, Mahatma Gandhi moved to Bardoli.

Shri Vallabhbhai wanted to keep the doors for negotiations open. He suggested that the request for an independent inquiry should be agreed upon, the arrested *satyagrahis* should be discharged, the right of the forfeited land should be restored to the occupants irrespective of the fact whether such lands are sold to some other party or not, the market price of confiscated movable property should be paid to the owners, dismissal and other punishments given to the *talatis* and other government servants during the struggle should be remitted.

Sardar Patel was willing to accept even an impartial *official* inquiry.

Several leaders like Shri Chunilal Mehta, Shri Daduabhai Desai, Shri KM Munshi, Shri Purushottamdas Thakurdas and others were anxious to bring a settlement. Outwardly, the government continued to put a brave front. It showed tough postures. Threatening statements were made by the Governor and senior officers. The government was aware that the situation was getting out of its control and a face-saving settlement was in their interest.

Negotiations continued and after several rounds of consultation, most of the demands asked by Shri Vallabhbhai were agreed upon. Shri KM Munshi played a key role in the matter, he went to Surat with other leaders to assist the Collector in arranging re-transfer of confiscated lands. The new Collector, Mr. Garrett successfully negotiated such transfers by persuading the buyers.

The government announced setting up of an inquiry on the terms suggested by Shri Vallabhbhai. Upon receiving the confirmation from Shri Vallabhbhai that he is satisfied with the negotiations, the government released the prisoners. The government also agreed to a draft prepared by Sardar Shri about the reinstatement of the *talatis* in government service.

This was a huge success.

Chamanbhai's joy knew no bounds. Jitenbhai called a meeting of the *satyagrahis* and congratulated them for their success. The news of the success of the Bardoli Satyagrah quickly reached every part of the country and messages of congratulations started pouring in. Leaders from all over India and abroad praised Shri Vallabhhai for his efficient handling of the non-violent *satyagrah*. Gandhiji congratulated the people of Bardoli and Shri Vallabhbhai saying that without their firmness as well as gentleness, the settlement would have been impossible. Leaders like Lala Lajpat Rai ji, Shri Subhash Chandra Bose, Shrimati Sarojini Naidu, Shri C. Rajgopalachari, Dr. Anne Besant, Pandit Madan Mohan Malviya, Shri Satyamurti, Shaukat Ali Sahab, Shri Srinivas Shastry and several others warmly congratulated Shri Vallabhbhai on the success.

Celebrations were held at Bardoli, Surat, Ahmedabad and many other places. This was the third success for Shri Vallabhbhai. But during the previous two *satyagrahas* of Kheda and Borsad, Gandhiji was in jail. This time he was a free person. He praised Sardar Patel for his leadership and observed that such a settlement would not have been possible without some change of heart of the government.

Sardar Patel responded very humbly to the praise showered upon him and said that he was just a follower of Gandhiji. The credit of success should go to Mahatmaji, to the people of Bardoli and to the selfless workers.

It was a wonderful atmosphere in Bardoli. The entire taluka was feeling proud of itself, there has been no violence and no ill-will. A major gain of the Bardoli Satyagrah was that the people were prepared to unitedly fight a longer battle with courage and determination .

However, the arrogant and defiant ICS lobby continued to create problems even after reaching an agreement. Sardar Patel saw their game and thwarted their attempts.

Chamanbhai took a break. He had not visited his home for quite some time. Uma was unable to come to Bardoli because their child was very young. At Ras, people asked him the details of the *satyagrah* and the general mood of the people.

Brisk preparations were afoot for the Navratri celebrations. On this special occasion, the festival was celebrated with greater fervour.

14

Chamanbhai returned to Bardoli for giving relief to Bhuvanbhai who had not been to Ras for quite some time. While Chmanbhai was busy with the *satyagrah* work, Bhuvanbhai managed the business almost single-handed with only occasional support from Chamanbhai.

"Take some rest at Ras. I will manage the work," Chamanbhai requested his brother.

Chamanbhai had developed useful contacts during the Bardoli Satyagrah. Now that the *Satyagrah* was over, business activities were resumed. New customers were coming. Some newly acquainted workers had opened small khadi stores in their villages. They used to come to his shop. A relationship based upon mutual trust and cooperation was being built up.

Jitenbhai was coming to Bardoli more frequently. He said, "Shri Vallabhbhai has developed a warm, emotional affection for Bardoli. He wants to spend more time here." Jitenbhai also brought the news that the members of the Inquiry Commission-Mr. Broomfield and Mr. Maxwell had commenced their work on the 1st November.

Jitenbhai informed that Shri Bhulabhai Desai would be presenting the case for the people of Bardoli. Mr. Broomfield had a prejudiced view about the farmers. On the very first day, when he commenced his enquiries in Afva village, he said that every where in the world, the farmers were in the habit of speaking untruth. The villagers asked him and his team to find out the truth. The Patel and the *Talati* told him that the Settlement Officer had never visited the village, the villagers had never seen Mr. Jaykar. His report was not based on ground enquiries. Even it was doubtful whether the other concerned officer, Mr. Anderson had visited the villages and examined the leases.

These preliminary enquiries reposed the Committee's confidence in the leaders who have prepared reports after making on the spot enquiries and carefully cross-examining the statements. Their valuable contribution was acknowledged in the report of the Committee.

At the beginning of the Bardoli Struggle, the villagers of Chaurasi Taluka had also requested for joining the campaign. Shri Vallabhbhai had showed his inability to manage the struggle in two talukas at the same time, however, he had assured them that once the problems of Bardoli Taluka are solved, their concerns will also be addressed. This came to be true.

The Committee reduced the increase in land revenue for Bardoli and Chaurasi Talukas from Rs. 1,87,492 to Rs. 48,648, thereby giving a benefit of Rs. 1,40,000 to the people which amounted to a benefit of about Rs. 45 lakhs over a period of 30 years. Some other tax relief was also recommended.

The weaknesses of the careless assessment were thoroughly exposed and the peoples' case was clearly upheld.

The Bardoli Struggle demonstrated that when the constitutional methods failed, peoples' struggle brought them relief. The peoples' confidence and their self-respect soared. People no longer meekly obeyed the unfair orders of the bureaucracy. They were prepared to fight for a just cause, which they hoped will ultimately bring *swaraj*.

"Our leader, Shri Vallabhbhai will lead us in our struggle for *swaraj*," Chamanbhai was convinced.

The mood in Ras was that of celebration. At the *choro*, Nandubhai wanted to listen about the next step. He said that now our Sardar is a national leader. His reputation has soared very high in the eyes of the people throughout India. Sardar Shri's efficient handling of the Bardoli Satyagrah has earned the praise of even his critics. He is being regarded as an expert in managing peoples' struggles on matters concerning unfair land revenue.

Jitenbhai had informed Chamanbhai, "This is going to be a year of preparation. We need to absorb the spirit of non-violence and khadi. Also we have to mobilise public opinion against drinking."

One afternoon Nandubhai opened the topic at the choro. He said, "Drinking is a big problem in the entire Surat District and neighbouring areas."

"Yes, and concerted efforts are required to handle the problem," Jivanbhai agreed.

Chamanbhai said, "A society has already been formed to convince people to stop drinking. Our Sardar Shri is the President of the Society and Mithuben Petit is the Secretary. They are already doing very good work."

It was a good opportunity for Nandubhai to make some comments. "Yes, Mithuben is very active. She looks so graceful in her simple *khadi* sari. She and her other woman colleagues will be able to persuade people to give up drinking."

Jivanbhai differed, "It is not an easy task. The liquor lobby is quite strong and some people in the villages are used to drink local liquor which does not cost much money."

Chamanbhai reminded, "The pickets were doing good work at Ahmedabad. Uma was also among them. But there was opposition from the shop owners as well as from the people who were used to drinking. The black market was thriving. Several volunteers were injured when the shop owners deployed goons to pounce upon them."

Nandubhai tried to convince, "That is true, But now the environment has changed. I have visited some villages after the success of the Bardoli Satyagrah. Thanks to Gandhiji and Shri Vallabhbhai, the people have developed a deep sense of sacrifice and self-respect. This is the right time to promote the cause of voluntary prohibition."

Chamanbhai commented, "Yes, now the workers are also free from the Bardoli Satyagrah. We can mobilise them for this work."

"Let us start our work from here, right from today," A co-villager said.

Uma was delighted. She was struggling with a sad feeling of just remaining a housewife during the Bardoli Satyagrah. On several occasions, she wanted to participate in the *satyagrah* and even Yashoda had offered to take care of her child but Damyanti was not in favour. "Nobody can be a substitute for the mother. The child will miss you and you will miss the child. Your mind will vacillate between *satyagrah* and home. Perform your duty as a good mother. Wait for a while, when the child grows then you put your heart and soul in the *satyagrah* work. Who stops you?"

Uma had agreed at that time. She should not escape from her duties as a mother. But now the opportunity has come when she can devote some time for the work.

She spoke to Chamanbhai about it who was supportive. He encouraged Uma to use her *khadi* spinning group as a messenger of prohibition. They selected some good singers among them and started practicing religious and patriotic songs. Uma suggested that every evening they should try to organise a *bhajan* session. This will create an environment for conveying their message. The spinning team took the lead. Women in their sweet voice started the *bhajans* while moving from house to house. Many women came forward to join.

Ashabhai himself led the gents' group. Chamanbhai assisted him. They used to target a few houses every day. Their work started early morning. Madhavbhai and several elders used to get up with *keertan* :

Jagne jadva Krishn govalia, tuj vina dhenuman kon jashe?
*Vansenne saath goval tole mally, vadore govalia kon thashe?**

Chamanbhai and his team tried to maintain a pious environment throughout the day. Though the people realised that they should stop drinking, in the beginning, they were unable to muster enough will-power to abstain. The success was slow but the response was positive. Slowly, the peoples' determination became stronger, and the collective encouragement helped them in strengthening their resolve. Ashabhai and Chamanbhai used to invite those people who had left drinking to persuade others.

Shri Vallabhbhai was regularly meeting and addressing the people. He was invited to preside over the Maharashtra Political Conference. The issue of unfair assessment was now being seriously studied by the social workers. A Land League was established under Sardar Patel's presidentship. A study of the land revenue situation in the Matar taluka was conducted by the Gujarat Vidyapith. The Taluka was hard hit by over assessment. As a result of the study, finally a concession of 25% was granted in the assessment.

The success of the Bardoli Satyagrah was very much appreciated and the leadership of Sardar Patel was admired throughout the country. Leaders from other provinces also wanted him to address meetings concerning land revenue issues and explain his successful Bardoli model to them. Shri Vallabhbhai travelled to Tamilnadu, Kanataka and Bihar. Wherever he went, he received a warm welcome. His reputation had preceded him. In Tamilnadu, his host was

* *Hindi text in the Appendix*

Shri C. Rajgopalachari, in Karnataka Shri Gangadhar Rao Deshpande and in Bihar Shri Anugrah Narayan Singh. His close friend Rajendra Babu was unwell at that time.

In Bihar, he reminded the people of their great struggle at Champaran, which he said, will constitute the first and the most important chapter in the history of Indian Independence. He said that the faces of the audience do not give the impression that they are the people who have carried out the memorable satyagrah. The European planters are no longer there, the tax imposed has been withdrawn, but the people are still afraid of the government. He asked them to shun the fear and develop the strength for carrying out the revolution.

Sardar Patel was warmly and affectionately hailed as a national leader.

The Year of Preparation, 1929, was swiftly coming to an end. The year had left an indelible mark on India's freedom movement. In December 1929, under the presidentship of Shri Jawaharlal Nehru, the Congress adopted the resolution for complete independence of India. The entire nation was full of enthusiasm and hope. Young people in particular were feeling impatient and wanted to join the struggle for *Poorn Swaraj*- complete independence. January 26, 1930 was celebrated as the Independence Day throughout the country. People in towns and villages had shed their inertia and were bubbling with enthusiasm.

Shri Vallabhbhai knew that he cannot remain confined to any particular location, he had to travel to many places in India. He had disbanded his establishment at Ahmedabad and, when not travelling, had chosen to live at Bardoli.

The government was trying to explain that the Round Table Conference was expected to meet most of the demands of the people. Gandhiji had placed some conditions for consideration of the government as a prerequisite for the participation of the Congress in the Conference. Abolition of the Salt Tax was one of the conditions mentioned. Several leaders and common people were approaching Mahatma Gandhi to launch the Civil Disobedience Movement. Gandhiji decided to break the salt law and asked Shri Vallabhbhai to select the route for the proposed *Salt Satyagrah*. Shri Vallabhbhai asked Shri Ravishankarji Maharaj and Shri Mohanlal Pandya to suggest the appropriate route. Shri Vallabhbhai examined their proposal and recommended the suitable route to Gandhiji. It was proposed that the Dandi March should start from the Sabarmati Ashram and cover places such as Aslali, Navagam, Matar, Nadiad, Anand, Borsad, Kanakpura, Ankaleshwar, Mangrol, Delad, Surat, Vaz, Navsari etc. The total distance was 241 miles. Gandhiji decided to start the Dandi March on March 12, 1930. He selected 80 *satyagrahis* living in the Ashram to join the March. Shri Vallabhbhai decided to raise awareness among the people living in the area of the proposed route about the Dandi March.

Chamanbhai was looking for an opportunity to join, but Gandhiji had personally selected his band of disciples for the purpose. He and other *satyagrahis* were talking to the people requesting them to adhere to non-violence during the March.

On 11 February, Shri Vallabhbhai addressed a huge public meeting in Bharuch. He said that the Civil Disobedience Movement will begin soon and the laws will be broken in a non-violent manner. Gandhiji may be arrested, his followers next, and then the turn for the common people will come. He asked them to remain firm and bravely face the consequences.

At the back of Shri Vallabhbhai's mind, there was a strong desire to give a befitting reply to a statement made by Lord Birkenhead in the British Parliament. When Gandhiji was arrested in 1922 and was sentenced for six years, Lord Birkenhead had made a statement in the Parliament that not a dog had barked in entire India when Gandhiji was arrested. Sardar Patel found it an appropriate occasion for giving a befitting reply to the curt statement and for bringing forward the truth. He asked the people to fill up the jails so that world should know whether the dog is capable of barking or not, if it so desires.

Chamanbhai was very active. He was in regular touch with Jitenbhai.

One afternoon, Ashabhai came to the *choro* in a very enthusiastic mood. Jivanbhai asked, "What has happened Asha bhai? You look so excited!"

"Jivanbhai, it is such a great matter that all of us should feel excited. Our Sardar is going to address a meeting at Kankapura. I will try to request him to address a meeting at Ras also on his way."

This was a windfall for the people of Ras and Chamanbhai felt that a beam of light has illuminated his body. He asked Ashabhai to give the details of the proposed journey.

"According to the programme, Shri Vallabhbhai will take his lunch here and then proceed to Kankapura. I have not received his confirmation for a meeting yet. Let us all request him to address us," Ashabhai said.

Sardar Shri arrived at Ras on the morning of 7 March 1930. He was accompanied with Shri Mohanlal Pandya, Shri Phoolchand Shah, Shri Gokaldasji and Shri Ravjibhai Patel. They camped at the Swaminarayan temple. A number of people from Ras, both men and women, called upon Shri Vallabhbhai and requested him to address them.

Sardar Patel asked, "How well are you prepared? How many people are ready to go to jail? "

About two hundred men raised their hands.

His next question was, "Whether women are also ready to go jail?"

Several women-old and young came forward and emphatically said, "Yes, Sardar, we are ready." Damyanti, Yashoda and Uma were among them.

Shri Vallabhbhai agreed to address the people who quickly assembled under the banyan tree at the outskirts of the village. Shri Vallabhbhai was welcomed at the speaker's seat at about 2 PM.

As he was preparing to deliver his speech, some government officials suddenly arrived at the scene. One of them, Shri Mansuklal, a first class magistrate from Borsad, served a notice prohibiting him from organising any meeting within five miles of Ras.

Sardar Patel consulted his colleagues, ignored the notice and said that he wants to proceed with the meeting and his speech. The magistrate politely ordered his arrest and the police superintendent Mr. Billimoria took him to the police car. Shri Vallabhbhai, bid farewell to the audience, asked them to remain peaceful and smilingly took a seat. He was taken to Borsad where he was tried by Mr. Alfred Master, the Collector of Kheda. In addition to Shri Vallabhbhai, and Mr. Master, the only other persons present were the magistrate and the police superintendent. Mr. Master wanted to remove Shri Vallabhbhai from the scene with a view to weaken Gandhiji, who was all set to launch the Salt Satyagrah. He sentenced Shri Vallabhbhai to three months' jail and a fine of Rs. 500. In lieu of the fine, an additional sentence of three weeks was ordered.

On the way, Mr. Billimoria stopped briefly at the Sabarmati Ashram to allow Shri Vallabhbhai to touch the feet of Mahatma Gandhi. Mr. Billimoria also offered him a cigarette, Sardar declined.

"But you do smoke Sir," Mr. Billimoria insisted.

"Yes, but I am stopping it now," Sardar replied.

Then and there, he gave up smoking for good. After bringing Sardar Shri to the jail, Mr. Billimoria wept like a child.

Sardar Patel was put in the Sabarmati jail as prisoner number 15170 where he served his sentence upto 25.6.1930.

At Ras, the entire audience was stunned and shocked. They had not expected this type of restriction on freedom of speech. It was a deliberate and determined mockery of justice. Since the meeting at Ras was decided at the last hour, the magistrate and the police had rushed from Kankapura.

At Ras, after Shri Vallabhbhai was taken away, Shri Ravishankarji Maharaj and Shri Gokuldas Talati addressed the meeting. Ashabhai, Gokaldasji and other leaders, had a difficult time in controlling the situation. Uma was crying her heart out. What a golden opportunity to listen to their own Sardar had been mercilessly snatched away by the insensitive administration! People were shocked and hurt. They wept and expressed their resentment. But following Sardar's advice, they remained peaceful.

The tree under which sardar Shri was arrested was named as *Vallabhvat.*

Although they were severely hurt, they resolved to take part more enthusiastically in the Civil Disobedience Movement. Some officers resigned, some shopkeepers surrendered their licenses and several people took a vow not to consume liquor. Chamanbhai was delighted when several persons volunteered for the *satyagrah.*

The Dandi March started as scheduled. Shri Vallabhbhai's arrest was resented throughout the country. Protest meetings were organised at many places. The lawyers of Ahmedabad asked that Shri Vallabhbhai had not made any speech, why he was arrested and sentenced without a proper trial? An account of the arrest was published by Shri Mavlankar who had met Sardar Patel in the jail as his lawyer. The matter was raised in the legislature and in the public fora.

On 21st April 1930, Ashabhai and Chamanbhai organised a meeting of the villagers to decide their future course of action. The people resolved that unless the government releases Shri Vallabhbhai and other leaders, no person from the village will pay the revenue assessment.

Mr. Jinnah asked whether Sardar Patel has violated any law? He said, "*No information was given on this matter. His arrest is a blow on the freedom of speech granted by law.*"

Sardar Patel spent his time in a cool and jolly mood in the jail. The inmates tried their best to keep him happy, the jail authorities and government officials were courteous to him. They offered him better food and some privileges which Shri Vallabhbhai declined to avail. Sardar had the company of Darbar Shri Gopaldas, Shri Gokaldas Talati, Shri Phoolchand Shah and others. Shri Vallabhbhai was very happy to see the enthusiasm of the young *satyagrahis* in the jail. They were eager to launch any purposeful struggle aimed at achieving independence. The Dandi March started as scheduled.

In a way, Sardar Patel was the first *satyagrahi* who was sentenced in connection with the Dandi March.

Ashabhai and Chamanbhai mobilised the people of Ras to come forward as volunteer. The village responded well by offering 300 volunteers comprising of both men and women. The people were very unhappy; their anger was contained only by Gandhiji's advice to remain non-violent. Yet, they were unable to digest the impertinent injustice of arresting Shri Vallabhbhai. They felt that they have a special responsibility of actively participating in the Civil Disobedience Movement. Chamanbhai had been visiting some neighbouring villages who also decided to launch a similar no-tax campaign.

When Gandhiji was consulted, he cautioned the people of Ras that if they wish to start the movement, they should realise that the government will retaliate strongly and will not hesitate in confiscating their movable and immovable property. Are they prepared for such a situation? Ras should develop strength and courage for this purpose. Other villages willing to follow Ras should also do likewise.

Paying compliments to his trusted colleagues, Gandhiji said that he understands the sentiments and the spirit of the people of a district which is the home of Shri Mohanlal Pandya and Shri Ravishankarji Maharaj. It is also the district where Sardar Vallabhbhai and Darbar Sahab were arrested.

Gandhiji's message was received with respect. The people continued with their resolve of not paying taxes. Gandhiji and many top leaders were arrested during the salt movement. When Shri Vallabhbhai was released after completing his sentence, he went to Ahmedabad and Bombay where he was given a warm welcome. He was again arrested in Bombay when he was participating in a procession on the death anniversary of Lokmany Tilak. Shri Vallabhbhai was sentenced for three months and taken to the Yaravda jail. On his release after completion of the sentence, he was again arrested in Bombay for giving a speech during the opening of the *Khadi Bhandar* there.

Though the top leaders were in jail, the enthusiasm of the people of Ras was never dampened. The leaders, in fact, got more support. Women came forward in big number and started picketing also. Spinning and wearing of *Khadi* clothes had become a regular habit of the people. Many enthusiasts were competing with each other in volume and quality of spinning. The government was going ahead with *Japti hukum.* In order to avoid the Japti, on 11.10.1930, some villagers moved to Jharola, Vasana and Sisva-villages which were under the control of Baroda Raj. Ashabhai and other leaders organised about 300 bullock carts for this purpose. Many people were living in makeshift shelters prepared from local materials.

Nandubhai was following the political developments. One day, he brought the news that some intermediaries are trying to bring agreement between the congress leaders and the government. The people were not happy at such a move because they were courageously-facing the confiscation of property and were accepting that. They wanted to see whether the government is willing to listen to their demands. One day, Nandubhai brought another news of the government officials' deplorable act of ransacking the house of Shri Vallabhbhai at Karamsad. Sardar Patel's mother was cooking, they took away the utensils filled them with kerosene and ransacked the whole house.

Jivanbhai was very angry. "Why the people of Karamsad did not break their head? Can any civilised government do that? Alas, I was not there, else, I would have taught them a lesson!"

Ashabhai tried to cool him down, "Our struggle in totally non-violent. We cannot respond violence with violence, Jivanbhai."

However, he did not get much support. Chamanbhai said, "That's true, but it is also a matter of self-respect."

One day, Chamanbhai was delighted to see Jitenbhai at Ras. He was in a cheerful mood. He said, "I had not met you and Uma for quite some time. I had been to Bardoli in connection with some work and felt a keen desire to meet you. But Bhuvanbhai told me that you have come to Ras for promoting no-tax campaign. Very good work is being done at Ras. Many people in Ahmedabad, Bombay and other places are talking about your village. Keep it up"

Chamanbhai and Uma explained the work they were doing. "You may be tired, take some rest. You can see the response of the people with your own eyes, tomorrow."

"I am fine. The tiredness was over the moment I saw you."

Nandubhai asked, "What about the negotiations with the government?"

"I have heard that it is progressing. Negotiations demand understanding and compromises. Gandhiji is always willing to negotiate for the sake of peace but the government is not sincere. In all negotiations, they adamantly refuse to investigate the excesses committed by the police and other officers. They shamelessly protect their guilty officers. This is very unfair but still Gandhiji wants to cooperate with them for the sake of peace."

Jivanbhai said, "What about confiscated property? They have already taken our buffalos and have attached lands of many people. What will happen to that?"

Jitenbhai told, "The government is willing to return the confiscated property including the unsold land. This is a departure from their officers' stand who had been telling all along that the confiscated land will not be returned."

Nandubhai asked, "But they have also sold some land to other people. How will they manage that?"

Jitenbhai informed, "They are working on a solution that somebody else, a third party, may buy the confiscated lands and return them to the owners. The return of land was promised by Shri Vallabhbhai."

Chamanbhai asked, "What about our friends who are in jail?"

"The government is willing to release those *satyagrahis* against whom there are no cases of violence. Cases of other persons will be examined." Jitenbhai said. "And the government officials who have resigned will also be reinstated."

He further added, "Gandhiji wants that peaceful picketing should be allowed and the people should get the right to prepare salt from the areas where possible."

After Jitenbhai's departure, Chamanbhai and other workers spoke to some people in Ras and other villages. Their reaction was not positive. Their standing crop had been mercilessly uprooted, their cattle had been taken away and above all, their pride was hurt. They were abused and insulted. An impartial enquiry on these misdeeds was called for. Why did Gandhiji agree not to have the enquiry for excesses committed by the government officials?

They had a hard time giving a satisfactory reply to the people. Gandhiji and Shri Vallabhbhai were aware of the peoples' discomfort at the settlement. When the agreement was reached, both the respected leaders travelled to several villages and tried to explain the situation to the people. They appreciated peoples' hard work, patience, their ability to undergo the sufferings, their sacrifice and selfless contribution to the movement. Chamanbhai and other fellow workers also went with them to some villages.

Some people had taken refuse in the Isnav village of Kheda district. Their make-shift cottages had caught fire and four people had died. Some cattle were also lost. Gandhiji asked Shri Vallabhbhai to provide some assistance to them. Sardar Patel, who had a great regard for the self-respect of the farmers did not agree.

Mahatmaji came to Ras on 12 March, 1931 after which arrangements were made to facilitate return of the villagers to Ras. This was done under the leadership of Khan Abdul Gaffar Khan and Shri Morarji Desai on 16 March, 1931.

Peasants returned to their dear village on their bullock carts, chanting sweet songs and carrying the portraits of Mahatmma Gandhi and Sardar Patel.

15

Amidst the gloom and despair, there was good news for Chamanbhai. His leader and the leader of the people was elected the President of the Karachi session of the Congress. It was a difficult session, people were unhappy at Congress's stand on the hanging of Shri Bhagat Singh and his colleagues. The situation created by the uncomfortable settlement and several other matters made the chairing of the session a very challenging task to perform. But Shri Vallabhbhai handled the issues with great confidence and aplomb. He was never flustered; he did not obfuscate the real issues. His views were clear, his speech inspiring.

In Gujarat, people in the villages in Bardoli and other talukas had suffered a lot, yet the local officials were issuing harsh notices and were troubling the peasants. When Gandhiji and Shri Vallabhbhai were away and busy with many other pressing responsibilities, the officials found it quite convenient to harass the peasants of Bardoli. Their houses were cordoned and the owners were prevented from entering their own house, the cattle were let out and captured, all sorts of abuses were hurled upon the poor peasants and they were beaten in front of women and other family members.

Shri Vallabhbhai was very angry. He sent several telegrams to Gandhiji who was in Shimla informing him of the happenings in Bardoli area. On the 29th August, Gandhiji left for England for attending the Round Table Conference.

After persistent efforts, the government agreed to hold an enquiry on the misconducts of the police officials and subordinates in Bardoli and on the revenue collection matters. The enquiry began on October 5th 1931 at Bardoli. Shri Bhulabhai Desai who was assisted by Shri Narhari Parikh and Shri Bhogilal Lala represented the case of *khatedars*. Shri Vallabhbhai was present in Bardoli during the period of enquiry, which lasted for a month. Unfortunately, it turned out to be a mockery of enquiry. On advice from Shri Bhulabhai Desai, Shri Vallabhhai agreed that the Congress and the *khatedars* should dissociate themselves from the eye-wash drama.

Jivanbhai was a tower of strength for his entire family. Ras was severely affected, the people had suffered a lot, yet they have stood like a rock during the entire period of Civil Disobedience. This was a matter of pride for Chamanbhai. The contribution made and the stand taken by his family was cited as an example to others. Ras had always held its head high with self-respect.

Shri Vallabhbhai was both sad and angry. He informed Gandhiji about the happenings in Gujarat and requested him to return to India as soon as the Round Table Conference was over. Barely after a week of his return to India, Gandhiji was arrested and so was Sardar Patel. Their arrest brought them together in the Yeravda jail for a period of 16 months. Shri Mahadevbhai was also with them.

This was a golden opportunity for the Sardar to remain with Mahatmaji and he made full use of the opportunity. He took care of his needs, served him as much as allowed by Gandhiji and kept him happy with his sharp satire and mordant humour. Unfortunately, the Sardar lost his dear mother while serving his jail term. The company of Gandhiji and Shri Mahadevbhai gave him much solace during this painful period.

In the villages, people were feeling Sardar's absence very much. In order to keep the spirit of the people high, his trusted colleagues were travelling in the rural areas. The *swayamsevaks* and *swayamsevikas* were working with patience and devotion. They were mobilising people and encouraging them to continue their struggle. The villagers of Ras used to sing the *Ransoor Ras* song which praised their courage and valour.

Thokay jang thanan, hushiyar graam Raas tun
Poojay veer vhana, tayyar gram Ras tun
Sharnayee ghor baje, ne aatmmgherun gaje
Veer ne viratv cha je, padkar gram Ras tun
Ek din rashtr name, jhukavyun julm same,
Tuj kirti tham thame, sardargram Ras tun.
Bhanu salil khenche, varsha adhik che,

Undhi rajniti vhe che, nij dhar gram Ras tun.
Swarth sadaiv dhumi, rasheen kidhi bhumi
Satyagrahe jhajhoomi kar, vahaar gram Ras tun.
Ladi satyni ladaee, dafnav dand shahi
Ho saach na sipahi, rakhval gram Ras tun.
Shuddh aatm Shakti, veri de vadra bikheri,
Kar pran ne vadheri, uddhar gram Ras tun.
Vayu sugandhi vashe, yash gaan dev gashe,
Te dhany-dhany thashe, avtar gram Ras tun
De rang jang lhanan, kirtar gram Ras tun,
Thokay veer thanan, tayyar gram Ras tun. *

While poets of repute wrote inspirational songs, many songs sung by the common villagers were created by local people-most of them were illiterate. The songs did not have much literary merit but they conveyed the message loud and clear. The songs appreciated the valour of the people and inspired them to remain firm in their resolve. The songs quickly became very popular and played a key role in mobilising people.

In Borsad also, people were full of enthusiasm. Patriotic songs written by local people in simple language were sung by the villagers. The entire area was determined to fight for Swaraj.

Hind yuddh ghant vagyo, sangram Borsad tun,
Jay shankhnad gajyo, bahadur Borsad tun;
Chalya rane shurao, Sarkar julm same,
Neeti yuddh aadaryun, ransoor Borsad tun.
Tun yuddh no rasilo, tuntyag no bharelo,
Swatantrya ne varelo, mashhoor Borsad tun,

---

* *Ransoor Ras*
O clever village Ras, you were forced to fight. The brave children whom you groomed were worshipped everywhere. The shahnai of struggle was sung, you sounded the trumpet. Eager to face the challenge, O Ras village, you inspired valour in the brave.One day, for the sake of the country, you raised your head against tyranny. O leader village Ras, your fame was spread everywhere. The heat of the sun increased, heavy rains disturbed, political situation was adverse, even then O Ras, you remained stedfast. Selfishness was tempting, the soil became devoid of its essence, yet following the path of satyagrah, O Ras, you progressed ahead. With a view to burry the punishment from the government, fighting for truth as a soldier of truth, O Ras, you became the sentinel.
See Appendix for the text in Hindi

Tuj aikya mugdh kartun, bhumi hind chek aaje,
Tak che mali amoli, shoorvir Borsad tun.
Topo, machinegano thi, Sarkar chek bhare,
Karto na pachee paani, bahadur Borsad tun,
Jene kare jameen, aaje ja khalsa te,
Ke top thee udave, dagto na Borsad tun
Vijay pooro bani tha amar Borsad tun. *

Gandhiji and Shri Mahadevbhai were released on the 8th May, 1933, Shri Vallabhbhai was left alone. His other colleague Shri Chaganlal Joshi was in the same jail but in a different barrack. Both Gandhiji and Shri Vallabhbhai felt the pain of separation. Gandhiji expressed it in a statement when he said that Sardar Patel's company in the prison was one of the greatest joys of his life. Complimenting him for his affectionate care, Mahatmaji said that Shri Vallabhbhai's love and affection overwhelmed him and reminded him of his mother.

Touched by Sardar Patel's sentiments about the problems of the farmers. Gandhiji said that he will never forget how much Shri Vallabhbhai was concerned about the anxieties and troubles of the peasants of Bardoli and Kheda.

Sardar Patel was shifted to the Nasik jail on the 1st August 1933. His brother Shri Vitthlbhai was seriously ill. He had been to the US and Austria. During this period, Shri Vallabhbhai wrote several letters to Shri Vitthalbhai, which did not reach him. While in the Nasik jail, Shri Vallabhbhai received the painful news of his brother's death on October 23 in Geneva. Shri Vallabhbhai was terribly shocked. The government offered to release him on parole for 48 hours on certain conditions to which he did not agree. His son Shri Dahyabhai performed the last rights.

These were difficult days for Chamanbhai. He and Uma were doing their work of khadi promotion. Chamanbhai was mostly living

* *O brave Borsad, you sounded the trumpet of Hindustan's struggle. The brave marched to fight, facing the tyranny of the government. O brave Borsad, you started the principle-based struggle. You are skilful in struggle, you are full of sacrifice. O famous Borsad, you have taken the vow of independence. Your unity charms Hindustan. O brave Borsad, you have given a wonderful time to us. You did not show your back while facing the government's cannons and machineguns. O Borsad, remain steadfast, even when the government oppresses, evacuates you from your land or blows you with cannon. O Borsad, you win completely and become immortal.*
See Annaexurefor text of the songs in Hindi

at Bardoli but Bhuvanbhai always spared him for doing his swaraj related work. Bhuvanbhai had brought his nephew, Jivanbhai's son Nanabhai to Bardoli. The idea was to groom him for taking over the business responsibilities. He also proved helpful when Chamanbhai was away.

Gandhiji had stopped the Civil Disobedience movement and had closed the Sabarmati Ashram on the 31st July, 1933. The Ashram was now the centre of the Harijan Sevak Sangh.

Gandhiji had said that the programme for individual *satyagrah* could be continued. Sardar Patel was released. He had undergone an operation for his nose that had been troubling him for quite some time.

Chamanbhai was feeling himself very lucky. He had chosen to be a *satyagrahi.* Uma was expecting her second child. Chamanbhai 's family was supporting him and Uma wholeheartedly. They had never given him any problem to worry about domestic matters. Damyanti and Yashoda were providing all possible help to Uma. Mukundbhai was also very cooperative. Some other families had also followed their example of supporting their members who joined the *satyagrah.*

Another important work was awaiting them. Since 1932, the entire Borsad Taluka was perpetually getting affected by plague. The government did not take any serious note of it and the people accepted it as fait accompli. On 9 March, 1935, Sardar Patel was informed about the outbreak of plague in Borsad Taluka. He immediately sent Dr. Bhaskar Patel to the areas where the epidemic had broken out. Shri Vallabhbhai visited twelve affected villages with Shri Darbar Saheb on the 13th March.

The situation was very bad. Medical assistance was almost non-existent. Patients were living in filthy conditions, no effective measures were taken to prevent the spread of plague. The most affected community of the *Barahiyas* was also very superstitious and accepted the disease as the curse of some imaginary goddess. Dirt and smoke surrounded the patients and the affected areas. Hygiene was a chronic casualty.

Dr. Bhaskar reported the matter to Shri Vallabhbhai. Realising the gravity of the situation, Sardar Shri came to Borsad on the 23rd March and immediately set up a relief camp and a temporary hospital. He also made an appeal for enlisting volunteers.

Fifty-seven male volunteers including Shri Vallabhbhai, Shri Darbar Gopaldas, Dr. Bhaskar Patel and others offered their services. There were eight female volunteers also. Except Sardar Patel and Maniben, everybody was given anti-plague injection. These two distinguished volunteers served the people without worrying about themselves.

The volunteers were assigned duties in the affected villages. They visited every house, unmindful of their personal safety. They sprayed disinfectant in the affected places, caught rats, cleaned the streets and the wells and provided all possible care. Daily Bulletins were issued and distributed to the villagers, advising them that it is necessary to keep their houses and surroundings clean. They were told that *the disease can be cured by medicine, not by offering goat to the goddess!*

Chamanbhai assisted them with great devotion. Sincere work by volunteers was well appreciated by the affected people and by the great leaders like Gandhiji, but the government's response was lukewarm. In some cases, even the *mukhis* had reported to the higher authorities that there are no plague cases in their area! The doctors, working on an honorary basis, had treated more than 3000 patients in March and over 2000 in April. Dr. Patel had himself treated 44 patients in their homes.

Gandhiji visited some affected villages in May and greatly appreciated the work done by Shri Vallabhbhai and his colleagues. On the other hand, the government tried to cover its negligence by blaming the relief workers in their typical bureaucratic manner. Sardar Patel appointed a committee of four persons which included two eminent doctors, to recommend measures to prevent the outbreak of plague in the future. The committee examined the work done in detail and concluded that the conduct of the officials of the health department in handling the plague epidemic was extremely callous and unscientific. On the other hand, the volunteers had worked in a professional manner and had rendered excellent service to the people.

Handling the relief work was a matter of great satisfaction for Chamanbhai. In assisting the volunteers, he completely forgot about his own safety and welfare. His main concern was to help the affected people. This he did to his satisfaction. Uma was delighted at her husband's silent contribution to the important work.

The wings of time know no rest. The political scenario in the country was changing rapidly. Provincial Elections were called.

Shri Vallabhbhai used to address several meetings, often travelling by bullock carts, sometimes addressing people in the moonlight. The people were excited. Chamanbhai and his friends were immensely delighted when in 1937, the Congress won provincial elections in many provinces. One direct and great relief to the villagers was the return of the confiscated lands to the farmers. This was an occasion of great joy for Chamanbhai. The promise given by Shri Vallabhbhai had been fulfilled.

Nandubhai and other workers were very happy." Chamanbhai, the restoration of land rights to the owners brings lot of satisfaction for us. The poor peasant had suffered heavily during the last few years,"

He paused for a while and reminded, "Chamanbhai, do you remember, the decision taken at the Faizpur Congress?"

He was referring to the 50th session of the Congress which was held from December 27-28, 1936 at Faizpur village near Jalgaon, Maharashtra. This was the first session of the Congress organised at a village. It was Gandhiji's desire that since India resides in its villages, the fiftieth session should be organised in a village.

At the session, which was held under the leadership of Pandit Jawaharlal Nehru, Sardar Patel had extended an invitation to host the next session in Gujarat. Gandhiji had asked Shri Vallabhbhai to make *khadi* and cottage industry as the main theme of the decoration and arrangements. Nandubhai was referring to this specific instruction from Gandhiji. In his opinion, this was a big challenging task.

He said, "Now we have to work for the successful organisation of the Haripura Congress. It is a matter of prestige for Gujarat."

Chamanbhai was very happy. He argued, "Lot of work has been done in the area. People have adopted *khadi* as a way of life and village industries are prospering. Why should we have any difficulty? Will it not help in promoting the *khadi* and cottage industry in the entire area ? Let the leaders decide what we are required to do, we will do our best."

He said, "The name of Ras was also proposed sites for organising the session-the other three proposed sites are in Bardoli district. Gandhiji and Shri Vallabhbhai have selected Haripura for the session."

"What a delight it would have brought if the session was held at Ras!" Chamanbhai said.

"A large number of people are likely to attend the session. The selection committee had to examine several things before deciding the venue," Nandubhai said.

Chamanbhai and other workers were full of enthusiasm. The site for the session was at the bank of the river Tapti. A total area of 400 acres was required for organising the session and the owners had offered their land without charging any rent. About half of the total area was owned by Muslims, who gladly offered their field for hosting the session.

The entire work was being organised under the guidance of Shri Vallabhbhai. Shri Nandlal Basu from Shantiniketan visited the site so that he can design the appropriate decoration. Engineers and other workers came from the Satyagrah Ashram.

On the Vijayadashmi Day, 15th October 1937, Sri Vallabhbhai laid the foundation of the Vitthalnagar, the venue of the congress which was named after his brother, Shri Vitthalbhai Patel.

The Haripura Congress brought forward the organisational skills of Shri Vallabhbhai. The place was not well connected with the rail network, the nearest station was 11 kms away and there was no market place nearby. Arrangements to repair the leading roads, to bring construction material, food supplies etc. required meticulous planning and careful execution. Transport was a major item that needed much attention. The roads were repaired, a temporary bridge was constructed on the Tapti river, about 500 buses were hired, post and telegraphs facilities were arranged, two huge RCC wells with a capacity of supplying one lakh gallons of water per hour were constructed. At the initiative and request of Shri Vallabhbhai the electric lighting was arranged by the Killick Nixon &Company and the Excelsior Electric Company. A dairy was established by purchasing 500 cows to ensure supply of pure milk, ghee and butter.

An impressive *khadi* exhibition was also organised. Bhuvanbhai, Chamanbhai and their colleagues gave dedicated support to the organisers. Likewise, care was taken to provide all facilities like drinking water, proper sanitation, accommodation, drainage, medical care etc. The art and design works were beautifully done by Acharya Nandlal Basu and his students. The entire Vitthal Nagar presented a very impressive look.

Shri Subhash Chandra Bose was the Congress President.

It was a huge task to organise the session, which Sardar Patel accomplished very efficiently. Under his guidance, all arrangements for successful conduct of the Session were made. The temporary township was capable of accommodating the stay of about 50,000 persons. Also, about two lakhs people could attend the Session.

The weather was rather unkind on two or three days and a sudden cold wave blew off the roof of a few cottages. Some people were also affected by cold. The volunteers provided the necessary support and maintained a high level of cleanliness.

An important outcome of the Haripura Session was the expression of the Congress stand on the Indian States. It was clarified that, *"The Congress stands for the same political, social and economic freedom in the States as in the rest of India and considers the States as the integral part of India which cannot be separated. The Purna Swaraj which is the objective of the Congress; is for the whole of India inclusive of the States, for the integrity and unity of India must be maintained in freedom as it has been maintained in subjection."*

This was the beginning of the making of a United India.

The arrangements made at the Haripura session were appreciated by everyone. People from every part of India and delegates from abroad saw and appreciated the management skills of Sardar Patel. But Shri Vallabhbhai gave full credit to the volunteers for the successful arrangements. He said that 8000 volunteers worked day and night, 2000 of them were exclusively responsible for sanitation and cleanliness. He specifically appreciated the service rendered by Mridula Sarabhai and her band of young girls and praised the work of Shri Ravishankar Maharaj who was the in-charge of the kitchen. Sardar Patel affectionately said that he is the *Maharaj of Gujarat.*

Participation in the Congress Session taught some very valuable lessons to Chamanbhai. He learnt several tips in crowd management, in maintaining discipline, in ensuring cleanliness and in understanding the varied requirements of the guests. It was a very satisfying experience.

16

Years rolled by. The fight for independence had gained momentum. A top priority for the British Government was to organise support for the war. They wanted to mobilise as much resources from India as possible, without committing to grant independence. At the same time, they were playing the game of divide and rule. They created rift where it did not exist and tried their best to widen the gulf between Hindus and Muslims and among various communities. It was a difficult task for Mahatmaji, Shri Vallabhbhai and other leaders to counter their manipulations.

Amidst hope and despair, the Congress workers were trying very hard to follow the directions given to them. On the 8th August, 1942, the congress adopted the Quit India Resolution, which asked the British to leave India. Gandhiji's message to the people was very clear- *Do or Die.*

Shri Vallabhbhai was frank in his views. He said that the British Government has never been sincere and transparent in matters concerning the transfer of power. In India, they asked the Muslim League-to whom they should transfer the power? They never asked the same question in Burma.

Sardar Patel said, *"This fight is going to be tough. We have to become free and we cannot tolerate subjugation anymore."*

Gandhiji, Sardar Shri and many important leaders were arrested on the 9th August. Shri Vallabhbhai was kept in the Ahmednagar jail.

Public reaction was strong and disruptive, the government's violent. People expressed their anger, the government showed its might. Thousands of people died, many more were seriously injured. The people stood firm amidst all these atrocities. Many people came forward to sacrifice their lives for the country. The fear of the government had vanished. The government had understood that its writ was no longer being honoured on several occasions and its control had weakened significantly.

At the same time, the scene in the World War was changing quickly. Germany surrendered in May 1945.

Chamanbhai asked, "Can we expect to get freedom now?"

"No guarantee," Jitenbhai said. "They are playing the divide and rule policy."

The government released the leaders in order to enable them to attend a meeting in Shimla. Sardar Patel was released on 15 June, 1945.

The British were successfully playing the communal card through Mr. Jinnah. An environment of mistrust and hatred between Hindus and Muslim was created and encouraged.

On a business visit to Bombay, Chamanbhai met Jitenbhai who was very sad and perturbed. He said, "The atmosphere of goodwill, sacrifice and peace has been vitiated. Shri Vallabhbhai is deeply hurt. He said that up to now we were fighting the British Government together. Now a solid wedge has been driven between the two comm-unities. The League treats the Congress as its enemy number one."

Chamanbhai asked, "Is the government really sincere in giving freedom to us?"

"They think it inevitable. The war is over and the Labour Party has won elections in England. The Prime Minister Mr. Atlee has announced that a Constituent Assembly will be set up for framing India's Constitution. Gandhiji, Jawaharlalji, Shri Vallabhbhai, Rajendra Babu, Maulana Azad and all leaders want the Muslim League to join but Mr. Jinnah is adamant."

Chamanbhai commented, "He knows that his 'No' is bringing more and more favours to him. He will continue to say No."

Jitenbhai became very emotional. He said, "Shri Vallabhbhai is not keeping a good health for quite some time. His nose was operated upon but is still giving him trouble, there are other problems also with his health. But Shri Vallabhbhai has never cared about himself. His attention is solely focussed on achieving independence. Chamanbhai, think what have we done for him? Can't we maintain communal harmony as we have done for several years? You have worked in many villages. Muslims and Hindus have lived together and have jointly fought for *swaraj*. All of a sudden, this rude change has over taken the warm sentiments of love and brotherhood between Hindus and Muslims."

Chamanbhai agreed, "True, Jitennbhai, I also wonder about that. Only a few years ago, nobody could have thought in terms of a communal divide. But now there is complete mistrust. We do not know what will happen tomorrow! However, our trust in Gandhiji and Shri Vallabhbhai keeps our hopes alive."

While Chamanbhai was in Bombay, about 3000 Indian naval ratings rose in mutiny, protesting against discrimination between them and their British colleagues in their service conditions. Other navy establishments and members of the Air Force also went on a sympathetic strike. Some people threatened that Bombay will burn.

Shri Vallabhbhai came forward. He had understood the situation clearly. The naval personnel had full trust in him. Finally, with his intervention the situation was saved.

Jintenbhai said, "It was only due to Shri Vallabhbhai that the situation was brought under control. Several forces were out to destroy Bombay. The British Army would have reacted with full vengeance."

A disappointed Chamanbhai returned to Ras, not knowing what is going to happen! He did not have to wait for long. The Cripps Mission arrived in India and presented a plan for India's future government, which could result in balkanisation of India. In the proposals, the Muslim League found an opportunity for establishment of Pakistan, the Congress rejected the plan but agreed to the proposal for the establishment of the Constituent Assembly.

One afternoon Nandubhai came to the *choro* in a very excited mood. He said, "Jinnah Sahab has called for Direct Action on August 16. The Muslim League Ministry has declared a holiday in Calcutta. It is going to show its aggressive face in a very defiant manner. The people are scared."

Jivanbhai commented, "Let us pray for good sense to prevail."

Unfortunately, good sense did not prevail. Hell was let loose and thousands of poor innocent people were killed.

The two terrible happenings-the blood bath during the Direct Action in Calcutta and the revolt of the naval ratings in Bombay shook the British Government. They invited the Congress President Pandit Jawaharlal Nehru to form an interim government.

Pandit Nehru tried hard to get cooperation from Mr. Jinnah who said "No" to almost every proposal, creating more and more obstructions in the united struggle for independence. The situation continued to be difficult. Many people felt that Mr. Jinnah was strongly supported in his demand for Pakistan by the British who had assured to give him more than what the Congress would offer.

The Congress Committees in the provinces had voted for Shri Vallabhbhai as the head but Gandhiji's choice fell upon Pandit Nehru. A disappointed Chmanbhai asked Jitenbhai, "Why did Gandhiji not choose Shri Vallabhbhai?"

Jitenbhai said, "I cannot say. However, it does not matter for Sardar Shri. He will not ask for anything nor will he question the decision taken by his leader. He will efficiently handle any work assigned to him."

Sardar Patel was given the heavy responsibility of Minister of Home, Information and Broadcasting.

Shri Vallabhbhai, many other leaders and the common people were convinced that the British wanted to break India into several parts. They were supporting the Muslim League and Mr. Jinnah, which encouraged violence in many parts of the country. Unfortunately, they succeeded in their machination of creating a situation in which the Congress had to reluctantly agree to the painful demand for creation of Pakistan.

This was a terrible blow for the country. All nationalists were shocked and severely disappointed. India was going to gain its independence in an atmosphere of gloom and violence.

Shri Vallabhbhai was not running a good health but he never cared for himself. His strong will power and an earnest desire to serve the motherland had kept him active and motivated. Gandhiji had been advising him to take care of his health. On one occasion, conveying his birthday greetings to Sardar, Gandhiji had said "*Remember, we are not to go until we have attained swaraj.*"

It was the time to prepare for welcoming the golden rays of long cherished freedom for which thousands of people had sacrificed their lives. The peoples' struggle bore fruit and the British Government decided that India will be made independent. With the creation of Pakistan, India's freedom came with a very heavy price, nevertheless, it was going to be a day when the dreams of millions of people would be fulfilled.

Chamanbhai and the fellow congress workers moved from house to house greeted each other and asked them to assemble for hoisting the national flag. Sweets were distributed and the houses were decorated. In the night, people lighted their houses and streets and sang patriotic songs.

At the *choro*, Jivanbhai said, "Now, it is time for Shri Vallabhbhai to take some rest and recover his health."

Little did he realise that much difficult and challenging tasks were ahead for Sardar!

PART - II

[1947-1952]

1

One afternoon, Chamanbhai and Uma received an invitation from Jitenbhai to come to Ahmedabad. He had invited his colleagues and some other workers for celebrating the announcement of India's independence. Chamanbhai was himself planning to go to Ahmedabad. Uma had not been out of Ras for quite some time. Jivanbhai's elder son Nanabhai was already helping Bhuvanbhai in his *khadi* and village industries business at Bardoli, which was growing well. His younger brother Nanubhai was helping Jivanbhai in farming.

Bhuvanbhai's elder son had moved to Bardoli. The younger had opened a small shop in Ras of cottage industry items. He was also selling ghee and milk products –a business which his father was doing before shifting to Bardoli. His small business, though not a substantial source of income, helped him in taking care of his family and in supporting his family farming.

The announcement of independence had brought a great sense of pride among the people. The evening gatherings at the *choro* were the source of joyous celebration. People were trying to put behind the tragedy of partition. However, their joy was frequently disturbed by painful descriptions of atrocities, violence and the tragedy of migration.

Chamanbhai's daughter Devki was married to a distant relative of Mukundbhai who owned a small shop in Hyderabad. His sons Kantibhai and Jayantibhai had already completed their high school and were looking for a career.

Kantibhai had been occasionally helping Chamanbhai for sourcing and transporting food grains and had acquired some experience in the work. His idea was to get associated with the chain of supplies to Bombay, which was a very big market. Some wholesale merchants of Ahmedabad, with whom Mukundbhai had business dealings, were, in turn, part of a bigger chain, which had major business deals in Bombay. Some of the wholesale traders were also successful exporters.

His younger brother Jayantibhai did not have much interest in business. He wanted to pursue further studies.

Chamanbhai was very keen to meet his friends in Ahmedabad. They had joined the *satyagrah* movement as workers and were not knowing whether the independence will be gained in their lifetime. They took part in the movement with devotion, enthusiasm and with full trust in their leaders. They were confident that the leaders especially Gandhiji and Shri Vallabhbhai knew how to strengthen the movement. They believed in the assurances given by Mahatmaji and Shri Vallabhbhai that their struggle will bring freedom, and this has come true. This was great moment of joy.

All workers were in a happy mood and were enjoying the get together. Jitenbhai had also invited Mukundbhai and some other friends for joining the celebrations. Jitenbhai greeted them with warmth and affection. Uma and Chamanbhai met many co-workers who had sacrificed the best period of their youth for the cause of the nation. The celebration gave them an opportunity to think of the future. The main task of securing independence has been successfully accomplished and the people were now looking for a suitable occupation.

During the celebrations, Chamanbhai asked, "How is our Sardar Shri? Have you met him recently? When is he coming to Ahmedabad?"

Jitenbhai replied, "He is very busy. Migration is taking place at a mass scale and the people on both sides are describing the atrocities committed upon them, which incites further violence. Shri Vallabhbhai has a heavy responsibility in maintaining law and order in the country. He is the Deputy Prime Minister, he has to control and manage many difficult matters-such as the refugee problem, the maintenance of law and order, the making of the constitution, the problems with the States, the establishment of a sound system of governance and so on. I do not know when he will be able to come, but we are very eager to meet him."

After the celebrations, Jitenbhai invited Uma and Chamanbhai for a dinner. People were enjoying the hard-won independence but the bitterness of communal divide was heavy on their heart.

After the celebrations, Mukundbhai asked Chamanbhai and Uma to stay for a couple of days with him. Mukundbhai's manager, Kailashbhai had become quite old, his eyesight was falling and he had developed knee problem. He wanted to be relieved of his work.

Mukundbhai asked Chamanbhai, "Can you shift back to Ahmedabad? You know the work and you are associated with our customers. They like you and trust you. Ahmedabad is a better place for your children. They can develop their career and Uma can also do some social work here."

This was a good suggestion. Chamanbhai did not see any difficulty in accepting the proposal. But he must consult Jivanbhai and Bhuvanbhai and seek their approval.

Jivanbhai was disappointed, but he did not want to come in Chamanbhai's way. Jivanbhai was getting old and he needed more support from family members for handling the farming work. His son and nephew were there to help him but he was missing the support of his younger brothers. Chamanbhai was liked by the entire village and by many people of neighbouring villages also. His presence at Ras brought more people at the *choro* and Jivanbhai's house was a centre of activity for the entire area. Damyanti and Yashoda treated Uma as their younger sister. Uma had a jolly nature. She used to cut jokes and fun, even amidst heavy workload she always remained happy and tried to keep others also happy.

But now it was a question of the career for the children. Jivanbhai reluctantly agreed on the condition that like in earlier days, Chamanbhai will frequently come to Ras with Uma and children.

Chamanbhai left Ras with a heavy heart. Damyanti, Yashoda and Uma could not check their tears.

Jivanbhai blessed them with moist eyes.

It did not take much time for Chamanbhai to settle down in the city which was so familiar to him. Ahmedabad was the city where he met his idol, the city where on the banks of the river Sabarmati he listened to Gandhiji's speeches, the city where he was initiated in the *satyagrah* as a worker, the city where he met Uma for the first time. He affectionately remembered all these important events in his life which were associated with Ahmedabad.

The situation was improving. Business had picked up and the workload had increased. Farmers were now concentrating on agricultural activities, people were free from the *satyagrah* and were returning to their occupation on a full time basis. Chamanbhai had to make changes in the management of the business, which had slumped during the intervening period.

Mukundbhai introduced Kantibhai to some friends in Bombay who were engaged in wholesale trading in food grains. With a reasonable cash deposit, some dealers from Ahmedabad agreed to offer supplies on a 15-day's credit. This was possible due to Mukundbhai's high reputation and Chamanbhai's goodwill.

Jayantibhai joined a course in journalism.

Jitenbhai used to call his former colleagues to his home. Uma and Chamanbhai never missed the opportunity to meet their friends of *satyagrah* days. It was also a very useful gathering for information exchange and updating on current events. Dineshbhai, a close friend of Jitenbhai was a regular visitor. He was planning to publish a Gujarati journal in partnership with Jitenbhai.

On one evening, Jitenbhai informed that Shri Vallabhbhai wanted to come to Ahmedabad, but he was busy with many important things at the moment. The Constituent Assembly had started its work under the able chairmanship of Dr. Rajendra Prasad who was unanimously elected president of the Assembly. The Muslim League had boycotted the Assembly. Sardar Patel was involved in key sub committees such as the Fundamental Rights Sub-Committee, the Minority Sub-Committee and the States Constitution Sub-Committee etc. His duties as the Home Minister during the troubled times were quite heavy, he had to restore peace when a virulent form of communal hatred had vitiated the entire atmosphere, vitriolic utterances and devilish behaviour were routine rather than exception.

But in spite of all this, Shri Vallabhbhai made several practical recommendations to the Assembly. By his sound logic, he convinced the Minorities Committee to abolish the provision of separate electorates.

Sardar Patel had made the integration of the States his top priority. The matter was very close to his heart. No amount of challenge or opposition could deter him. His goal was clear and his approach practical. The Chamber of Indian Princes which was led by the Nawab of Bhopal was opposing the Cabinet Mission Plan and was advising the States not to send any representative to the Constituent Assembly. But thanks to the convincing lobbying by Shri Vallabhbhai, several States agreed to send their representatives to the Assembly. On 28 April, Baroda, Bikaner, Patiala, Rewa, Cochin, Jaipur and Jodhpur joined the Assembly.

Mr. Jinnah was negotiating with Jodhpur and some other States to accede to Pakistan. He offered them any facilities they desired. In addition to Mr. Jinnah and his team, Sir Conrad Corfield and sympathisers of Pakistan in the British administration and political system were a regular source of problems and anxieties to the Indian leaders Pandit Nehru and Shri Vallabhbhai. The leaders also had to manage several influential but difficult personalities concurrently.

Chamanbhai requested Jitenbhai to organise a weekly briefing session for the workers and other friends on the developments concerning the integration of Indian States. Jitenbhai readily agreed. Things were changing fast and the people were very eager to know about the latest situation. He invited some other persons also who were keeping track of the developments to join the meetings, which were held on every Saturday.

On June 3, 1947, just two months before the due date for independence, the British Government had announced that the Paramountcy would be over on the 15th August. This meant that from 15th August, the Princely States would be on their own; they will be free to choose whether they want to accede to the Indian Dominion or to Pakistan.

A Ministry of States was created for handling the matter and Sardar Patel was made the Minister of States. This was a huge challenge for Shri Vallabhbhai who was the Deputy Prime Minister and was already handling two crucial ministries. There were as many as 565 States spread over the entire country. Many large States were nursing ambitions to become totally free after the lapse of paramountcy and it was a very challenging task to integrate them with India within such a short time. Pakistan was making desperate attempts to woo them; it had its eyes set on the bordering and the Muslim majority States.

Some rulers were also trying to establish unions by joining together. On the 17th June, Sir CP Ramaswamy Aiyar, the Dewan of

Travancore made a surprising and shocking announcement that the State will not join any dominion, it will remain independent. He even appointed a trade representative to deal with trade and commerce matters with Pakistan.

While at Delhi, Jitenbhai had spent some time with Shri Vallabhbhai there. On his return to Ahmedebad, he invited his colleagues and conveyed Shri Vallabhbhai's greetings to them. Sardar was not running a good health but ignoring his personal care, he was working from morning until late night without taking rest. His keen desire was to build a united and strong India for which unification of princely States was critical. Gandhiji had given compliments to him saying that only Shri Vallabhbhai was capable of handling the highly complex issue of integration of the Princely States.

With his astute moves, which included building personal relationships and gaining confidence of the rulers, Sardar was planning to implement his ardent desire of having a united India. He invited several rulers and their high officials to his residence and tried to rouse the spirit of patriotism among them. These included the rulers of Patiala, Jodhpur and the Jamsaheb of Navanagar among them. The Jamsaheb was highly respected among the princes and it was important to have his support for integration of several States.

Unfortunately, during the Rajkot Satyagrah in 1939, there was a threat on Sardar's life. Sardar's life was saved due to a last minute change in his travel route. Forgetting the bitter memories of the past, Sardar sent an invitation to the Maharani Saheba and Jamsaheb to have lunch at his residence at 1, Aurangjeb Road in Delhi through Jamsaheb's brother Shri Himatsinhjee. The Jamsaheb and Maharani Saheba were overwhelmed by Sardar's warmth and hospitality. In a spirit of patriotism, they promised their best support in integration of various States, especially from Kathiawad.

Jitenbhai said, "Shri Vallabhbhai had already taken control of the States department on 27 June. He has appointed an efficient officer, Mr. V.P. Menon as the Secretary of the Department on July 5. A competent ICS officer Shri C.C. Desai has been appointed as Additional Secretary. Some other officers have also joined and they have already started working at vigorously for achieving the difficult task."

"Sardar Patel has selected Shri V. Shankar, a capable ICS officer as his personal secretary. Mr. Shankar's name was recommended by

Shri Morarji Desai, under whom Shri Shankar had worked. Shri. Shankar is playing a valuable role in implementing Sardar Patel's decisions."

Prabhubhai, a lawyer colleague of Jitenbhai commented, "I have heard about them. This is a very efficient team which is capable of cutting the Gordian knot."

Jitenbhai said, "Time is running fast, the Muslim League is trying desperately to lure some rulers, some states are extremely difficult to handle and there are challenges and hostilities all around."

Jitenbhai's colleague Dineshbhai said, "It is true, but tell me when our Sardar Sahab was given any easy task to perform? He has always been given heavy and challenging responsibilities. He is a practical leader. He possesses a sharp acumen, strong organisational and negotiation skills. He will succeed."

Jitenbhai took out a piece of paper from his file and said, "I have a copy of the policy statement made by Shri Vallabhbhai on the subject."

Dineshbhai said, "Thanks very much for bringing this important document. Can you tell us the main points of the statement?"

"Of course," Jitenbhai said, and continued, "He has started by reminding people that due to the political fragmentation and our inability to make a united stand, India has succumbed to successive waves of invaders. Our mutual conflicts, internecine quarrels and jealousies have been the cause of our downfall and our falling victims to foreign domination a number of times. We cannot afford to fall into those errors or traps again."

"Very true," Chamanbhai said. "This is a very timely warning to our people. We became slaves only due to our disunity."

"Yes," Jitenbhai said, "Shri Vallabhbhai says that the safety and preservation of the States and the as well as that of India, demand unity and mutual cooperation between its different parts."

Prabhubhai said, "Some Princely States feel that the lapse of paramountcy will make them free from all obligations and they will be free to opt as an independent state or form a union of their own."

Jitenbhai clarified, "The system of paramountcy was designed by the British to regulate their relationship with the States according to their wishes. Shri Vallabhbhai reminds that the doctrine of paramountcy has remained undefined, but in its exercise, there has undoubtedly been more subordination than cooperation."

Jitenbhai continued, "Shri Vallabhbhai says that the country, with its institutions is the proud heritage of the people who inherit it. It is an accident that some live in the States and some in British India. We are all knit together by bonds of blood and feeling no less than of self-interest. None can segregate us into segments; no impassable barriers can be set between us."

Shri Vallabhbhai has made a very friendly gesture to the rulers, *"I invite my friends, the Rulers of States and their people to the councils of the Constituent Assembly in the spirit of friendliness and cooperation in a joint endeavour, inspired by common allegiance to our motherland for the common good of us all."*

"Very right. Shri Vallabhbhai is magnanimous in his approach," Chamanbhai said.

Jitenbhai said, "He has already clarified that *the sovereignty rests with the people and not with the individual ruler."*

Jitenbhai agreed, "But he is a leader of practical wisdom. He says, *"We are at a momentous stage in the history of the India. By common endeavour we can raise the country to a new greatness while lack of unity will expose us to fresh calamities."*

He has cautioned the States, *"alternative to cooperation is anarchy which will overwhelm great and small in a common ruin."*

"He has invited them to leave a legacy of mutually beneficial relationship which would raise this sacred land to its proper place amongst the nations of the world and turn it into an abode of peace and prosperity." Jitenbhai's friend, Prabhubhai, the lawyer, said, "The best option for the States is to join the Union of India. It is in their own interest. The people of these States are no different from those living in the British India. In fact, most of them have taken part in the freedom movement."

Jitenbhai said, "Shri Vallabhbhai's team is working very hard. The team is in regular touch with Lord Mountbatten who appreciates the leadership qualities of Shri Vallabhbhai. Shri Vallabhbhai is making personal contacts with the rulers and their representatives and is trying to convince them to sign the Instrument of Accession. His speeches have roused the feeling of patriotism in the hearts of several rulers who are inclined to join the Indian Union. There are difficulties but he is determined to have their integration."

Jitenbhai said, "Although I am with you here, my mind is in Delhi with our leader. I am again going to Delhi to ask him what help we can give to him at this crucial moment. I have to tell him on behalf of all of you, that we are solidly behind him and are ready to make any sacrifice for the motherland."

Chamanbhai requested, "But return before the 15th of August. We need to celebrate our independence day on a grand scale."

2

Jitenbhai returned after two weeks. He said that Shri Vallabhbhai has shown great skill in dealing with the rulers and their subjects. He has maintained warm friendly relation with them and at the same time has convinced them that they do not have much option in this matter, they will have to accede to the Indian Union. His persuasion was strong, so was his advice.

Jitenbhai said, "His health is not good, but like *satyagrah* days, he does not bother about himself. He knows that the intentions of many rulers to stay away from the Indian Union or to create their own exclusive dominion, has to be nipped in the bud. Any delay in their accession will create more problems."

Chamanbhai said, "Shri Vallabhbhai talks in a straight forward manner. He is a very frank person and people respect him for his patriotism and sacrifice."

"Yes, this was the reason that most of the princes, have confidence in him and have a high regard for him, "Jitenbhai said." He has invited them to join him in building a strong and united India."

Chamanbhai asked, "How did Shri Vallabhbhai proceed in the matter?"

Jitenbhai replied, "By sound management, personal touch and great leadership. He is an excellent planner. He invited the rulers of Patiala, Baroda, Gwalior and Bikaner at his residence on the 10th July and requested the States participating in the Constituent Assembly to immediately accede for matters concerning External Affairs, Defence and Communication. After a series of meetings with the rulers, the drafts for the Instruments of Accession and Standstill Agreement were approved. The rulers of Bikaner, Gwalior and Patiala took the lead in signing it which inspired others."

"This was a great achievement within such a short time." Chamanbhai said.

"Yes, initially there were serious difficulties. But now the progress is rapid. When Shri Vallabhbhai started the work of integration of the States, people were having doubts about its success. But within a very short time, their perception has changed. Shri Vallabhbhai is working with his dedicated team in a well-planned manner to achieve the objective of integration."

A worker asked, "What about Bhopal?"

Jitenbhai said, "Initially, the Nawab of Bhopal was not willing to accede to the Union of India. He tried various options-to establish a separate Dominion of States, to have an independent State, or to accede to Pakistan. The Nawab was also hobnobbing with the some other States. He was trying to gain time and had asked for an extension of date.

"Special efforts were made by Lord Mountbatten who secured his signature on the Instrument of Accession before the midnight of the 14th August. Lord Mountbatten *promised to lock them up in his private case and undertook not to deliver them to the States Department until 25th August or unless authorised by the Nawab to deliver them earlier.*"

"So, finally the Instrument of Accession was signed. The Nawab and Sardar Patel are good friends. The Nawab has also promised to help in handling the refugee problem."

Prabhubhai said "By God's grace, Shri Vallabhbhai has succeeded in achieving his cherished goal to a great extent. We owe him a lot. May God grant him all success and a long life."

Jitenbhai agreed, "Yes. Let us all pray for his success. It will take some more time but Shri Vallabhbhai will certainly achieve his goal of having a united India...."

Prabhubhai interrupted, "If he is given freedom to do so."

Jitenbhai paused for a moment and said, "Now it is time to prepare for the celebrations. Let us celebrate our independence with joy and enthusiasm. We have achieved it after a prolonged struggle and precious sacrifices."

Though saddened by the unfortunate partition, communal divide and violence, the people celebrated their hard earned right to breathe in the free air. No pleasure could equal the freedom from the British rule, which had dampened the spirit of India and had generated an inferiority complex among the people. The people adored leaders like Gandhiji, Sardar Patel, Pandit Jawaharlal Nehru, Dr. Rajendra Prasad, Shri C. Rajgopalachari, Maulana Azad and others. They also remembered the unknown people who were not alive to see the fruit of their sacrifice. With tears in their eyes and flowers in their hands, the grateful people remembered the unsung martyrs. What a great price our people had to pay for the freedom!

The enthusiasm of Chamanbhai and his friends knew no bounds. A new India-full of hope and confidence was born.

After the celebrations were over, Jitenbhai gave the good news that on the 15th August most of the States except Junagarh, Hyderabad and Kashmir had signed the Instrument of Accession.

His friend, Prabhubhai advocate said, "Shri Vallabhbhai must have developed a very powerful strategy to deal with the various aspects of the work involved."

"Yes," Said Jitenbhai, "He has successfully convinced them that the congress is not their enemy, they will retain their personal property and the loss of income will be compensated by a privy purse. He also assured them that they will be eligible for election or selection to public offices."

Prabhubhai said, "I am amazed at the speed with which Shri Vallabhbhai and his team has worked. It is a miracle. Within such a short time, they have achieved something that is unique and perhaps the greatest gift to the motherland. Their strategy is superb."

"The leader inspires. His team is also full of enthusiasm and patriotism." Prabhubhai asked, "What about the remaining three States?"

Jitenbhai said, "Kashmir is being handled by the Prime Minister and Hyderabad by Lord Mountbatten. They consult Sardar Shri in the matter."

Junagadh was of immediate interest for many persons sitting there. Jitenbhai understood the silent question and replied, "Junagadh is a big problem, the Nawab wants to accede to Pakistan."

"This is very serious. How can he do it? "Chamanbhai asked.

"Perhaps he has been advised by his Dewan Sir Shah Nawaz Bhutto who is a confidant of Mr. Jinnah. Mr. Jinnah is working very hard to secure Junagadh's accession," Jitenbhai said, "Everybody is shocked."

"The people of Junagadh will never like to join Pakistan." Chmanbhai said.

Prabhubhai added," I am confident that Shri Vallabhbhai will handle the problem quite successfully."

Chamanbhai asked, "What will happen to States which have already signed the Instrument of Accession?"

"There are two important tasks ahead-complete integration of States and making them homogenous with the rest of India."

Dineshbhai announced that he, Jitenbhai and Prabhubhai have decided to launch a news magazine in Gujarati. Chamanbhai's son Jayantibhai, who has become a qualified journalist has joined the team. The team was closely following the developments of integration of States. Jayantibhai will be visiting the various States and will be sending updates for publication in the journal. Dineshbhai promised to join the weekly briefings and disseminate the updated information.

Sardar Patel was very perturbed due to the communal divide. He always asked the people to forget the communal differences and work together for the development of the country. He said, "*There can be no communal feeling among the peasants. An agriculturist, a day labourer, to whatever religion he may belong, is in the last analysis a peasant. All peasants are in the same boat. All of them will have to swim or be drowned together.*"

On 29 December, 1947, addressing a gathering of villagers near Mehrauli he said, "*Internal peace and communal harmony are essential if the government are to go ahead with their plans for improving the lot of the common man in India. Disturbed conditions are detrimental to your own interests.*"

He said, "*The need for industrial and communal peace in the country is imperative. Peace is necessary for stabilizing the newly won freedom and for leading the country on the road to progress and prosperity.*"

Chamanbhai always missed Ras-his dear village where he was born and had enjoyed his childhood days. He remembered the sacrifices of his brothers and other family members. He missed the soothing love and care of his family. Although the transition from an agrarian family to a trading one was ineluctable in the changing circumstances, his hands were in the business, heart was in the village.

He knew that Jivanbhai, Damyanti and Yashoda must be waiting for him and Uma. His brothers and sisters-in-laws had made their family a unique one. The lead was given by Damyanti who herself came from a large joint family. She was aware that she has to create an environment of love and affection in the family.

Chamanbhai and Uma went to Ras and spent a week there. The topic of discussion at *choro* was partition and the communal tension. Many families of Gujarat had business and social relations with Karachi and they were unable to comprehend how Karachi can be a part of a different country! How the traders of Karachi will do business with the people of Gujarat? Many small traders, barbers, carpenters and technicians had their shops and dealings in Karachi.

One afternoon Nandubhai brought the shocking news that the Nawab of Junagadh has decided to join Pakistan. Although some local newspapers had earlier published news about the possibility of Junagadh's accession to Pakistan, yet many people found it very difficult to believe. How can Junagadh be cut away from India? Geographically Junagadh was so situated that it was an inseparable part of India. Soon after the publication of the news, the Dewan of Junagadh, Khanbahadur Abdul Kadir Mohammed Hussain had dispelled the news as rumour and had categorically denied that Junagadh was thinking along those lines. He even published a news to this effect in the gazette.

His brother Mr. Nabibaksh had represented the State in the meeting called by Governor General on the 25th July, 1947, and had asked several questions which were clearly replied by Lord Mountbatten. He had then confided to Lord Mountbatten that he would advise the Nawab to accede to India. He had told the same thing to Shri Vallabhbhai and to the Jamsaheb of Nawanagar whom he met in Delhi. But unfortunately Abdul Kadir Mohammad Hussain went abroad for treatment and his brother Nabibaksh was eased out. The new Dewan, Sir Shah Nawaz Bhutto was a staunch Muslim League leader who had come with the determination of acceding Junagadh to Pakistan. The Nawab, who was well-known for his love for dogs and other odd habits, was a typical person who easily fell into the octopus clutches of his Dewan.

When Nandubhai broke this terrible news, Jivanbhai asked, "Is it true or just a rumour which was floated a few months back?"

"No, no, Jivanbhai, unfortunately this is true. You can read the news here."

Jivanbhai read the news and threw the paper aside, "How it can happen? Will our Sardar allow that?"

"He is our last resort. Our hope lies with him. Let us pray that he succeeds in retaining Junagadh in India," Nandubhai said.

On his return to Ahmedabad, Jitenbhai said that the Nawab was in regular touch with Pakistan and the announcement of accession was pre-planned. The Dewan had played a crucial clandestine role in the matter and they were trying to win time. Telegrams and letters from the Government of India were either not replied or replied in the typical bureaucratic fashion evading a pointed reply. The Jamsaheb of Navanagar and other rulers of Kathiawad were very upset at this move and they strongly protested Junagadh's accession to Pakistan to Pandit Nehru, Shri Vallabhbhai and Lord Mountbatten. Shri V.P. Menon was sent to Junagadh for making a last minute effort to save the situation.

Prabhubhai said, "We have heard that after listening about Junagadh's accession to Pakistan, several Hindus are leaving the state. This has created further problems in other parts of Saurashtra."

Jitenbhai said, "It was anticipated that the Nawab will avoid meeting Mr. V.P. Menon and so he did. His Dewan informed Mr. Menon that the Nawab is very sick, he cannot meet Mr. Menon and the prince is busy playing cricket!"

Prabhubhai commented, "Not surprising for the Nawab who spent large sums of money for celebrating his dog's wedding!"

Jitenbhai reminded, "He had also declared a state holiday to celebrate the function."

He continued, "Mr. Menon had conveyed the Government of India's views in clear terms to the Dewan. He also explained that the people of Kathiawad are very agitated and they will not tolerate the accession of Junagadh to Pakistan. Mr. Menon also met the Khan of Manavdar and the Sheikh of Mangrol. The Khan admitted that he has already signed the Standstill Agreement with Pakistan and pleaded that he should be allowed to accede to Pakistan. He was being asked by Pakistan to remain firm."

"This was an encroachment into the Indian territory," Prabhuhai said.

"Mr. Menon explained the consequences of these drastic actions. The Khan promised to see him the next morning after re-considering the matter. He did not turn up." Jitenbhai said.

"What about Mangrol?" Chamanbhai asked.

Jitenbhai said, "After some hesitation, the Sheikh showed his willingness to accede to India provided the State was made independent of Junagadh. This was agreed upon, and he signed the Instrument of Accession. Later on, under pressure from Junagadh Mangrol pressed them to retract the letter. But by that time the accession was already accepted by the Governor General."

Prabhubhai said, "Shri Samaldas Gandhi, Shri U.N. Dhebar and other leaders are under pressure from the people of Kathiawad to act. They wanted to form a parallel government. But Shri Vallabhbhai advised them to have some patience."

Jitenbhai explained, "Actually all these problems are caused by the ill-advised Nawab who is under the clasps of Mr. Bhutto. Junagadh claims that Mangrol, Babariawad and Manavdar are all under its suzerainty. This is not a fact. With the lapse of paramountcy, these small states are free. The Nawab of Junagadh does not have a control over them now."

"Does the Nawab understand the situation?" Chamanbhai asked.

Prabhbhai tried to answer, "He is busy playing with his pets. He does not find enough spare time for other matters!"

"But his Dewan should give him the correct advice," Chamanbhai said. "His Dewan is a staunch Muslim League leader from Sindh. He has come with a set agenda to ensure the accession of Junagadh to Pakistan. He is not concerned with the peoples' sentiments or with the logical conclusion that Junagadh should accede to India."

Jitenbhai continued, "Shri Vallabhbhai understands the situation very well. He does not want to precipitate the matter. He will certainly have a balanced approach. As we all know, our Sardar has a special knack of combining personal touch with practical wisdom. I am confident that he will solve the problem soon. Let us wait for a while and see what happens."

He added, "I have also heard that Lord Mountbatten, Lord Ismay and Pandit Nehru are trying to convince the Prime Minister of Pakistan Mr. Liaqat Ali Khan not to press for Junagadh's accession to Pakistan. But Mr. Khan is adamant. It clearly means that now our hopes rest only with Shri Vallabhbhai."

Jitenbhai again gave disturbing news that the Nawab of Junagadh has sent forces to Babariawad, which was a cluster of 51 villages inhabited by *Moolgarasiyas*-the original inhabitants. In order to prevent internal conflicts, the Political Department had brought them under Junagadh. After the lapse of paramountcy, they became independent of Junagadh and signed the accession to India. Sending force to Babariawad was a seen as an attack on the Indian Territory.

Jitenbhai tried to collect more information on the matter and informed his friends that Shri Vallabhbhai wanted to give a befitting reply to this aggression but was advised by Lord Mountbatten to exercise restraint. He even suggested that the matter be referred to the United Nations to which Sardar Patel disagreed.

The Nawab, under the influence of his Dewan, was regularly creating problems through the Khan of Manawadar and the Sheikh of Mangrol. The entire population of Kathiawad was disturbed. In order to control the situation, the Government of India decided to send a brigade for protecting those states, which had acceded to India. The brigade, designated as the Kathiawad Defence Force was placed under the charge of Brigadier Gurdial Singh. The Kathiawad Defence Force comprised of the forces from the Indian army and those of the States such as Bhavnagar, Porbandar and Nawanagar.

Jitenbhai said, "Shri Vallabhbhai is a great leader. He wants to handle the issue very cautiously. The Government of India is constantly corresponding with the Government of Pakistan on the matter, but the latter is very adamant. The people are very much disturbed and the leaders of Kathawad are in Bombay discussing the situation with the concerned persons in the government and among themselves."

He informed, "I am going to Bombay tomorrow. Hectic activities are going on in matters relating to Junagadh."

On his return from Bombay, Jitenbhai gave an account of developments in the political circle about Junagadh. Jayantibhai had just returned from there and he had collected first-hand information about the developments in the area. Jitenbhai said that several top leaders like Shri Shamaldas Gandhi, Shri U.N. Dhebar, Shri Balwant Rai Mehta and others discussed the developments in Junagadh with Shri Morarji Desai and other Congress leader in Bombay. A huge public meeting was organised on the 25th September in which the *Arzi Hukumat* was established. The proclamation issued by the public of Junagadh displaced the Nawab and established an interim government under the leadership of Shri Shamaldas Gandhi. After the meeting, Shri Shamaldas Gandhi and his colleagues went by train to Rajkot. They were given a tumultuous welcome at every station and at Rajkot, where the headquarters of the *Arzi Hukumat* was set up.

Jitenbhai said, "The Nawab and his Dewan are left with no other choice but to acceded to the Union of India. Pandit Jawaharlal Nehru and Shri Vallabhbhai are regularly reminding them and about the legal situation and are requesting them to withdraw their troops from Babariawad and Mangrol. The people of Sardargadh and Bantwa have also requested the Government of India to take possession of the tiny estates because upon lapse of paramountcy, the State of Junagadh no longer has any right to keep them attached."

Jayantibhai said that the situation was becoming volatile. Everywhere there was anger against the Nawab, his Dewan and the Government of Pakistan. The leaders were having a difficult time in convincing the people to remain calm amidst regular provocation.

Jitenbhai was making frequent trips to Delhi. He was confident that the Sardar would solve the problem soon.

And so it happened. The Government of India decided to send force for taking control of Mangrol and Babariwad. The Sardar refused to accept a suggestion from Lord Mountbatten that the contingent of the Central Reserve Force should be deputed for this purpose. Shri Vallabhbhai did not want to take any chances. In his view, it was necessary to deploy the Indian army for taking control of Mangrol and Babariawad. However, he sent a small police force headed by a DIG to take control of Manavdar.

Chamanbhai's business friends were very much perturbed. They did not want to do any business with Junagadh and other disturbed neighbouring areas. Trading had come to a standstill and in spite of some food supplies from Pakistan, the situation had not improved. It was obvious that the administration of Junagadh had collapsed.

One evening Jayantibhai brought the news that the Nawab has fled to Karachi with his family, cash, jewellery and his prized possession-most of his favourite dogs!

Jayantibhai also narrated an interesting incident. A Begum of the Nawab had forgotten to bring her child when the family was leaving for Karachi. The Nawab refused to wait for her, later she had to go via the Portuguese settlement of Diu.

Chamanbhai asked, "The Nawab must be very careful in taking his dogs and not the cash!"

Jitenbhai said, "Perhaps he was careful enough in taking away both cash and several dogs."

Jayantibhai confirmed, "Indeed. He took away as much as he could."

The situation was changing rapidly. The volunteers of the *Arzi Hukumat* were moving fast and they had taken over the town of Nawagadh. The Dewan Sir Shahnawaz Bhutto informed Mr. Jinnah that the people of Junagadh, including Muslims, have requested him to solve the problem urgently. They are apprehensive that if the problem is not settled quickly, it will result in heavy bloodshed which nobody wants.

Jitenbhai informed that the Dewan had agreed for a negotiation, which was going on with Shri Shamlaldas Gandhi but the local Muslim leaders advised Sir Shahnawaz Bhutto to hand over the administration to the Government of India and not to the *Arzi Hukumat*. Sir Bhutto wrote to the Regional Commissioner Mr. Buch seeking his assistance in administration of the State. On 9 November 1947, Captain Harvey Jones, Brigadier Gurdial Singh and Mr. Buch took over the administration of Junagadh. The *Dewan* had already left for Karachi the previous day.

This was the news for which the entire people of India were waiting eagerly. They all knew that the smooth accession was made possible by Shri Vallabhbhai who combined his administrative, diplomatic and personal skills remarkably well.

Jitenbhai said, "Shri Vallabhbhai tried to persuade the Nawab, his Dewan and the Pakistan Government but they refused to see the reasoning. They should have realised that Shri Vallabhbhai will not bow to pressure, he cannot be bullied. He did not want to use force unnecessarily but was left with no other option. He used the force in a very discriminate manner. There was no gunfight. The accession of Junagadh is another feather in his cap."

Jayantibhai added, "The people of Junagadh are very happy."

Jitenbhai informed his friends in a joyous mood, "Shri Vallabhbhai is coming to Rajkot and Junagadh. Let us go and listen to him."

This was wonderful news. They had not met him for quite some time. Chamanbhai asked his brothers and other family members to join. Jayantibhai was already there covering the memorable event.

For Jitenbhai, Chamanbhai, their family members and friends, it was a thrilling moment to meet Sardar Shri after a long time. Although Shri Vallabhbhai was very busy, he spared some time for them.

The audience at Rajkot gave a lusty cheer to Shri Vallabhbhai. Sardar Shri began his speech by thanking Thakore Saheb, who, on that day itself, had instructed his Dewan to implement the agreement reached between Shri Vallabhbhai and the late Ruler of Rajkot on the 26th December, 1938.

He was referring to an agreement reached during the Rajkot Satyagrah which was launched against reckless administration, extravagance, palace intrigues, arrogance and manipulations by the officers which had emptied the state treasury. The State had resorted to impulsive and unfair measures such as heavy taxation, grant of monopolies, selling of the State's resources etc. for increasing its income. This was the State where Shri Kaba Gandhi, the father of Mahatma Gandhi had served as Dewan. Shri U.N. Dhebar and his colleagues were arrested during the *satyagrah*. The deteriorating situation had even compelled Mahatma Gandhi to undertake a fast.

After referring to the Rajkot Satyagrah, Shri Vallabhbhai said that the real purpose of his visit was solve the thorny problem, which has cropped up due to the sudden collapse of administration in Junagadh. This has affected the whole of Kathiawad.

Shri Vallabhbhai said, *"You know how the Nawab of Junagadh had left the State without a shot being fired. The trouble had been brought upon the Nawab's head by the wrong advice which he received from the people who were bent upon mischief and by the mechanisation of the Pakistan Government itself. Pakistan had no business to meddle in Junagadh."*

His hurt came out, *"When we accepted partition, we did so in the hope of a final settlement of a brotherly dispute. We felt that by satisfying the obstinate demand of a brother, who had been part of the joint family, we would bring peace to both of us and prosperity to all."*

Sardar Patel mentioned about the situation in the Punjab and Pakistan's malevolence in Rampur, then referring to Junagadh, he said, *"We warned them, we begged them, we reasoned with them but obstinacy was not conquered."*

Shri Vallabhbhai said that the troops were sent to Manavdar,

Mangrol and Babariawad for safeguarding the rights of the acceding States and for maintenance of peace in Kathiawad.

The Dewan's decision to hand over the administration of Junagadh had the approval of the Nawab of Junagadh and the backing of the people.

He called upon the people-Hindus and Muslims to forget the past and live happily together.

The next day, on November 13, Shri Vallabhbhai was given a very warm welcome at Junagadh. A big public meeting was held at the Bahauddin College, Junagadh. Jitenbhai, Dineshbhai, Prabhubhai, Chamanbhai and their family members went there ahead of time for finding a comfortable place among the front rows.

Shri Vallabhbhai congratulated the people, the Kathiawad Defence Force and the members of Junagadh Administration. He said that the Nawab has paid dearly for listening to the ill-intentioned and ill-omened advice.

He asked the people whether they accept the conclusion of the Junagadh's problem. Thousands of people raised their hands in response.

Sri Vallabhbhai also mentioned about the situation in Hyderabad and warned that *"Hyderabad's fate will sooner or later be the same as those of the other Rulers and dynasties who had attempted to thwart the popular will only at the cost of their existence. He said that the problem of Hyderabad is the affair of India and India alone."*

After the meeting, Jitenbhai went to see the organisers. He brought the news that Shri Vallabhbhai will be visiting Prabhas Patan the next day. Jitenbhai and his entire team also went there. Sardar Patel decided to construct a new grand temple at Somnath. The Jamsahab of Nawanagar announced a contribution of one lakh for this purpose and Shri Shamaldas Gandhi contributed ninety one thousand. The people were very happy at this announcement.

Chamanbhai was delighted. He and his friends asked Jitenbhai to celebrate this event. Jitenbhai said, "Of course, let us celebrate the occasion, but we should not forget that there are other major problems which require tactful handling."

Prabhubhai commented, "If the problems are given in the hands of Shri Vallabhbhai, he will solve them efficiently."

Soon after this, the administration of Junagadh was streamlined.

Jayantibhai brought the news that the Reserve Bank of India issued notes worth about 1.29 crores, which were taken by the Nawab. The dogs left behind by the Nawab in Junagadh were sold. The government saved Rs. 16,000 per month of dog maintenance cost!

Later, on the 20th February, 1948, the Government of India arranged a referendum under the supervision of Mr. C. B. Nagarkar ICS who was neither a Hindu nor a Muslim. There were 2,01,457 registered voters, out of them 1,90,870 voted. Only 91 voted for accession to Pakistan, the rest all voted for India. In a similar exercise held for Mangrol, Manavdar, Bantwa and Sardargadh out of 39,434 votes only 39 voted for Pakistan.

Later, an Executive Council comprising of Shri Shamaldas Gandhi, Shri Dayashankar Dave and Mrs. Pushpavati Mehta was constituted which did commendable work under the able leadership of Shri Shamaldas Gandhi. When the Saurashtra Union was formed then Junagadh and the States like Mangrol, Manavdar etc. were integrated with Saurashtra.

This was a great contribution from Shri Vallabhbhai who worked with tact, dignity and utmost devotion for integration of Junagadh and other States into Indian Union.

Jayantibhai brought the news that Shri Vallabhbhai is working on a plan for integration of the Sates from Orissa. He told that after the Haripura Congress *Praja Mandals* were formed in several States and people were trying to assert their democratic rights. Such *Praja Mandals* were organised in the states of Talcher and Dhenkanal also. A committee formed under the chairmanship of Shri Harekrishna Mahtab had recommended the integration of 26 States with Orissa. On 26 April, 1946, he had also written to the Cripps Mission requesting the integration of the States with the Province of Orissa.

The rulers were trying hard to prevent integration. They were obstructing the *Prajamandals* and were encouraging rifts among their members. As a counter measure to integration, at a meeting held at Raipur, thirty one States of Orissa and Chattisgarh formed the Eastern States Union which started functioning on 1 August, 1947. The secretariat of the Union was financed by contributions from the States. Some rulers even encouraged rift between tribal and non-tribal people. In Nilagiri, the Santhals attacked the non-tribals with bows and arrows. The situation soon became out of control.

Jitenbhai said, "Shri Harekrishna Mahatab, who was heading the Government of Orissa, had sought Shri Vallabhbhai's permission to take over the administration of Nilagiri."

Prabhubhai commented, "Shri Mehtab is a respected leader. He is a close associate of Shri Vallabhbhai."

Jayantibhai informed, "The Government of India gave the permission and on the 14th November, the Government of Orissa ordered the District Magistrate of Balasore to take over the administration of Nilagiri."

Jitenbhai said, "Shri Vallabhbhai called a High Level meeting in the office of Shri V.P. Menon. Shri Harekrishna Mahtab and the Regional Commissioner of Samabalpur attended the meeting. The meeting decided that the Eastern States Union will not be recognised, the B and C class of States will be brought under the Provincial Government for a common administration of certain subjects. It was also decided to call a meeting of the rulers of B and Class states in Cuttack."

Jayantibhai informed, "Shri Vallabhbhai is going to Orissa on the 13th with his team. He has a trusted colleague in Shri Mahtab. They will make all possible efforts to persuade the rulers to join the Indian Dominion. I have also been assigned to cover the visit and to report the developments for publication in the next issue of the journal."

Jayantibhai meticulously followed the situation and kept on sending reports about the developments. Jitenbhai compiled the information and briefed the people about the progress of the integration process.

Shri Harekrishna Mahtab and his colleagues had handled the situation well. On the 14th December, the Conference with the rulers of class B and C States began at 10 A.M. at the Government House. It was attended by twelve of the fifteen rulers of class B and C states including Raja Hruday Chandra Dev Birabar Hari Chandan of Talcher, Raja Brajendra Narendra Mahapatra and his mother Rajmata Manjari Devi of Ranpur, Raja Harihar Singh Mardraj Bhramarbar Ray of Khandapara, Raja Bahadur Kishore Chandra Deo Bhanj of Daspalla and others. The twelve States participating in the conference were Athgarh, Baramba, Daspalla, Hindol, Kharsavan, Khandapara, Narsinghpur, Nilgiri, Pallahara, Rairakhol, Ranpur and Talcher.

Sardar Patel explained the main objective of the meeting and said that the discontent among the people is growing, the law and order situation in the States is deteriorating and the safety of the rulers and the common people is in jeopardy. In a warm persuasive tone, Shri Vallabhbhai said that he has come to Orissa as a member of the family for finding a solution to a family problem. He explained that a strong Orissa was essential for ensuring peace and development. The small States did not have enough resources.

The Sardar requested the rulers to voluntarily relinquish their authority in the interests of Orissa. He assured that the Government of India will guarantee their privileges and honour.

He frankly said, "If you do not accept our proposal, I do not take responsibility for law and order in your State. You have to take care of yourself."

The rulers raised some questions which were answered by Sardar Shri and his team. When the young ruler of Ranpur enquired whether he could contest the election to the Orissa Assembly, Shri Vallabhbhai replied in his characteristic manner, "Why to attempt diving in a well? You will be entitled to swim in an ocean!"

The rulers were concerned about the privy purse and wanted it to be enhanced. The formula for deciding the amount was explained to them.

After some discussion, the twelve rulers agreed to sign the merger agreement. It was decided to contact the three States, which were absent to sign the agreement later. These states were Athmallik, Bonai and Tigaria.

In the afternoon, a meeting of the rulers of class A states began. Sardar Patel explained the situation and advised them to sign the merger agreement. He said that the States were like ulcers in the body of Orissa *which either need to be cured or eliminated. If they acted according to his advice they could be cured otherwise they will be removed by the people."*

The Raja of Mayurbhanj said that he has already established a ministry and he must consult his ministers before taking any decision. He left the Conference. The other rulers also avoided signing of the merger document. They wanted to gain time. However, Shri V.P. Menon diplomatically handled the situation well and he could convince the Raja of Dhenkanal, who agreed to sign the merger document with some conditions. He also convinced some other rulers to do so. Finally, ten rulers signed the merger document. Subsequently others also did so. Later on, the Raja of Mayurbhanj realised his mistake and signed the merger agreement.

At a public meeting on the 14th December, the Sardar thanked the people of Orissa for remaining unaffected by the communal trouble. He said that with united will and hard work, Orissa could become prosperous. He called upon them to sink their differences and follow the lead of Mahatma Gandhi by eradicating untouchability and fostering inter-communal unity.

Jayantibhai informed that on the next day, Shri Vallabhbhai also addressed ten rulers of the Chattisgarh States at Nagpur. He gave them an account of the developments at Cuttack and advised them to sign the merger agreement. He had an interactive session with the rulers and replied to their queries. Convinced, the rulers of the ten States signed the merger agreement.

After reaching Delhi, Shri Vallabhbhai issued a statement on the developments in Orissa and Chattisgarh States. It was focussed on Integration and Democratization. He thanked the rulers of the States *who showed commendable appreciation of the realities of the situation and a benevolent regard for the public good. To all of them, the decisions they have taken, have undoubtedly, involved considerable sacrifice of powers and fortunes. They have accepted this sacrifice cheerfully and voluntarily in the interests of the people and the country at large.*

Sardar Patel believed that the people would appreciate their sacrifice and generosity.

3

The onset of the winter had curtailed the working hours due to which, Chamanbhai had to spend some nights away from home on his routine business travels. His son Kantibhai was gaining valuable business experience in Bombay. The developments in Junagadh, Orissa, Chattisgarh and elsewhere had affected other parts of India also. After the accession of Junagadh, the demand for popular government was picking momentum in many States. In Kathiawad, the Congress Organisation, the *Kathiawad Rajakeey Parishad* was a well-organised unit, which had been benefitted with the guidance of Mahatma Gandhi, Sardar Patel and other leaders.

The States of Kathiawad were of a varying size and influence. There were 14 salute States, 17 non-salute States and 191 other States of various sizes. There were several small constituents also.

Chamanbhai was puzzled how these states will be integrated! This matter was discussed several times in the past but no body was able to give a satisfactory reply. They were unanimous in their understanding that with Shri Vallabhbhai at the helm of affairs, the problem will be solved. They had seen the accession of Junagadh and were told about the merger of states of Orissa and Chattisgarh. They were hopeful.

Chamanbhai raised his doubt, "But the situation in Kathiawad is different. We have salute States like Bhavnagar, Dhrangdhra, Dhrol, Gondal, Jafrabad, Junagadh, Limbdi, Morvi, Nawannagar, Palitana, Porbandar, Rajkot, and Wadhwan. There are so many small States..."

Prabhubhai interrupted, "And what about Vejanoness which had a population of about 200 people and an area a little over a quarter square mile? We have many tiny States."

"This is an interesting challenge. But don't you agree that Shri Vallabhbhai likes to handle difficult tasks! He has already galvanised his team which is working very hard. Shri V.P. Menon and his colleagues must have forgotten the difference between day and night!," another friend said.

Prabhubhai commented, "But after the lapse of paramountcy, there is an upsurge in the demand for popular government in the States. The rulers must be reading the writing on the wall."

Jitenbhai arrived. His smiling appearance indicated some good news. He said, "The ruler of Bhavnagar has taken the lead. He had been to Bapu to seek his guidance. Mahatmaji advised him to see Shri Vallabhbhai. Sardar Patel was very clear in his approach and he frankly suggested him to respect the peoples' demands for installation of a popular government. The ruler agreed to any amount of privy purse decided by Gandhiji."

The news transmitted a frisson of delight to the audience present. They clapped their hands and cheered Jitenbhai.

Jitenbhai said, "Don't clap for me, clap for the Maharaja of Bhavnagar who has demonstrated his leadership. We must express our gratitude to him for his foresight and sacrifice."

He continued, "It has been decided that the leader of the *Prajamandal,* Shri Balwantrai Mehta will be the Premier and the responsible Government of Bhavnagar will be inaugurated by Shri Vallabhbhai on January 15."

"This is the beginning of consolidation in Kathiawad." Chamanbhai commented.

Jitenbhai said, "Shri Vallabhbhai is handling the matter with great aplomb. He has already sought Bapu's blessings, is guiding Shri. V. P. Menon and his team but is keeping himself in the background. The respected Maharaja of Bhavnagar has given the lead. Things will improve quickly."

Prabhubhai said, "You will see, soon the brilliant Maharaja of Dhrangdhra will come in support of a united Kathiawad."

January 15 was a red-letter day for Bhavnagar. The popular government was installed there under the premiership of Shri Balwantrai Mehta. That day Sardar Patel addressed a huge meeting at Rajkot. He made a very powerful speech in Gujarati and said that small pools of water become stagnant, but if these are combined together, they can constitute a lake of cool water for everybody's benefit.

Shri Vallabhbhai's subtle, precise and effective guidance bore fruit. The Jamsaheb of Nawanagar came forward in support of a United Kathiawad and the rulers unanimously supported of the proposal.

A United Kathiawad was born.

Unfortunately, on the black day of 30 January 1948, the great tragedy struck the nation. The tragic death of Bapu shook the entire world. The Mahatma who devoted his entire life spreading the message of love, non-violence and peace, the respected leader who successfully led India's freedom struggle, the beacon light of millions was shot dead. At a crucial time when the country was facing serious problems on many fronts, India's Bapu was no longer available to guide them.

Chamanbhai and his family did not know how to absorb the shock.

He asked Jitenbhai, "How will Sardar Shri adjust himself to this situation?"

"It is a very difficult situation for him. I am afraid, he may even lose interest in his life," a worried Jitenbhai replied.

Prabhubhai said, "You are right, Jitenbhai. I have similar feelings. But I am also confident that Sardar Shri will handle his responsibilities with utmost devotion and efficiency."

It took several days for them to recover from the shock.

Shri Vallabhbhai inaugurated the United States of Kathiawad and Jamnagar on February 15th. The Jamsaheb was installed as the Rajpramukh. Bapu was no longer alive to see this great event. But the achievement was possible due to his influence and blessings, Sardar Patel's brilliant handling of the situation and dedicated efforts by Shri V.P. Menon and his colleagues.

Congratulations started pouring in. Congratulating the Jamsaheb, Pandit Nehru hoped that *this far-sighted act of statesmanship will be fully justified in growing economic prosperity and happiness of the people of Kathiawad.*

The Jamsaheb made a very impressive speech. He said in a candid manner, "*It is not as if we were tired monarchs who were fanned to rest. It is not as if we were bullied into submission. We have by our own free volition pooled out our sovereignties and covenanted to create this new State so that the United States of Kathiawad and the unity of India may be more fully achieved and so that our people may have that form of government which is today most acceptable to them and which I hope and pray will prove beneficial to them."*

Later, the new United States of Kathiawad was renamed as the United States of Saurashtra. Sardar's lake of coolness was created by merging the small pools.

"What a great achievement!" Chamanbhai said.

Jayantibhai continued to send good news about merger of states. The Deccan States and Kolhapur had been integrated into the Bombay Province. These mergers were examples of the negotiating capabilities of Sardar Patel and his practical guidance to his capable team led by Shri V.P. Menon. Subsequently, under Shri Vallabhbhai's guidance, Vindhya Pradesh was formed.

Driven by the love and devotion to the motherland, the Maharaja of Gwalior, achieved the honour of being the first ruler with 21-gun salute to agree to the integration of the State with India. After initial hesitation and falling in the group created by the Nawab of Bhopal, Indore also joined. Due to persistent efforts by Sardar Patel and Shri V.P. Menon, on 28 May, 1948, the Madhya Bharat Union was formed and was inaugurated by Pandit Jawaharlal Nehru.

Jitenbhai gave the bad news that the stress has taken a toll of the Sardar's health. He had suffered heart attack and was convalescing in Dehradun. But even during his convalescence, he was regularly giving directions to Shri Menon and his team and was advising the Prime Minister on various matters. On his directions, Shri Menon convinced the Maharaja of Patiala and secured his agreement for the establishment of a Union of the States of East Punjab and Patiala. In spite of his poor health, Sardar Patel went to inaugurate the Union at Patiala on 15th July, 1948. The Maharaja of Patiala played a key role in convincing the other rulers to sign the agreement.

In his address at the opening ceremony, Shri Vallabhbhai said that *a new chapter in the history of India is opening before us. This is the first time in the history after centuries, that India can call itself an integrated whole in the real sense of term. But we must all resolve that whatever mistake we might commit, we should do nothing that which would be calculated to send India back into the slavery of the past. We must also realize that if we have to take our due place in the comity of nations, it will not come to us for the asking, we shall have to strain every nerve for it.*

Shri Vallabhbhai reminded the audience of his own statement made in the past that *if we approach the princes in the right fashion, they themselves would be willing to surrender their power.* He also reminded the people of his request *to give an undisturbed passage to the refugees going to Pakistan.*

He reiterated that his only desire is that *India should be well protected and that it should be for every Indian to see that there are no loopholes or weak links in the whole system of security, both external and internal.*

Sardar Patel addressed the Maharaja of Patiala as his friend and brother and *appreciated his notable contribution made to the unity and integrity of India. He reminded the people that the Maharaja took up the case of the country at a time when there were few friends amongst the Princely Order and when serious attempts were being made to balkanise India by means of one or more "Raja-sthans." It was his patriotic lead that contributed in a large measure to a change in the attitude of the Princes to the problem of accession to the Indian Dominion.*

Shri Vallabhbhai completed his speech by telling that *the future is now with the people, they themselves can make or mar it.*

During his address Shri Vallabhbhai also mentioned about Hyderabad. He said, *"Many have asked me what is going to happen in Hyderabad? They forget that when I spoke at Junagadh, I said openly that if Hyderabad did not behave properly, it would have to go the way Junagadh did. Those words still stand and I stand by those words. The former Governor-General, Lord Mountbatten thought that he would be able to secure a peaceful settlement. I let him try. He tried his best. But although up to the last Lord Mountbatten was hopeful of settlement, that hope never materialised owing to the intransigence of the Nizam and the fanaticism of the forces at his back."*

He continued, *"But I should like to make one thing clear. The terms and the talks which Lord Mountbatten was hopeful of settlement, those terms and the talks which Lord Mountbatten had, have gone with him. Now the settlement with the Nizam will have to be on the lines of other settlements with the States."*

Shri Vallabhbhai was almost prophetic when he said, *"No help from outside, on which he seems to rest his pathetic hopes would avail him."*

Kantibhai's wholesale grain traders had business dealings in Jaipur, Udaipur and Alwar. They brought some disturbing news about the violence in Bharatpur and Alwar. It was alleged that the Meos, started the disturbances, which affected both the States.

Although Sardar Patel had cautioned them against the violence but the two States were unable to maintain peace. The Government of India took over the control of Alwar and the Maharaja of Bharatpur decided to hand over the administration of the State to the Government of India. Subsequently the neighbouring States of Dholpur and Karauli also agreed to join a proposed union of these States, which was known as the *Matsya Union*- a name suggested by Shri K.M. Munshi which was based upon the name of a kingdom in the area during the Mahabharat era.

This was another achievement for Shri Vallabhbhai and Shri V.P. Menon. On 25.3.1948, Banswara, Bundi, Kota, Dungarpur, Jhalwar, Shahpura, Partabgarh, Kishangadh and Tonk took the initiative to form the Rajasthan Union. The Union was inaugurated by the Prime Minister Pandit Nehru on the 11th April 1948. Thanks to their efforts and driven by his love for the country, on 18.4.1948, the Maharaja of Udaipur decided to join the Union and the United States of Rajasthan was formed.

Jayantibhai who covered the celebrations on behalf of his news magazine, brought first-hand reports of the jubilation of the people of these States. There was unprecedented enthusiasm all over. Even the most vitriolic critics were astonished at the speed, efficiency and smoothness of the integration.

Jitenbhai celebrated the event with his friends. Prabhubhai was the first to comment, "This is a very good example for other States to follow. Now only Bikaner, Jaipur, Jaisalmer and Jodhpur are remaining out. These are big States and their integration is essential. Bikaner, Jaipur and Jodhpur want to maintain their identity. They have borders with Pakistan and are being enticed by them. This is a serious matter because key security issues are involved."

Jitenbhai said, "We know his nature well. He will not take rest when he has such major responsibilities to handle. He wants to have a Greater Rajasthan Union for which he is actively working with his team. Shri Vallabhbhai has already announced that the four States will be integrated with the Rajasthan Union."

It was a difficult task, which required continuous discussions in a spirit of mutual understanding, cooperation and goodwill. Technical details had to be worked out and the rulers needed to be convinced about their privileges. Jayantibhai was regularly sending updates on the developments in the Rajasthan Union and in other states. Finally, he gave the good news that the States of Bikaner, Jaipur, Jodhpur and Jaisalmer joined the United States of Rajasthan to form Greater Rajasthan which was inaugurated at Jaipur on March 30, 1949.

On 15 May, 1949, the Matsya Union was merged into Greater Rajasthan.

Shri Vallabhbhai never failed to pay his compliments to the princes for their sacrifice and patriotism. Addressing at the inauguration of the Rajasthan Union on May 30th, 1949, he said, *"Now for the first time, India is integrated and bigger than ever before in the history. This we now have to consolidate and our freedom must be made so deep-rooted as to be unshakable."*

He also had a word of advice for his fellow Congressmen. He said that their claim to power and authority springs from their being followers of Mahatma Gandhi in the fight for India's freedom. "*Any further and future claim or honour that we find shall also be through sacrifice for the poor and the downtrodden. Our proper place is not at the vantage points of power but at the vantage points of service.*"

Shri Vallabhbhai was trying to find a solution for the States of Travancore and Cochin. Sir C.P. Ramaswamy Aiyer the Dewan of Travancore had earlier surprised and pained the people by announcing independence for the State. As a result, there were violent protests and political disturbances in the state. There was a feeling among the people that Sir CP was given too much authority. Public opinion was against him.

One day Jitenbhai brought the news that there was an attempt on Sir C.P. Ramaswamy Iyer's life on July 25, 1947. He said, "When Sir CP was attending a music function in Trivendrum, an unsuccessful attempt was made on his life. He received several injuries and subsequently left Travancore and went to Madras."

Somebody asked, "Who has succeed him?"

"He has been succeeded by Shri P.G.N. Unnithan."

Jitenbhai commented, "Now we can expect good progress in the integration of Travancore and Cochin."

He was right. Under the guidance of Sardar Patel, Shri V.P. Menon had several rounds of discussion with Sree Chithira Thirunal, the

Maharaja of Travancore. As a result of these negotiations, the ruler of Travacore agreed to accede to the Indian Union.

Jitenbhai said, "It was a very difficult task to perform but due to persistent efforts and deft handling by Sardar, the Union of Travancore and Cochin was formed on the 1st July, 1949."

Chamanbhai commented, "This is another important achievement of Sardar Shri and his team."

The Maharaja of Mysore had signed the Instrument of Accession and Standstill Agreement in August 1947. At a later date, when Sardar Patel was sick, he called Shri V.P. Menon and asked him to settle his privy purse. Shri V.P. Menon went to Mysore, discussed the matter and settled the matter. An agreement was signed by both the parties.

Jitenbhai commented, "Although Shri Vallabhbhai was not well, he asked Maniben to call Shri V.P. Menon. Shri Menon was worried about Sardar Shri's health. When he reached Sardar Shri's residence, Shri Vallabhbhai asked him to settle the privy purse of the Maharaja of Mysore."

Chamanbhai said, "Sardar was sick but his mind was busy in managing important matters."

Jitenbhai informed, "Just after Independence, on a visit to Kanyakumari, Sardar Shri took a bath in the holy place and resolved to work for a strong and united India. He has a vision and an image of united India in his mind. I am sure that in spite of his poor health, Sardar Shri will manage the difficult issue of integration of Hyderabad into the Dominion of India."

Chamanbhai agreed, "Our hopes reside in him."

4

Since June 3, 1947 when the Mountbatten Plan of giving freedom to India on the 15th August, 1947, was announced, like the rulers of many other States, the Nizam was nursing the ambition of ruling Hyderabad as a sovereign State. He was actively supported by his courtiers and sycophants, the militant and fanatic Razakars and a section of the British politicians and press. The entire country was worried and concerned about the developments there.

Jayantibhai had made several trips to Hyderabad and other areas. He had talked to many people in the cities and in villages. Out of about 1.6 crore people living in the State, more than 86% were Hindus, about 12.5% Muslims, about 1.5 % Christians and others. About 7 million people spoke Telugu, 4 million Marathi and about 2 million Kannada. Urdu was the language of the ruling elite and aristocracy.

The Nizam-ill advised by his impractical and some fanatic advisers wanted to make Hyderabad an independent Islamic State.

Shri Vallabhbhai had decided to request Lord Mountbatten to handle the negotiations, who consulted the Sardar on the matter. Although Shri Vallabhbhai was not maintaining good health, he was closely monitoring the situation and was giving necessary directions to Shri V.P. Menon for handling the negotiations in the best interests of the country.

Jitenbhai was bringing disturbing news about Hyderabad.

Chamanbhai and his friends were seriously disappointed when the Nizam issued a *Firman* on the 26th June 1947 that Hyderabad will not participate in the Constituent Assembly and it will not join the Dominion of India. He also proclaimed that with the lapse of Paramountcy, he is entitled to declare his independence.

Jitenbhai informed, "The Nizam has an understanding with a rabidly fanatic organisation Majlis-e-Ittehadul Musalman, headed by hate-monger Kasim Razvi, which is spreading communal fire in a most irresponsible manner. With not so covert support of the State machinery, the organisation was fermenting trouble through the Razakars who were dangerously militant. They were bent upon disturbing communal harmony. In his misguided frenzy, the Nizam wants to treat Hyderabad on an equal footing with India! Even flying of the National flag has been banned by him."

A fellow advocate Prabhubhai said, "Some people say that the Nizam has assigned all key positions in his government to the members of this communal organisation Majlis-e-Ittehadul Musalman."

"Yes. The situation is very dangerous."

The lion-hearted Shri Vallabhbhai showed his magnanimity in offering many concessions for maintaining good relations with the Nizam and communal harmony in Hyderabad. Several relaxations were offered and a Standstill Agreement was signed, the Government of India even agreed to a seriously unreasonable demand from Mr. Laiq Ali, the Prime Minister of Hyderabad, that instead of the Instrument of Accession, an Instrument of Association should be singed between Hyderabad and the Government of India.

Jitenbhai said, "While the diplomatic activities were going on, arms and ammunition were being stored for fighting India. A Gun Factory was established and various related preparations were in the full swing. At the same time, Kasim Razvi was delivering ferocious speeches against India and Hindus on a regular basis."

Prabhubhai reminded, "At the time of Independence, the population of Hyderabad was about 1.6 crores, comprising of 86% Hindus, 12.5% Muslims, 1.5% Christians and others. But all the key positions in the government were held by Muslims."

Jitenbhai added, "When the question of appointing a Political Agent for Hyderabad had come, Shri Vallabhbhai had selected his trusted colleague Shri K.M. Munshi for this extremely onerous task. Before leaving for Hyderabad, when Munshiji had gone to seek Bapu's blessings, Mahatmaji had said that he will face problems from Ittehad and Razakars. Knowing the difficulties fully well, Shri Munshi, willingly accepted the difficult responsibility and he is facing serious problems in Hyderabad. He was not even given an appropriate accommodation, he does not have freedom of movement. But as a true disciple of Gandhiji and a devoted lieutenant of Shri Vallabhbhai he is bravely managing a very difficult situation there."

Prabhubhai said, "On the 27th August, the Nizam had quoted his earlier speech, made on the 14th August in which he had said that after the departure of the British, he should become an independent sovereign. He said that on the 15th August, 1947, he has assumed that status."

Chamanbhai commented, "What a fantastic fantasy! And to think that Shri Vallabhbhai will allow that to happen!"

Prabhubhai Observed, "He seriously underestimate Shri Vallabhbhai's skill and strategy. You will see, Sardar Patel will show his finesse in handling the situation at the appropriate time."

Jitenbhai added, "The Nizam is being pampered by Pakistan, a section of the conservative British politicians and the press. But remember what did Shri Vallabhbhai do on the 29th November when he submitted the agreement and other correspondence to the Constituent Assembly? He was magnanimous in his approach. He said that the agreement for a period of one year has been signed for forging closer relations and for creating an environment of mutual understanding and goodwill."

Prabhubhai lamented, "But what happened thereafter! Instead of reciprocating the goodness shown by the Government of India, the Nizam, upon the advice of his short-sighted advisors issued disturbing ordinances declaring that the Indian currency was no longer a legal tender in Hyderabad. He also banned *export* of precious metals from Hyderabad to India!"

"What a strange thing to do!" Chmanbhai said.

Prabhubhai added, "These were potentially dangerous ill-advised decisions. In addition, the Nizam advanced a *loan* of twenty crores to Pakistan in the form of Government of India securities. This was done in a clandestine manner by his minister Nawab Moin Nawaz Jung who was also the brother-in-law of Mr. Laik Ali."

Jitenbhai said, "The Government of India came to know about another dangerous step taken by the Nizam. His Government had appointed trade representatives in some countries like UK, USA, Canada, Egypt etc. Mr. Laik Ali announced that Hyderabad's case would be referred to the UNO. The Nizam also requested the

President of the USA to intervene but the President declined to do so."

He added, "The Nizam has banned the national flag, even photographs of great leaders could not be displayed, singing of Vande Matram was prohibited and Congress was declared a communal organisation."

Chamanbhai said, "They have gone too far. Something must be done now. There is a limit to patience!"

Prabhubhai said, "The Congress leaders Swami Ramanand Tirth, Shri B. Ramakrishna Rao and others were defying the orders and were mobilising public protest against the atrocities committed by notorious Razakars and Ittehad. Many Muslim nationalists such as Mr. Abdul Hassan, Mr. Syed Tirmizi and others were actively supporting the Congress."

Jitenbhai added, "On August 22,1948 Mr. Shoebullah Khan, the young editor of *the Imroz* weekly was brutally murdered in front of his house. His hands were chopped-off. His earlier paper *the Taj* and the *Rayyat* were banned by the Nizam. Shoeb had clearly understood that the future of Hyderabad lied in its integration with India but the fanatics won't listen to reasoning."

"This was very unfortunate. On one hand, the Nizam's government was tacitly encouraging the Razakars and Ittehad, on the other hand, they were also trying to gain time by engaging the Government of India in fruitless discussions, parrot-like homily and repetitive correspondence ad nauseam. The Nizam was hopeful that his advisor Sir Walter Monkton would be able to influence Lord Mountbatten in his favour. That could not happen. Sir Monkton left for England but was again called back by the Nizam."

Prabhubhai said, "I have heard that in a meeting with Mr. Laik Ali, Shri Vallabhbhai had clearly said that the Hyderabad problem has to be decided in the same manner as has been done with the other states."

"You are absolutely right," Jitenbhai said. He looked at Jayantibhai who referred to some papers in his folders and read from the paper- *" Shri Vallabhbhai told Mr. Laik Ali that the Hyderabad problem will have to be settled as has been done in the case of other States. No other way is possible. We cannot agree to the continuance of an isolated spot which would destroy the very Union which we have built up with our blood and toil. At the same time, we do wish to maintain friendly relations and to seek a friendly solution. This does not mean that we shall ever agree to Hyderabad's independence. If its demand to maintain an independent status persists in, it is bound to fail."*

"What a clear statement," Chamanbhai said.

Terrorised by the Razakars, many people had left the Hyderabad State and had taken shelter in the bordering states. Law and order situation in Hyderabad was deteriorating fast. The Razakars were concentrating on the borders with other states and were attacking the lives and property of innocent people on one pretext or the other. Armed raiders had created terror in several villages and along border areas.

Jayantibhai was sent by his management to Delhi for getting more details. Jitenbhai had given a letter of introduction addressed to a friend who was in a position to help Jayantibhai. Jayantibhai met journalists from other parts of India and some other countries of the world. He found that a section of foreign press was very sympathetic to the Nizam. They were made to believe that the situation in Hyderabad is normal and the Ittehad is only involved in genuine political activities. He was told that some influential media persons are being treated to lavish hospitalities by the Nizam's government, they are not allowed to see the situation in the areas where atrocities have been committed by the Razakars. Many correspondents had not visited the place, they were printing what the Ittehad wanted them to publish!

Jayantibhai came to know that Shri Rajgopalachari, the Governor General of India who replaced Lord Mountbatten, was alarmed at the situation. He had written to the Nizam requesting him to ban the Razakar's organisation and to control the situation. The Government of India again reminded the Nizam, drawing his attention to the violence in the neighbouring States, holding of trains, loot, arson and other atrocities which were occurring on a daily basis. The communal peace was shattered But it was maintained by the Nizam's government that no atrocities have been committed, the reports are biased and exaggerated.

In order to clarify the situation, the Government of India, on the 26th July, 1948, issued a White Paper on Hyderabad which gave the complete details of the correspondence and of the atrocities committed by the Razakars. Shri Vallabhbhai said, *"Hyderabad had become an ulcer in the heart of India and this ulcer had to be operated."*

Jayantibhai reported, "The Government of India has already posted army at the border states. Despite his poor health, Shri Vallabhbhai, has returned to Delhi from Dehradun and is handling the situation."

"He will not remain a silent spectator, he will do something," Prabhubhai said.

Prabhubhai was not wrong. The situation was going completely out of control. Jayantibhai rushed to Hyderabad. He reached there at the correct time.

In order to maintain peace in Hyderabad and in the neighbouring Indian States, the Government of India decided for police action and sent troops into Hyderabad. A meticulous plan was drawn and *Operation Polo* was launched under the direction of GOC-in-Chief Southern Command Lt. General Maharaj Sri Rajendra Sinhji. Major General J.N. Chaudhry commanded the force. On wee hours of September 13, forces marched towards Hyderabad from Sholapur and from Bezwada. Hyderabad was 186 miles away from Sholapur and the distance between Bezwada and Hyderabad was 160 miles.

The Razakar tried to put up a fight in the beginning but their much swaggering resistance collapsed after two days. On the very first day, the Indian troops captured Lieutenant T. T. More, a retired officer of the British Army, who was employed in the Nizam's army. Lt. Moore was on a mission to destroy the Naldrug and other bridges and was carrying heavy ammunition in his jeep. He was acting on an information that the India army was expected to start operations on the 15th and not on the 13th September.

There was some resistance at Zaheerabad where a bridge at Ekhelli was blown up but the Indian army was able to construct the bridge and captured Zaheerabad on the 16th September.

The Nizam asked his forces to surrender on the 17th September. The ministry of Mr. Laik Ali resigned on the same day.

Addressing the people on the 17th September, the Nizam announced that he has sent a message to HE Shri C. Rajgopalachari, Governor General of India, informing him *that he has ordered cease fire to his troops and have also ordered to disband the Razakars. He is allowing the Indian troops to occupy Bolaram and Secundrabad Barracks.*

The message said that *he has issued orders to release the Congress President Swami Ramananda Tirth, who he was sure will help, Hyderabad in this crisis.*

Addressing Shri K.M. Munshi as *his friend*, the Nizam said that he had had consultations with him and thanked him for his help.

The Nizam hoped that once law and order is restored in Hyderabad, *it would not be difficult to arrive at an arrangement with the Government of India under which my people, whose welfare is my only concern, can live in integrated harmony with the rest of the people of India.*

He said that he *has asked his ministry not to press for the appeal in the Security Council. He wanted to open a new chapter of friendliness with India.*

Mr. Mir Laik Ali's broadcast on the 17th September was that of a battered enemy which did not show any friendly sentiments for India. But the Nizam, in his second broadcast, made an appeal to the people not to panic. He said that *the entry of troops will take place in a spirit of friendliness. The Indian army is India's Army in which I include Hyderabad. It is your Army, an Army of friends to rescue the life of Hyderabad from the nightmare of the past twelve months.*

Major General Chaudhry entered Hyderabad on the 18th September and was designated as the Military Governor. The entire operation was completed in 108 hours. Kasim Razvi was arrested from the house of his relative on the 19th September. Some other Razakar leaders were also arrested.

The sabre-rattling was left behind, there was no communal violence. A proclamation issued by Lt. Gen Rajendra Sinhji asked the people to maintain peace and order. On the 23rd September the Nizam sent a cable to the Security Council withdrawing his complaint. On the 23rd November, the Nizam announced the integration of Hyderabad with the Union of India.

The successful solution of the knotty Hyderabad problem sent a wave of jubilation throughout the country.

Jitenbhai and his friends were exuberant. Their period of exultation lasted for several days. They were all full of praise for Shri Vallabhbhai. Thanks to his determination and able guidance, the knotty Hyderabad problem was finally solved.

Jitenbhai said, "Shri Vallabhbhai has made several important contributions to the country, but Hyderabad's is the crowning one. We do not know what would have happened otherwise..."

Prabhubhai interrupted, "Yes. The situation had sharply deteriorated. It was the right time to enforce police action there."

So far, Chamanbhai had been more a patient listener than a vocal speaker in the group meetings, but today he felt that this was the appropriate time to appreciate Shri Vallabhbhai's contribution in the entire Hyderabad episode. He listened to the bits of information brought by Jayantibhai which was narrated and analysed by Jitenbhai. Prabhubhai. Dineshbhai, Chamanbhai and other friends have been discussing the matter for quite some time. Chamanbhai was now having a clear idea of the situation.

He said, "We have to understand the nuances of the situation and the brilliant handling of the matter by Shri Vallabhbhai. He first kept himself in the background and let Lord Mountbatten handle the matter. When Shri Vallabhbhai differed with him, he placed his views frankly and openly. He went out of the way to accommodate the ever-increasing demands of the Nizam and his team. He gave an open option for the establishment of a popular government which the Nizam did not agree. Shri Vallabhbhai continued giving more and more concessions. The situation was deteriorating sharply but Sardar Patel waited for the good sense to prevail. When all options were exhausted then only he ordered police action."

Prabhubhai added, "His health was not good. As soon as he recovered, he came back from Dehradun and guided his team."

"Our grateful thanks to him. India will never forget his great contribution," Chamanbhai said.

"Alas, the task of integrating Jammu and Kashmir should also have been given to him!" Jitenbhai lamented.

Subsequently, when India became a republic on the 26th January, 1950, Hyderabad became a class B State of India. The Nizam was appointed the Rajpramukh of the State.

News about disturbances in Kashmir was coming right since independence. The Maharajah was unable to decide about the accession for quite some time. Perhaps the vacillating attitude or his compulsion gave some advantage to Pakistan which tried its best to exploit the situation in its favour.

There was an uncomfortable view among the workers that if the responsibility of securing the integration of Jammu and Kashmir was given to Sardar Patel, the problem would have been solved. While the States department was tasked with the responsibility of integration of all States, the integration of Jammu and Kashmir was handled directly by the Prime Minister. Shri Vallabhbhai's followers were finding it difficult to understand the reasons for making this fateful exception!

In a weekly meeting, Uma asked Jayantibhai to explain the situation in Kashmir. Jayantibhai had not followed the developments, he checked with his fellow journalists who were also not updated on the matter. It took him some time to gather authentic information. Jitenbhai invited some other leaders to his weekly meetings to explain the situation. This was particularly informative for Uma and the women workers who wanted to know the latest situation in Jammu and Kashmir but were unable to get it at one place. The explanation was precise and once again showed that a decisive and effective approach was necessary in the matter which the Sardar would have certainly taken.

Jitenbhai briefed, "After independence, Maharajah Shri Hari Singh had decided to sign the Standstill Agreement with both India and Pakistan. Pakistan signed the agreement, India waited for some time. The Government of Jammu and Kashmir was complaining that Pakistan was not honouring the agreement and was bullying them to sign the Instrument of Accession. They had stopped the supply of petrol and some other essential items and were creating problems in the smooth transit of travellers to Pakistan. The Government of Jammu and Kashmir had approached the Government of Pakistan to supply 50000 gallons of petrol, which was not supplied by Pakistan. Upon request, India sent 500 gallons."

He continued, "When the news of the invasion of Kashmir by the frontier tribesmen in October 1947 had reached Jitenbhai, everybody was quite surprised at Pakistan's move of attacking the State of Jammu and Kashmir which had not acceded to India at that time. The attack was purely communal in character, the Muslim staff of the J&K's battalion had deserted and had joined the invaders. Brigadier Rajendra Singh, who was the Chief of Staff of the J&K Forces, fought valiantly. With just 150 men, he defended Uri, destroyed the strategic Uri Bridge and kept the invaders engaged for two days. He and his soldiers were brutally cut to pieces. On the

24th October, the invaders had captured the Power House at Mahura and had cut off power supply to Srinagar. The invaders had boasted that they would celebrate Eid at Srinagar Mosque on 26th October."

Jitenbhai had informed his friends that on the 24th October, the Maharajah had sent an S.O. S. to the Government of India for help; but the Governor General Lord Mountbatten said that since J&K had not acceded to India, it would be improper to send Indian troops there. By that time, the invaders had almost reached Baramula and were likely to enter Srinagar in a day or two. Shri V.P. Menon was immediately sent to Srinagar to assess the situation. He met the Maharajah and saw that the administration had collapsed, people were in panic and rumours were afoot that the invaders have already infiltrated Srinagar.

Mr. Menon returned to Jammu where the Maharajah had shifted with Mr. Mehar Chand Mahajan, the Prime Minister of J&K. The Maharajah was desperately waiting for Shri Menon. He signed the Instrument of Accession to India and requested immediate help from the Indian Army.

Although the matter was handled directly by the Prime Minister and Lord Mountbatten, Sardar Patel was waiting for Shri Menon at the airport. They straightway went to the meeting of the Defence Committee, where after prolonged discussions, the Instrument of Accession was accepted.

It was a Herculean task to organise the air lifting of the troops to Srinagar within a very short time and to push the invaders back. This was done with remarkable swiftness. Shri Shankar, Shri Sarin and his other colleagues worked very hard within a critically short time to facilitate the availability of aircraft for air lifting of troops.

Meanwhile Mr. Jinnah had invited Mr. Mountbatten and Pandit Nehru to Lahore to discuss the situation. Shri Vallabhbhai did not like the proposal. He was of the view that since Pakistan was the aggressor, Mr. Jinnah should come to Delhi for discussion. The matter was referred to Mahatma Gandhi but coincidently Pandit Nehru had developed high fever, Lord Mountbatten and Lord Ismay went to Lahore and held discussions with Mr. Jinnah. Lord Mountbatten asked the invaders to go back to Pakistan.

Sardar Patel and the Defence Minister Sardar Baldev Singh visited Srinagar on November 3 and discussed the situation with the ministers and with the defence officers. Shri Vallabhbhai and Shri Baldev Singh asked the forces to take back Barmula which they did on the 8th November under the command of Major-General Kalwant Singh. Uri was recovered on the 11st November.

Meanwhile, the meetings between India and Pakistan, Pakistan always raised the issue of withdrawal of Indian troops, which Pandit Nehru objected. Lord Mountbatten and Pandit Nehru were insisting that Pakistan should call back the invaders.

Several rounds of inconclusive high-level meetings took place. Finally, Lord Mountbatten requested Gandhiji and Pandit Nehru to agree to his previous suggestion of refereeing the dispute to the UNO.

"Sardar Patel strongly objected to this proposal. In his opinion, it was a blunder to refer the dispute to the UNO. The Maharajah had signed the Instrument of Accession, a popular government under the Prime Ministership of Sheikh Abdullah was installed, the Indian Army was in a strong position to push the invaders back to Pakistan and retrieve the lost territory. What was the wisdom in referring the dispute to the UNO?" Jitenbhai commented.

"But the matter was being handled by the Prime Minister's office."

Shri Vallabhbhai was very upset when the Kashmir issue was referred to the UN.

Jitenbhai commented, "I read somewhere that Bakshi Gulam Mohammad wanted that Sardar Patel should handle and solve the Kashmir issue. But that did not happen."

"We know the result," said Prabhubhai in a dejected mood.

Uma was trying her best to help Chamanbhai and her children settle in their respective roles. Situation in the country was unstable, people were reluctant to take risks and recovery of debts was a problem. Yet there was an undercurrent of hope and enthusiasm among the workers and the general public. They were already groomed to make sacrifices, they had adopted a simple living and their needs were few. This was a major contribution from Gandhiji, Sardar Patel and other leaders to the people.

When the accession of Hyderabad was secured, Sardar Patel was the acting Prime Minister. Pandit Nehru was abroad and Shri Vallabhbhai was in Bombay. Streams of visitors were coming and congratulatory messages were pouring in droves.

In a weekly meeting, Jitenbhai discussed the situation in Baroda. Baroda was the first State to sign the Standstill Agreement and the Instrument of Accession. In fact, Baroda inspired other states to follow integration in the Indian Union. However, the credit was marred by their subsequent actions.

When Shri Vallabhbhai was handling the difficult problem of accession of Junagarh, the rulers of Kathiawad had given their full cooperation to Sardar Patel. But at that time, on the 2nd September, 1947, the ruler of Baroda had written a letter to Shri Vallabhbhai, in which he said that *Baroda was ready to shoulder the responsibility of maintaining law and order as well as peace and tranquillity of the entire Kathiawad subject to several conditions.* These conditions were aimed at expanding the hegemony. There was an uncomfortable impression that the ruler of Baroda wanted to place himself in the same position as the Nizam.

This suo motu offer was responded by Sardar Patel in a befitting manner who retorted that Government of India had not asked for, and does not need his help. Shri Vallabhbhai had admonished him that the territorial ambitions of the ruler will bring disaster. Realising the gravity of the situation, the Maharajah had adopted a conciliatory tone by putting the blame on his Dewan Sri B.L. Mitter. But it was Shri Mitter who had advised the Maharajah to sign the Instrument of Accession!

The matter was put behind. However, one evening, some business associates of Chamanbhai from Baroda brought the news that the Maharajah was withdrawing huge amount of money and from the state treasury. Shri Vallabhbhai had directed Shri V.P. Menon to convince the Maharajah for agreeing to the merger of Baroda with Bombay.

Jitenbhai tried to get further information on the matter. He came to know that the Maharajah had visited Delhi and had a meeting with Shri Vallabhbhai. The Maharajah had told Sri Vallabhbhai that he will take a decision on the matter after consulting the Maharani Sahiba.

Jitenbhai said, "Initially the Sardar wanted to announce the merger of the State of Baroda with Bombay, but he was requested by the Maharajah not to do so. After several rounds of discussion, he had finally agreed for the merger and signed the merger document.

The Maharajah himself announced about the merger on the 31st January, 1949."

A few days later, Jayantibhai brought the news that the Government of Bombay will take over the administration of the Baroda State on the 1st May, 1949. He said, "I plan to attend the public function in Bombay."

Jayantibhai said, "Last week I had been to Baroda. There are matters pending about the amount of money, jewellery and other movable wealth taken by the Maharajah. The issue of Privy Purse is yet to be decided to mutual satisfaction. Several other legal matters which need to be sorted out. Things are not going well there. People feel that the situation needs another intervention by Shri Vallabhbhai."

The loss of territory to Pakistan had given a rude shock to the people. Even greater was the shock of communal conflict in various parts of the country. Was it necessary to divide the country? The number of Muslims in India outnumbered those in Pakistan, which demolished the much pampered but unrealistic two-nation theory. If the creation of Pakistan was agreed in the interest of peace then the assumption was belied. Why should India lose its territory? India had lost about 3.6 lakh square miles of its territory and 81.5 million people to Pakistan. It was impossible to convince the common person about the logic of partition.

However, with passage of time, people had reconciled to the situation. After the integration of the States, they had the satisfaction of living in a united India-their country devotedly united by her great son.

In a weekly meeting, Jitenbhai said, "With the integration of the States, India has added about 5 lakhs sq miles of area and 86.5 million people to united India. Apart from being a matter of compensation and consolation to us, it is also a matter of pride for every Indian."

Prabhubhai said, "The integration of States is a great achievements for our Sardar. He has used his negotiating skill, his art of persuasion, the force of his strong personality and the practical application of his sound judgement to achieve it."

Chamanbhai added, "He had adopted a very friendly approach in convincing the rulers. But he also said that States should maintain cordial relationship with their people, should recognise their rights and encourage the establishment of popular governments."

Jitenbhai said, "It was a miracle. Only our Sardar was capable of integrating the States within such a short time. His art of persuasion was so convincing! He never failed to thank and congratulate the rulers for their cooperation which brought about the integration."

"We are proud of him, every Indian is proud of him."

Uma shouted, *"Sardar Patel ki Jay."*

Everybody joined her in repeating it.

Chamanbhai said, "Jitenbhai, When you meet him next, please request him to take some rest. After the heart attack, he is not running a good health, he is suffering from acute pain in his stomach but he continues to work hard."

Prabhubhai said, "You are absolutely right . After Bapu's death, he has become more serious. I read somewhere that he had told Bapu that he does now want to live after Bapu is gone. When the negotiations about Hyderabad were in progress, one afternoon at the lunchtime he had suffered heart attack. When he regained consciousness he had asked his doctor '*Why did you stop me, I was going to Bapu?*'

Jitenbhai added, "Did he ever care for his health? He has been travelling to various places solving one critical problem after the other."

"What about Ahmedabad? Will he find time to come here?" Asked Uma.

Her desire came true. The people of Ahmedabad wanted to present him a purse of fifteen lakhs to him on his birthday. It was a momentous occasion for Chamanbhai and his friends. People had lined up along the roads and had showered flower petals on him. They cheered him all the way and expressed their love to him in a jubilant manner. It was a very happy day for Chamanbhai and Uma.

The last time they had seen Sardar Patel was in 1949 when he had visited the Swaraj Ashram, Bardoli. He was in a poor state of health at that time also. His Ahmedabad visit was a memorable one for Chamanbhai.

The Sardar said, "I am a peasant and a humble congress worker."

Shri Vallabhbhai was satisfied that he was able to convince the peasants to take pride in themselves.

This statement touched Chamanbhai's heart. The son of the soil was back!

Chamanbhai and his family regularly visited their family home at Ras. Jivanbhai had become quite old but he was still supervising the farming work. He was the head of the family and all family members were following his instructions without asking any questions. Chamanbhai always used to feel like a child in his presence.

The news of integration of various States had reached the villages and there was excitement and joy among the people. The architect of the unification was their own Sardar who had visited their village and was arrested during the Dandi March. Whenever Chamanbhai came home, the gathering at the *choro* was bigger. Nandubhai always used to ask several questions to Chamanbhai. The weekly briefing by Jitenbhai had equipped Chamanbhai with the current updates and he enjoyed telling the details of integration of States to them. Uma was equally popular among the womenfolk.

One afternoon, Nandubhai said, "I am unable to understand what made Shri Vallabhbhai change his life style. Initially he was not impressed with Gandhiji. In fact, when Gandhiji came to the Gujarat Club, Shri Vallabhbhai was busy playing bridge and he even scoffed at Mavlankar Saheb who was rushing to see Mahatmaji. He said *Gandhiji would ask you to pick up stone particles from wheat. And he believes that such actions will that bring independence!*"

Jivanbhai was very practical in his response. He said, "Gandhiji's courageous reply to the district authorities at Champaran must have brought the change in Shri Vallabhbhai's thought process. He is a brave man and a man of action. Gandhiji's bold leadership at Champaran had struck a chord in his heart."

Nandubhai added, "Around that time, Shri Vallabhbhai was getting interested in doing public service. He did not want to become an armchair social worker. He must have felt that in Gandhiji, here was a role model for doing public service at the grass root level."

Jivanbhai said, "Shri Vallabhbhai is a man from a rural area. He has suffered the pains of the peasants, their struggle for survival. That's why he could inspire others with his message to fight for self-respect."

Nandubhai commented, "Many people in rural areas were struggling for their meagre survival, they had not thought of standing up for their self-respect. Shri Vallabhbhai almost taught them to fight for their self-respect even at the cost of remaining in abject poverty."

Jivanbhai said, "And how well he has conveyed this message to them! It is this spirit which built up the courage and resilience in them. He watched Gandhiji's actions carefully and became convinced about his efficacious method of work. He placed his services at the feet of Gandhiji. As the years passed by, the *Guru-Shishya* relationship became stronger."

Chamanbhai commented, "This has proved to be a great asset for the country. See, how they set up an example for the workers and for the common people. How successfully they have inspired the people! Even in the States, people came forward to set up *Praja Mandals.*"

Nandubhai reminded, "Remember our own Bardoli Satyagrah? Sardar tested the power of *satyagrah* at Bardoli. I had attended the Surat Conference, where farmers from the entire Bardoli Taluka gathered and heard him in rapt attention. They had come prepared to sacrifice everything; in fact sometimes there was some sort of an inherent competition among the farmers-who is willing to sacrifice more?"

Jivanbhai observed, "It was possible only for Mahatmaji and Shri Vallabhbhai to make such an impressive impact upon the people. See the result! Our Vallabhbhai became *Sardar* there. And who gave this title to him?-our brave womenfolk from Bardoli!"

Nandubhai asked the people present at the *choro*, "Do you remember the election campaign of 1935? Sardar used to travel on bullock carts-sometimes he travelled the whole night. He had covered several villages without taking rest. Even some meetings were held in the open-in the moonlight. He infused great enthusiasm among the people. In his characteristic style he asked to people to vote for even a lamp post if he is from Congress for he will do something for the people."

He added, "Shri Vallabhbhai became a leader due to his special abilities and hard work. He has never wanted to have the aroma of fame or soothing comforts of power."

Jivanbhai remarked, "Shri Vallabhbhai was magnanimous in dealing with the rulers. He harbours no bitterness against anybody. He convinced many rulers to voluntarily integrate their States with India."

Chamanbhai said, "Sardar Shri wants to achieve economic and social integration also. His approach is Political Integration, Democratisation, Social and Economic integration."

"Yet, lot of work is required to be done." Nandubhai said, "May God grant a long life and good health to our Sardar. We have full confidence in him."

Jivanbhai said with a worried look, "I heard that recently there was an emergency landing of a plane in which he was flying to Jaipur."

Nandubhai told, "Yes, thanks God, finally all went well. The plane had developed some fault soon after it took off from Palam and was brought back. After checking the plane, the pilot decided to fly again but within 30 minutes of taking off, one of its engines failed and the pilot forced landed the plane on a riverbed near Shahpur. Incidentally Shri KB Lall, a senior ICS officer who was travelling on the same route, came to know about the incident. He rushed to the site and found Shri Vallabhbhai sitting in a chair. Mr. Lall brought Sardar Patel and his party in his car to Jaipur."

He added, "The news was spread all over the country and the anxious public were relieved to know that Sardar Shri was safe."

Nandubhai continued, "When Sardar Patel came to the Parliament, the members gave him a standing ovation shouting *Sardar Patel Zindabad*. They continued to express their relief and showered their respect for a long time. It was a difficult task for the speaker to maintain order in the house."

"The speaker narrated the anxious moments in the country during those difficult hours. The anxiety that enveloped the entire country shows his affectionate place in the hearts of the people. He thanked God for saving Sardar's life and wished him a long life."

Sardar Patel voice was drowned in emotions when he said, "The *demonstration of love and affection which I have seen today will have an abiding place in my memory as long as I live. The three or four hours which I spent on the river bed were filled with thoughts of anxiety caused to my countrymen.*"

Jivanbhai said, "You see, he was not worried about himself, his concern was for us."

Nandubhai added, "Jivanbhai, the people have tremendous love and affection for Shri Vallabhbhai. Later, the Members of the Parliament organised a party to celebrate his safe return and presented him a silver trophy with the replica of the plane that flew him. Shri Vallabhbhai gave it to the Air Force as a souvenir."

It was a winter afternoon in Ahmedabad. Chamanbhai was not feeling comfortable for quite some time.

As he was immersed in his thoughts, Jitenbhai came rushing to him, "Sardar Shri is not well. His health has again deteriorated and he has been advised by Dr. B.C. Roy to take some rest in Bombay. Today he is being brought to Bombay by a special IAF plane. When top leaders like Nehruji, Rajendra Babu, Shri Rajagopalachari and others went to see him off, he waived a parting salute to them with a sad smile."

Jitenbhai's voice was choked with emotion, "I am going to Bombay. Will you also come?"

Several other workers joined them. The situation at the Birla House, Bombay was very grave. Sardar Shri was put on oxygen. The expression on the faces of the attending doctors Dr. Misra, Dr. Gilder, Dr. Nathubhai Patel was quite disappointing. Maniben, Shri V. Shankar and those present there could understand the gravity of the situation. The night of December 14-15 was seriously alarming. Sardar suffered another attack in the wee hours of the morning and became unconscious for some time. After regaining his consciousness, he asked Maniben to give him some water. She gave him some *Gangajal* sweetened with honey. He sipped it and said, "It is sweet."

He became unconscious again. Those were his last words.

The tragedy struck at 9.37 A.M. of 15 December, 1950.

Sardar Shri's death shocked the entire nation. Chamanbhai and Uma were unable to control their tears. He was a friend of all-whether the person was a common man, a poor peasant, a congress worker, an office staff, a petty businessman, a rich industrialist, a senior officer, a top business executives, a well-known politician, a media person, an artist-everybody belonged to him and he belonged to them all.

Soon on getting the sad news, a grieving Pandit Nehru said that they had seen him off for Bombay only three days ago with the hope that he will recover his health in Bombay. *His health has been grievously shattered by the hard work and continuous worry.*

Paying tributes to him Pandit Nehru said, *"It is a great story that all of us know and the whole country knows. History will record it in many pages and call him the builder and consolidator of the New India and say many other things about him. By many of us he will perhaps be remembered as a great captain of our forces in the struggle for freedom and as one who gave us sound advice both in times of trouble and in moments of victory; a friend, a colleague and a comrade on whom one could invariably rely, as a tower of strength which revived wavering hearts when we were in trouble."*

Rajendra Babu, Panditji, Shri Rajgopalachari, Shri Purushottam Das Tandon, the Service Chiefs, Sri K.M. Munshi, Governors, Chief Ministers and several dignitaries rushed to Bombay.

Chamanbhai and Uma joined Jitenbhai and other colleagues to the Birla House from where the body of his beloved leader was laid in state for the public to pay homage. Millions joined the funeral procession which was carried through the main streets of the city which he loved and the city which loved him so much.

According to Sardar Shri's wishes, his body was taken for cremation at the Public Cremation Ground at Sonapur. Sardar wanted to be cremated like a common man at the same place where his wife Jhaverba and his brother Shri Vitthalbhai were cremated.

Rajendra Babu had travelled to Bombay. He, Pandit Nehruj, Shri Rajgopalachari wept at the loss of their close colleague and warm friend. They were unable to check their emotions. Later, Rajendra Babu composed himself and managed to speak a few words, *"Sardar's body is consumed by fire but no fire on earth can consume his fame. We grieve for ourselves, not for him. The achievements of Sardar Patel obtained in the field of Satyagraha, in attaining freedom and his service to the nation in the first years of freedom, will be written in letters of gold and will occupy an immortal place in the history of India."*

Rajaji said, *"What inspiration, courage, confidence and force incarnate Vallabhbhai was! We will not see the like of him again."*

In Delhi Maulana Azad, paid rich tributes to Sardar and so did other dignitaries.

It took several days for Uma and Chamanbhai to regain their composure. The shock was too terrible to absorb. The leader who guided their life and that of lakhs of people was no more. Sardar's was a household name and everybody felt that he is their own Sardar.

Jitenbhai, Prabhubhai, Dineshbhai and others were themselves reeling with shock. It took several days for them to compose themselves.

In their weekly meetings, Jitenbhai read some condolence messages which were pouring in large numbers from several places in

India and abroad. They realised how much respect Sardar Patel commanded from dignitaries, friends, political colleagues and adversaries and the common man whose great friend he was.

Prabhubhai raised the question, "Shri Vallabhbhai has done so much for us. What are we going to do for him?"

Uma suggested, "The first thing for us should be to help in completing his unfulfilled tasks. Although most of the work has to be done by the government, we need to play our role as required by Sardar."

Chamanbhai said, "We should continue the weekly meetings and from time to time decide what we should do."

Jitenbhai agreed, "We will do so. Now the most important task for us is to maintain peace and harmony in the country and continue to make sacrifices for the nation. We also need to involve our next generation in the task of nation building. This will be a befitting tribute to our leader."

Prabhubhai took out a piece of paper from his pocket and read, *"On February 23,1949, Shri Vallabhbhai had said at Madras that the first requisite for building a strong, free India is unity and peace. If there is no unity in the country, it is bound to go down. Therefore, we must first of all adjust our differences and behave in such a manner that there is complete harmony and peace in the country. You cannot expect the government continuously to maintain peace by force. Today we are passing through a period of crisis and our young men have, in their impatience not realised that the freedom which has been obtained with great difficulty is likely to be lost or give no benefit, no advantage, if we do not appreciate that our present duty is to unite and consolidate our freedom."*

He looked at the audience which was listening to him with rapt attention and continued, *"For unity, we must forget differences of cast and creed and remember that we are all Indians, and all equal. There can be no distinction between man and man in a free country. All must have equal opportunities, equal rights equal responsibilities. We cannot function if the government is to be challenged day after day by groups of people who want to have their own way. We are living in very difficult times; yet the heart of the country is sound. The whole country knows that we are carrying an unbearable burden. Everyone in India has to realise that as a free citizen of India, he must shoulder graver and greater responsibility, if India is to take its proper place amongst the nations in the world."*

Chamanbhai was trying to come out of the shock. Surprisingly, Uma was more composed than Chamanbhai. She argued, "We cannot bring our Sardar Shri back. Can we? But we can certainly give ourselves some comfort by contributing towards the fulfilment of his dreams.

Chamanbhai said, "You are right. But we need direction; we need a leadership of his calibre."

"Remember what he said on his last Independence Day. She took out her diary and said quoted, *If we have survived, it is because of our own intrinsic efforts, in whatever directions they may have been exerted. We have relied on ourselves, whether in the external or in the internal domain, and it is the self-reliance which has enabled us to achieve consolidation at home and prestige abroad. Today, I have faith in the future, it is based on this spirit of self-reliance."*

"He also raises his apprehension that *certain tendencies and developments in our administrative and public affairs fill me with disquiet and sadness of heart."*

Uma stopped for a while. Her eyes had become moist. She said in a voice overwhelmed with emotions, *"The country can realise the feeling of one who has spent the major part of his public life in witnessing epics of sacrifice and selfless endeavour and feats of discipline and unity, and who now finds enacted before him scenes which mock at the past."*

She continued, "See his anguish. He was very much disappointed with the deterioration that has come into our public life. He says that the tasks confronting us are complex and taxing as ever. They demand the best in us. We seem to devote too much time on trifle things and less time on important matters. We talk, while the paramount need is that of action."

Jitenbhai commented, "How true. Shri Vallabhbhai was always very frank. He was a man of action and he wanted others also to act, not to just talk only. I remember that on his 75th birthday on the 31st October, 1949, at a reception in Delhi, he had said that seventy-four years is fairly long life span in India and he does not have much time left in the world. He had also said that what departure could be better than to depart with all the love that the people have shown to him."

Uma continued to read from his Independence Day Message, *"I have reached a stage when time is of the essence. Age has not diminished the passion which I bear to see my country great and to ensure that the foundations of our freedom are well and securely laid. Bodily infirmity has not dimmed my ardour to exert my utmost for the peace, prosperity and advancement of the Motherland. But the bird of time has a little way to fly and Lo !it is on the wing."*

Everybody was immersed in thoughts.

After a while, Chamanbhai broke the silence, "Jitenbhai what should we do for fulfil his dreams?"

Jitenbhai said, "We must love our nation. For Shri Vallabhbhai, it was the nation that came in his thoughts first. He devoted his life for the country. He wanted that the people also should continue to make sacrifices in the manner as they have made during the freedom struggle. The task of nation building is still incomplete. This can come from unity, honesty and hard work. Remember he said that *we are wasting our energy on trifle matters. We must work hard and make the country self-reliant."*

Prabhubhai added, "He was a fearless leader. We must be courageous. Courage requires sacrifice and honesty. He wanted harmony among the people, he denounced provincialism and factionalism. He has given us a united India and it is our duty to strengthen our country."

Uma was taking notes in her diary. Jitenbhai asked, "What are you writing Uma?"

"I have taken several notes during our weekly meetings. I want to hand over the diary to our children with an instruction to follow Sardar's footsteps and pass on this to their next generation with the same advice."

PART - III

[2016 and beyond...]

1

It was the suggestion for organising a family [illegible] triggered the initiative for contacting [illegible] generations of family members of Jivabhai [illegible] were living in many different cities in [illegible] the potentials and popularity of the world [illegible] quickly established their family network.

The initiative was taken by Abha and [illegible] father [illegible] used to [illegible] several [illegible] Chunnibhai at a [illegible] Sardar [illegible] a junior executive [illegible] Ahmedabad. He [illegible] required approval [illegible] tourism market. In order to prepare her [illegible] immediate family first. She also had [illegible] cousins, sons of Kantibhai were in the [illegible] family had settled down in Bardoli.

It was by no means a simple job [illegible] different places and there was not much [illegible] Most of them had not visited Ras for [illegible] was unaware of its native village. Contact [illegible] relatives. Some of them used to meet on [illegible] or a family tragedy.

Sometimes Abha's grandfather Jayanti [illegible] his relative Sumanbhai who was living in [illegible] contact their family had initially. One evening [illegible] mother Madhuri and told her that her [illegible] her from the US. Mayurbhai's young daughter [illegible] task in her school to prepare a family [illegible] parents were unaware about their family [illegible]

1

It was the suggestion for organising a family gathering at Ras which triggered the initiative for contacting the third and fourth generations of family members of Jivanbhai and his brothers who were living in many different cities in India and abroad. Thanks to the potentials and popularity of the social media, the youngsters had quickly established their family network.

The initiative was taken by Abha, and her brother Amit. Abha's father, Pavanbhai used to tell several stories about his grandfather Chmanbhai and grandmother Uma who were close associates of Sardar Patel. Abha was a junior executive in a travel company in Ahmedabad. Her job required approaching potential clients for the tourism market. In order to prepare her data base, she looked at her immediate family first. She also had relatives in Mumbai. Other cousins, sons of Kantibhai were in the US. Another branch of their family had settled down in Bardoli.

It was by no means a simple job. The family had dispersed to different places and there was not much contact among the off-springs. Most of them had not visited Ras for years. The younger generation was unaware of its family lineage. Contacts were limited to immediate relatives. Some of them used to meet on special occasions like marriage or a family tragedy.

Sometimes Abha's grandfather Jayantibhai used to mention about his relative Sunanda. Who was living in Mumbai. That was the only contact their family had initially. One evening Sunanda called Abha's mother Madhuri and told her that her relative Mayurbhai had called her from the US. Mayurbhai's young daughter was assigned a summer task in her school to prepare a family tree. The young girl and her parents were unaware about their family lineage. Mayur knew that his grandfather, Kantibhai had migrated to the US. He was also aware that Kantibhai's parents Chamanbhai and Uma were associated with Sardar Patel during India's freedom movement.

The young girls' summer assignment generated an interesting query in the family circle. Madhuri herself did not know much, but she provided some scattered information which she had picked up from desultory conversations in the past, to Abha. Abha and her brother Amit tried to collect further details. They used the power of technology, posted some information on the social media and asked the concerned persons to respond. They were surprised to get a quick response from the family circles. Within a month, a sizeable number of persons had joined their family group and the number was increasing. Thanks to the young girl's summer assignment, a family network was soon established.

"That's the power of technology, see our family network is ready!" exclaimed Abha. Mayur inspired those in the US to join the chat group.

"Sometimes they start chatting at midnight. There are some compulsions of the time zone also, but nobody minds being disturbed," Amit said.

Once thy were on the network, they found that there were three main branches of their family-One at Ras, the other at Bardoli and the third one at Ahmedabad. From there they had spread to other parts of Gujarat and to other cities. Some had gone abroad.

The proposal to have a family get-together was initiated by Mayur. He wrote, "The only places I have seen in India are Mumbai, Ahmedabad and Delhi. My children and most of the cousins living in the US have not been to India! Can you plan a get together? Let us know our family."

Abha gave them several options. Being an executive in a travel agency, she was able to explore economic packages. It was impossible to get a plan that could suit everybody's requirements. Finally a compromise was reached. Those living in India will meet at Ras during Navratri celebrations. A larger get-together will be arranged during the summer holidays when the children are free from their schools and colleges.

It was not easy to make the arrangements for a big gathering in the village. Abha requested her parents to accompany her to Ras.

Thanks to the social media, she was no longer a stranger to her cousins, but she herself had never been to Ras. It was necessary to discuss the arrangements with her relatives at Ras. They travelled via Anand... It took about an hour to reach Ras. The road was excellent and the journey exciting.

Ras was no longer a village-it was a small city undergoing rapid urbanisation. Buildings on both sides of the road were well built and there was brisk movement on the road. Before entering the village, they saw the boundary wall of the Ras high School. A bust of Sardar Patel was erected at the gate. A sign indicated that the *Vallabh Vad* is located in the school campus. They stopped at the school gate. It was a holiday, the school was closed but upon their request they were allowed to enter the campus.

Abha and her parents went to see the historical tree and its surroundings. A small *choro* was constructed around the tree. Some benches were placed in front of the tree. The school building was a few yards ahead. The serene atmosphere of the clean and well maintained campus gave them much satisfaction.

As they proceeded ahead, they saw the Swaminarayan temple. The road to the village became narrower. It was Sunday, the pace of life was slow. Several people were gossiping in front of their houses, children were playing and womenfolk busy in their daily chores.

Curious villagers came out to see them.

Ras was now almost a small town inhabited by about 6600 people. The population had slightly increased when Pavanbhai had visited there about 15 years ago. There were about 1500 houses.

Jivanbhai's descendants, Basant and his cousin Ashok were living at Ras. They were successful farmers and were also running a dairy business. Basant was in the home when the car stopped there. He came out to welcome the visitors. Abha was already in touch with them. It did not take him much time to establish the linkage with Pavanbhai.

Word went around in the village by the two-legged newspapers that Basantbhai's relatives have come to Ras. Some co-villagers soon arrived at his house. Somebody informed Ashok, who was supervising farming activities in the nearby field about their arrival. Ashok hurried home in a pleasantly excited mood.

The house was reasonably clean and well maintained. The women of the house quickly got busy offering snacks and tea and preparing meal for the visitors. Meanwhile Pavanbhai, Madhuri, Abha, Basant and Ashok started discussing the arrangements. Abha felt that the family members would not mind sleeping on the floor. However, two important things will have to be organised-provision of running water to supplement the water input from the public supply system and at least two western style toilets. There was a boring in their adjacent field. It was difficult but possible to bring water from the tube-well by hose pipes. Another important requirement was to enhance the degree of cleanliness and hygiene.

Basant, Ashok and the other family members gave useful information about other family members they knew. Some members of Bhuvanbhai's family used to come to Ras from Bardoli. A few years' ago they came to sell their share of land-they wanted to buy some land in Bardoli for expanding their dairy. The land was purchased by Basant who was happy that the deal was finalised in the family itself and it did not disturb the ownership boundaries of the family land. His father and grandfather were very keen about consolidating and expanding their holdings. Cash flow from sale of grains, milk and other dairy products allowed them to maintain a reasonable standard of living in the village. Basant and his cousin Ashok lived in the village, others were engaged in service or business in Ahmedabad, Nadiad, Bardoli Anand and other places.

The family members were very excited about the reunion. Basant and Ashok assured them about the arrangements. After making a general appreciation of the arrangements to be made, they went to have a look around the village. The villagers were very happy to see them.

One of them complained, "You have forgotten your own village. Ours is a historical village. Gandhiji and Shri Vallabhbhai came here many times. Ras had played an important role in the freedom movement."

Another person commented, "You should remember that your own family had actively taken part in the movement."

Women were also complaining to Madhuri in the same vein.

An old woman asked, "Our elders used to mention about your family with respect. Why all of you have not visited us earlier?"

Pavanbhai tried to soften the tone, "You did not invite us! Next time when we come, will you prepare delicious *mohanbhog* for us?"

Basant assured them, "Now they will have to come frequently."

The woman said, "We will prepare delicious sweets for all of you!"

Abha returned home satisfied. Pavanbhai told her that there is always a shortage of extra cash even in affluent agriculturist families. She realised that she had to arrange some money for construction of western style toilets and bathrooms, she also had to augment the running water supply in the house. She informed about her visit to Ras to her relatives. They were very pleased to know about the enthusiasm of their relatives who were eagerly looking forward to their visit.

Some relatives offered financial support for the making the additional constructions and other necessary arrangements. Initially Basant and Ashok refused to accept the money, Pavanbhai had a hard time in convincing them.

"We still have about four months to go. We have sufficient time. Don't worry, the arrangements will be made," Basant assured.

Abha was requesting for confirmation. About sixty persons confirmed themselves for the get together.

"Not all of them will be able to come," said Madhuri.

"But we will make arrangements for all of them," Basant said.

And so they did. When Pavanbhai and his family reached Ras, they were very happy to see the arrangements in place. Basant showed the separate boring he had made for the house, two western style toilets had been constructed and the existing bathrooms were renovated. An engine generator was kept as a standby.

An aqua guard unit was also installed for drinking water.

"Perfect!" exclaimed Pavanbhai.

Although the main interest of the family was to meet each other, but most of them came prepared for the *garba* and *dandiya*. The large open space in front of their ancestral house was decorated. Men and women, boys and girls in glittering attire danced to their satisfaction. It was a splendid combination of devotion, dance and entertainment. The entire village came out to participate with vigour. They danced to songs old and new, traditional and mixed.

He Mari Mahisagar Ni Aare Dhol Vage Se
Vage Se Dhol Vage Se
Gam Gam Na Sonida Aave Se

Aave Se Hhu Lave Se
*Mari Mahisagar Ni Aare Dhol Vage Se**

Some youngsters also sang Bollywood songs–

Piya ka Ghar Pyara lage

and, several others. They were shoved into ecstasy. The arrangement made by Basant and Ashok were very nice. Youngsters and children were enjoying it most. The women were busy preparing delicious food. Although many of them were observing fast, it did not dampen their enthusiasm. They were full of energy and worked tirelessly with a smile on their face.

It was a memorable experience for them for their family members at Ras and for the entire village. The visitors developed affectionate relationship with many people. Wherever they went, they were received with warmth and affection. It appeared that many of them were knowing each other for a long time. Life was slow and simple, there was no mad rush of busy cities. People had time to socialise and they were eager to participate in such get togethers.

"We will come every year during Navratri," a youngster said.

"And before that, we are meeting again during the summer in a larger group," another person agreed.

The summer gathering was organised on a much larger scale. The number of family members attending the get together had increased. Twelve persons came from the USA. Abha had planned the itinerary well. Those who had not visited Ahmedabad went there first and after spending three-four days they visited Vadodara and then came to Ras.

Although it was not the time for the Navratri festival, yet the mood was festive. Mayur and his family members were particularly enthusiastic. It was a relaxed family environment. For the inhabitants of Ras, the gathering was a matter of attraction, curiosity and enjoyment. Many persons from the village-old and young came to meet them.

An old man suddenly threw an open question, "Do you know that Ras has an important history? Our great leader, Sardar Vallabhbhai Patel, the Iron Man of India was arrested here. Gandhiji had visited our village. Ras had played an important role in our freedom struggle."

* *See Annexure for Hindi text*

Some persons had faint idea about the role of Ras but they kept quiet. They wanted to listen.

Basant introduced the person, "Madanbhai was the history teacher at our village school. He knows about the history of Ras and its contribution very well."

He then requested Madanbhai to continue.

Madanbhai narrated the incident of Sardar Patel's arrest and the spirited contribution of the village in the *satyagrah*. Some youngsters were unaware of the meaning of *satyagrah*. It was explained by Pavanbhai.

Madanbhai briefly told them about the Bardoli Satyagrah and the Dandi March.

Hemant from Bardoli said, "All of you are coming to Bardoli. We will take you to Sardar Patel National Museum and to the Ashram where Shri Vallabhbhai used to stay."

Hemant was a great grandson of Bhuvanbhai. He was managing the Khadi and Cottage industry shop which Bhuvanbhai had started at Bardoli. Though the profit was not so high, he was emotionally attached to his family business which he had inherited from his father. His grandfather had also continued his dairy business. Hemant's father had sold his share of land at Ras and had purchased some land near Bardoli where he ran his dairy business.

Madanbhai said, "Our village had also contributed towards the various movements organised by Gandhiji and Shri Vallabhbhai. You can see the photographs of some *satyagrahis* at the school. Tomorrow I will bring you there."

The next day, they went to the Ras High School. The Principal Shri Sanjaybhai Kantibhai Patel welcomed them and enthusiastically showed the *Vallabh Vad* and the school campus. They also saw the photographs of the *satyagrahis* from Ras. The school was managed by the Ras Kelavani Mandal.

Shri Sanjaybhai gave the details about the school.

He said that Ras was an important centre of national activities in the Kathagara region of Borsad Tehsil. Ras had the honour of receiving Gandhiji as early as on the 17th April 1918. During his speech, Gandhiji had insisted that the people must follow the path of non-violence even at the cost of personal hardship.

Madanbhai complemented, "During the freedom struggle,

Shri Vallabhbhai, Shri Ravishankarji Maharaj, Jeevabhai, Asha Bhai and several other leaders used to visit Ras."

"I have heard that with a view to prevent profiteering, Ashabhai was able to collect hundred *maunds** of grains from traders of *Kathagara* region," Sanjaybhai said.

Sanjaybhai narrated the details of Shri Vallabhbhai's visit to Ras before the Dandi movement and his subsequent arrest under the *Vallabh Vad.*

Sanjaybhai said, "The British Government was upset by the huge success of the Dandi March. The people of Ras faced the atrocities of the revengeful government with courage and determination for a long period of nine years. Many peasants of Ras left their village, many were imprisoned but they bravely faced all these hardships in the hope of getting independence."

"What a great sacrifice," Pavanbhai said.

Madanbhai added, "Once Mahatmaji had said that out of total revenue loss of Rs. 13 lakhs for the Borsad Tehsil, Rs. 6.5 lakhs was from Ras alone!"

Madhuri exclaimed, "Half the amount!"

"Yes," Sanjaybhai confirmed.

Sanjaybhai gave details of various visits by Bapu, Sardar Shri and other leaders.

Abha said, "The people of Ras were brave."

Mayur said, "How lucky we are that our forefathers belonged to this place!"

Everybody was in a thoughtful mood.

The visitors spent two days at Bardoli, met their relatives, saw the Bardoli Museum and the Ashram before returning to Ras. Mayur had visited the Sardar Patel Museum in Ahmedabad a few days ago and was greatly impressed by its exhibits, the information content and the efficient management of the premises. He was absorbed in thoughts about Sardar Patel.

"I have requested Abha to plan a trip to Karamsad. Those who wish to come, join us."

The trip was both interesting and informative. They saw Sardar Patel's ancestral house and the beautiful impressive Museum, which was maintained in an excellent condition. Mayur observed the exhibits

* *Old unit of weight for grains. One Maund=40 seers, 1 seer=960 grams.*

minutely. He saw the making of Sardar, his great contribution to the nation and various aspects of his towering personality.

On his return to Ras, he said, "What a great man Sardar Patel was! We are very lucky that we belong to a family and a village which had some association with him."

Madanbhai said, "The young generation has not filly understood his great contribution to the nation. The India in which we live today, is his making. The British were not much keen on giving us a united India. Pakistan was created due to their policy and the States were groomed to remain subjugated to them under the paramountcy. They were left free after the lapse of paramountcy."

"It was the grit, determination and foresight of Sardar Patel and his excellent management that he could bring about the merger of the Sates in the Indian Union within a very short time."

Pavanbhai lamented, "In spite of that, we do not seriously recognise his contribution. Sardar Patel was very keen to have a united and strong India. See what are we doing! Are we following his advice?"

Madanbhai said, "During the freedom movement, many people followed what he said. They had complete faith in Sardar and they made huge sacrifices for the country. As you know, our village itself had taken very active part in the *satyagrah.*"

Mayur's wife suddenly remembered something and left the audience.

Mayur asked, "We get mixed news about India-progressing yet not progressing at the desired pace, developing but developing very slowly. Negative news about friction in the society and corruption keeps on coming. Seldom we get any news which makes us proud. And when we get such news, we feel immense pleasure."

Pavanbhai said, "We have won our freedom but we have not been able to progress at the desired pace. We are not united in our purpose and in the mission of nation building. We waste our energy in trifle things."

Madanbhai commented, "Ours is a large country. We are much engrossed in issues relating to religion, caste, communities, language, regions and provinces. We are facing serious problems of terrorism, naxalism, provincialism, corruption, poverty, sickness and several others. These can be handled efficiently only when we are united. Our ancestors have made sacrifices for achieving independence. Our people have quickly and comfortably forgotten the sacrifices made by our freedom fighters."

Pavanbhai said, "Today our people have plenty of complaints. They are dissatisfied with our leaders, our bureaucracy, our business community and with several other sections of society. Some public leaders are facing serious criminal charges. Although the political parties vouchsafe a vision of clean politics, they give tickets to the people who are known to have a criminal background. It is politics without morality. We wonder whether they have shortage of candidates without a criminal record!"

Madanbhai added, "Our bureaucracy works on a system left by the British. We are strengthening it on one pretext or the other."

Pavanbhai said, "How can you expect that the country can progress with a bureaucracy which works on an age old system established by the British and a mind-set of the Moghul era!"

"But it is acknowledged that India is making good progress. It is a leading economy of the world and commands respect for its economic resilience and progress," Mayur said.

"This is despite the disadvantages of a corrupt and insensitive bureaucracy and a leadership which has not done much for society building," a young family member commented.

"Sardar struggled for having a united India. Some of our politicians are seriously engrossed in the vote bank politics. They act in a manner which creates, maintains and expands the differences of religion, caste, states and language. Many of them do not think of the national interest as a whole," Hemant said.

"What can we do to solve the problem?" a young man asked.

Nobody came forward with an answer.

Abha asked, "Sardar Patel has made several significant contributions to the country. He taught the people to live and strive for self-respect. Can we progress and get self -respect without struggle?"

"Absolutely not, we need to work hard, the work of strengthening the nation demands our dedication. We have to look beyond our own world of comfort and luxury," Madanbhai said.

"The nation faces many problems. Can we pick up one matter which was dear to Sardar Patel and try to work for it?" Mayur asked.

"Yes, I think it is unity," Abha said. "Sardar Patel wanted to have a united and strong India. If we are able to strengthen our unity, other things will follow. A strong united India will be relatively free of corruption, it will be an India where people will come forward to invest and do business. A strong united India will be a confident India which will command respect from every country."

Mayur's wife came with a very old dairy, "I found this dairy in an old box which my mother–in-law gave to me. This is dairy which our great-grandmother maintained. She has mentioned several things about Shri Vallabhbhai. She used to attend weekly meetings at Ahmedabad where they discussed about the contribution made by Sardar Patel."

She gave Uma's dairy to Mayur.

"This is a precious asset for us. I will pass it on to you for having a look."

Madanbhai said, "Please allow us to make copies of this valuable dairy. I will circulate one for the reading and will also keep a copy in the school library."

The question triggered a thought process in everybody's mind. They had seen the family home of Shri Vallabhbhai and the museums at Karamsad, Bardoli and Ahmedabad. They were in Ras where Shri Vallabhbhai was arrested. They were filled with the feeling of pride that their ancestors had enjoyed the privilege of working with the great son of India.

Is today's India, the one which Sardar Patel had strived for? The country is struggling with its problems of poverty, terrorism, violence, corruption, provincialism, insensitive governance and several other knotty issues. Almost everybody is affected by one problem or the other. The family members from the US were also thinking of filth, beggars and lack of basic amenities.

The next day Sanjaybhai came with Madanbhai and thanked them for their visit to the school. Discussions centred on Ras and the contribution of Sardar Patel.

Sanjaybhai asked Mayurbhai, "Have you heard about the statue of Unity which will be erected at Kevadia?"

"I have read briefly about it in the newspapers," Mayurbhai said.

"Why don't you visit the famous Sardar Sarovar Dam and Kevadiya?"

This was an interesting suggestion. Most of the family members agreed to visit the place.

"Can you make necessary arrangements Abha?" Mayur asked.

Abha replied, "Let me try to obtain permission for the visit. Making travel arrangements will not be a problem."

With her knowledge and contacts, Abha was able to make the necessary arrangements. She contacted the concerned authorities and was surprised to receive an immediate reply from Shri Sanjay Joshi of the Sardar Sarovar Narmada Nigam Limited, who was very helpful. Abha called him. Shri Joshi gave him the details of the project and advised her to visit the concerned website for further information. The website was well-designed and it was very informative. A look at the website further prompted their desire to visit the place. She briefed them about the project.

The journey was comfortable, they enjoyed travelling together. Upon arrival they were warmly received by Shri B.N. Patel of the Sardar Sarovar Narmada Nigam Ltd. Shri Patel took them to the site of proposed Statue of Unity and explained the project in detail. A man of eminent goodness, Shri Patel proved to be an encyclopaedia of the Sardar Sarover and the Statue of Unity projects.

Shri Patel said, "the project is our humble and befitting tribute to the great son of India who devoted his entire life for the nation. The Statue of Unity is our dream project. We are putting our heart and soul in the work for this project of national importance. Our objective is that the Statue should be a permanent source of inspiration for the generations to come."

Pavanbha said, "This is a very commendable work and we are grateful to those who conceived this project and also to those who are implementing it."

Madhuri added, "Yes. Many people in our country are not fully aware of Sardar Patel's invaluable contribution to the nation. This statue should become a symbol of national unity and progress."

Mayur introduced himself and informed about the family get together and visits to various places associated with Sardar Shri. He said, "This has been a very useful visit for us. We have come to know about many valuable contributions made by Shri Vallabhbhai Patel. His life was full of sacrifice and devotion. We need to raise awareness about his great contribution, among the people. The Statue of Unity will certainly convey the message of unity and self-respect among the people."

Shri Patel showed the Sadhu-Bet island lovingly affectionately located between the Vindhya and Satpuda ranges. He said that the Statue of Unity will be 182 meters tall and—"

Pavanbhai interrupted, "That's very appropriate for a towering personality like Sardar Shri."

Madhuri added, "The beautiful location also symbolises the beauty of his heart."

Shri Patel continued, "This will be world's tallest statue, almost double the height of the Statue of Liberty New York and much taller than other famous statues of the world. The project area for the Statue will be about 20,000 sq meters. It will have an exhibition describing the history of the independence movement, a memorial and Visitor Centre, a Memorial Garden and many other places of attraction. A bridge will be constructed for connecting the Sadhu island with the mainland."

Shri Patel showed the sites and described the surroundings and described several associated infrastructure projects which have been planned. The visitors will be treated to an enjoyable boat ride of about 3.5 kms for reaching the Statue.

He said, "The planning is very environment–friendly. It is planned to create research facilities in the areas of bio technology, clean energy and other related fields will be created."

Amit said, "This will create good job opportunities for the local people."

Shri Patel nodded in the affirmative. He said, "A number of educational institutions will be established here which will improve the living conditions of the local people."

Abha said, "This will be a very important place of tourist attraction. That will also generate many business activities here."

Mayur smiled, "Abha ia an executive in the tourist agency. She is looking for future business."

Abha replied, "I am looking for business opportunities for the local people. There is immense potential for promoting local handicrafts and agriculture produce."

Amit added, "That will also create job opportunities in several sectors."

Shri B.N. Patel said, "The Statue premises will be able to accommodate 15,000 visitors per day. About 200 people can see the surroundings at the same time from the upper observation deck at a height of 500 ft., and about 3000 visitors from the observation level which can be reached by stairs."

Pavanbhai said, "Visitors can also see the Sardar Sarovar Dam."

Shri B.N. Patel said, "The visitor can get a memorable panoramic view of the Dam and the beautiful surroundings."

He then gave details of the various other attractions which have been planned. He said that the Statue area will be about 3 acres, 1 acre has been earmarked for Support and utilities."

Shri Patel mentioned about the provision for education, research and other facilities. He said, "An area of about 445 acres have been allocated for Education and research, about 200 acres for Recreation and Tourism, 120 acres for hotels, resorts and Housing, 90 acres for Health and related facilities."

"Wonderful!" Mayur said.

Everybody was full of appreciation for the planners of this project. Shri Patel was a huge reservoir of information. He smilingly answered various questioned asked by the visitors. He said that it has been planned to construct a modern Convention Centre which will be known as the Shreshtha Bharat Bhavan.

Pavanbhai said, "A befitting tribute to our great leader who devoted his life for the nation. The persons who have conceived the idea and are working for the successful implementation of the project are doing a great service to the nation."

Shri B.N. Patel said, "Sardar Patel was a farmer and he had great regard for the peasants, he successfully led several peasant movements. The farmers of our country held him in a very high regard. Farmers of about 172,000 villages have contributed iron implements for use in the project."

Mayur complimented, "Great! History is being made here."

Madhuri was immersed in thoughts. She said, "It is not only making of history, it is an expression of respect, love and affection for the great leader who gave us the united India."

Shri Patel also showed him other areas and gave further details of the project.

All family members were full of appreciation for the work being done.

"I will come here again," Mayur said.

On their return journey, they were thinking of Sardar Shri and the Statue of Unity.

Mayur and other family members were thinking about Sardar Shri. Mayur was feeling lucky that their family get-together had provided them an excellent opportunity to know about the great leader and about his contributions to the country. He sacrificed his flourishing practice and an assured life of luxury for the sake of the nation.

In the evening gathering, Madanbhai asked about their visit to Kevadiya.

Mayur said, "It was a memorable experience. This is a great project which has been very well planned."

Pavanbhai agreed, "What a wonderful idea! This Statue will attract and inspire millions of people. The entire project has been conceived with a sentiment of love and regard for Sardar Patel."

Abha added, "The Iron Man of India deserves our gratitude, love and respect in abundance."

Amit exclaimed, "What a great personality Sardar Patel was!"

Madanbhai said, "Sardar Shri was a great man-a leader of common masses, a leader who never cared about himself, a leader who only thought about the nation, a leader who fought for *swaraj* and tirelessly worked for national unity."

Pavanbha added, "And for self –respect of the people."

Madanbha agreed, "You are right. Shri Vallabhbhai was inspired by Mahatma Gandhi's bold reply to the District Magistrate of Champaran Mr. W. B. Heycock. In Gandhiji they found a courageous leader who stood for the self-respect of the peasants, for truth and for justice. Sardar Patel also stood against an arrogant and insensitive bureaucracy during the Kheda, Borsad, Nagpur and Bardoli *satyagrahas.* He inspired the people to stand against injustice and be prepared to make sacrifices. He had forewarned them of the repercussions, he was aware of the weaknesses of the people-their timidity and willingness to accept the servitude. Yet he filled up their heart with courage and mobilised them to resist the unfair taxation imposed upon them."

He paused for a while, "See what he did at Borsad and at Bardoli. Our forefathers fought unitedly against injustice and finally they were successful in their struggle."

Pavanbhai said, "And who can forget his contribution of giving us a united integrated India? Many leaders believed that it was only due to him that the integration of States was achieved almost in a miraculous manner. What a great gift the brave son of India has given to us!"

He continued, "If we fulfil his dream of strengthening our united India, it will be the best tribute to him."

Abha asked, "But there are several other problems like terrorism, violence, corruption, poverty etc…"

Pavanbhai interrupted. "If we feel pride in our country, if we love our nation and have self-respect as an Indian, we will be able to handle all these problem of effectively. Some problems will vanish altogether. There are many countries in the world whose citizen are having a strong feeling of self-respect and love for their country. If we are united and love our country deeply, we will not do anything that will harm our nation."

"How can we do that?" Hemant asked.

Pavanbhai replied, "Work for a strong and united India. Spread the message of Sardar Patel to mobilise public opinion, use the social media to promote his views and follow his advice in your own life. Work for making a Strong United India!"

Abha suggested, "Let us start it right now. We will establish a group of the *Admirers of Sardar Patel.* The Group will contribute towards strengthening the national unity and strength. The Group will help in its humble way to realise the vision of Sardar Patel of an India where narrow feelings based on religion, caste, province and language etc. will not exist. Our foremost duty will be to think of India, to love India and to struggle for our self-respect. That will be our tribute to our great leader."

Pavanbhai said, "Our approach to have a strong united India will promote the feeling of patriotism and self-respect which are the prerequisites for development and progress. Let us work for it, let us promote it whole-heartedly."

2

The warm fraternal company of ten sweet and memorable days was coming to an end. It was parting time for all family members. Everybody was sad. Initially, Basant and Ashok were a bit apprehensive about the first-time visitors-they had not met them earlier. Twelve of them had come from the US. The siblings were born there, they were not used to the climate and conditions of India-that too of a village. But, they cheerfully enjoyed the gathering and appreciated the hospitality of their family members at Ras. Basant and Ashok refused to accept any further financial contribution. For Mayur and his family it was a pleasure which they never had the privilege of enjoying. The family bondage had become stronger.

Ever since he visited Ahmedabad, Karamsad, Bardoli and Kevadiya-Mayur was thinking of Sardar Patel. The discussions at Ras and Kevadiya were very informative. The more he came to know about Sardar, the more he admired him. His previous knowledge about Sardar Patel was mainly an overview of his contribution in integration of Princely States. Here he got an opportunity to know about the details. He strongly felt something must be done in India to fulfil Sardar Patel's dreams.

He asked Abha to take the lead," Abha, you have the knowledge, skill and the initiative for promoting our drive. Take the lead."

Hemant supported, "We will all help you."

Abha said, "What am I supposed to do?"

Family members started offering suggestions. Hemant suggested, "Do not think too far. One good step will draw more people and will ensure the success of our mission. Start a group and request like -minded persons to join. Begin with our family members present here."

"And what will be the name of the group? Any suggestions?" Abha asked.

"Keep it simple-*Admirers of Sardar Patel." "Madhuri* suggested." Our moto should be – *Strong India-United India.*"

"And how should we proceed?" Abha asked.

"Let us start with our family group and request others to join. Sardar Patel has made many important contributions to the country. We just pick up his one contribution and see how we can contribute towards fulfilment of his dreams. We take a pledge that we will think of India first-as desired by Sardar." Pavanbhai suggested.

Madhuri was watching the people. She read the feelings and said, "Do not bother much about the result at this stage. Let us start sincerely our work now, let us promote the message among our family and friends first and request them to do likewise."

"And when are we going to meet again?" Hemant asked.

Mayur replied, "Every year. We will try to invite all family members to Ras and spend at least a week here."

In the late afternoon, Madanbhai came with Sanjaybhai, an energetic young man from the village and some other persons.

He introduced Amit, "He is another Amit from our village. He wants to say something."

Amit said, "Your Amitbhai has organised this event. My name is also Amit. I am from Ras. We thank you for your initiative. You have created an environment of joy and fraternity here. We want to bid farewell to you tomorrow."

Basant smiled, "Yes, they had approached me earlier. This was kept as a surprise. A small function will be organised tomorrow afternoon near the Banyan Tree where Sardar Patel was arrested before the Dandi March."

About four hundred people gathered for the function. Some chairs were kept in the front. Others were sitting on the ground.

Sanjaybhai welcomed them and gave a brief description of the contribution made by Ras in the freedom movement. He mentioned about the visits of Gandhiji and Sardar Patel, about the sacrifice of the people of Ras in the satyagrah movement. He said that even a question was raised about Ras in the British Parliament-*Where is Ras?*

He said "The people of Ras are lucky that their forefathers had set an example of sacrifice and courage and had struggled for a long time for the cause of national freedom."

He also spoke about the school and introduced his associates. In spite of its meagre resources, the school was making good progress.

The school was of a historic importance. Its venue was scene of several important activities during the freedom struggle. Many persons were not much informed about the contribution of Ras. This visit gave them a good opportunity to know about the details of the proud history of the place.

They thanked the organisers for arranging the function at the school.

Some students dressed in white khadi, sang patriotic songs with much fervour. Their spirited rendering of the song with synchronous action created an atmosphere of patriotism and the audience cheered them lustily.

Ke danko vagya ladyaiya shoora jagya re
Ke shoora jagya re, kayar bhagya re
Mathu melo hay baba haee tekne re
Hayee takne h oho hayee takne yu
Gaje khetar bhadee ne gaje gaamda re
*Gaje gaamda re, gaje gaamda re**

He also spoke about the school and introduced his associates.

Pavanbhai and Basant thanked them on behalf of their family members.

Madanbhai said, "We are very grateful to you for your visit. You are not a visitor, you belong to our village and you have revived the family ties. I am sure that other families in the village will also organise similar family unions. We want an assurance from you that at least once a year, all of you will come to Ras."

Pavanbhai replied, "We will try to come at least twice a year-during Navratri and in the summer. In addition, some people will come whenever they find time."

He continued, "We want to show you a short clip of Sardar Patel's speech."

Quickly a screen was fixed and Abha opened her laptop. She projected some snippets of a speech from Sardar Patel on the screen

---

* *The trumpet of struggle has been sounded. All braves will wake up, and the cowards will flee. It is important to be ready for making sacrifice for the country. The farmers working in the fields and other villagers should come forward for the struggle. (See Appendix for the text in Hindi)*

in which he called for unity among the people. He said that unity and peace are prerequisite for building a strong India. He also urged them to make sacrifices for the country. He said that unless everybody in the country–businessperson, labourers, industrialists, students, government all combine and cooperate, we are not going to make progress. He appealed to agriculturist to work hard and make India self-sufficient in food.

Abha then described the details of the Statue of Unity which is being built as a tribute to the great son of India. She said that the Statue will inspire millions and will further strengthen national unity.

Then Pavanbhai said, "What Sardar Patel had said earlier is true even now. This is the place where our leader was arrested before the Dandi March. He was a charismatic leader and wielded strong influence among the people. At his call, the farmers came forward to sacrifice their assets-even their fields. Many of them lived with their cattle for weeks together."

"He has done many great things for our country. He has given us a united India. It is our duty to complete his unfinished tasks. We have decided to begin with one task which he wanted us to accomplish-to make a strong united India. We need to contribute towards that. We should forget the differences of religion, caste, province and language. We must think of India first."

Somebody from the audience asked, "But our leaders are not united in this matter. They talk of specific religions, castes, groups and provinces. They want to maintain the exclusive influence so that they can have their core clientele."

"You are right," Madanbhai said. "We must oppose this as strongly as Shri Vallabhbhai did. Whenever anybody comes with any proposal which tries to create differences among the people, we should oppose that in the manner in which Sardar Patel did."

He person queried, "But what can we do from our village? Who will listen to us?"

Pavanbhai replied, "All big movements start from a small initiative by a few people. Let us begin, people will join and support us. A common person is very much interested in building a strong united India. We will get the support. Madanbhai, can you take the lead here?"

"Yes," Madanbhai said and asked the audience, "Are you ready to do what Pavanbhai has said?"

"Yes," shouted the audience.

"Let us begin with our village. Take a pledge under this historic tree that you will think of India first, you will harbour no prejudice of religion, caste, province or language. You will not listen to the leaders who try to create rift among us on these lines, you will bravely oppose any move to perpetuate and support these differences."

Mayur got up and said, "Thanks very much. We are overwhelmed with your love and affection. We are proud that our ancestors belonged to this village."

He smiled, paused a little and said, "You have given us so much of love and affection. Thank you very much. I feel that we must reciprocate your warmth with the same feeling and we should also work together with you to bring prosperity to this area."

He waited for a moment and said, "I have decided to open a large Agriculture Market-*Krishi Mandi* at Ras. This area is known for its excellent agricultural produce. The *Krishi Mandi* will offer an opportunity to the farmers of the area for selling their products efficiently."

The audience applauded him for a long time.

Mayur elaborated, "I have been visiting the houses in the village. I have met many people and have discussed about our family business here. Our family has been involved in grain and dairy business for several generations. I am myself running grain business for many years. I have business contacts in big cities in India and in many countries of the world. Many companies do not show much interest to invest in India, they prefer other investment destinations. But things are changing. I will myself take the lead and convince other partners to invest in good business in India."

"I have decided to open a *Krishi Mandi* here with a view to help all of you in producing, managing and selling your products. The proposed Mandi will have modern arrangements for providing necessary supplies-seeds, fertlisers, tools, weighing and packaging materials, warehousing facilities, marketing channels–everything you need. It will have reliable and modern communication facilities. I want to empower everybody present here with modern business tools. I will arrange training for Basant, Ashok and others."

Again people cheered him for a long time.

He added, "I have consulted some business associates and they are positive about the proposal. I will ensure efficient communication links from the *Krishi Mandi* to my business associates in India and abroad. You will not have to rush to big cities for every small sell or purchase. The *Krishi Mandi* will attract buyers and sellers here."

"Each one of you can avail the facilities at a reasonable cost. I will also explore the possibility of making Ras a solar village. We will install solar panels which will meet the energy requirements of the Mandi, of the entire village and its neighbourhood. It will facilitate irrigartion and will reduce cost of production. The surplus electricity can be sold also. Every house in Ras can have an *e-agriculture* related business."

He looked around and said, "We have heard about the great history of this place and its proud association with India's freedom movement. Mahatma Gandhi came to this very place, Sardar Shri Vallabhbhai Patel was arrested here. This is a very historical place. We need to do something for Ras."

He continued, "I will try to support the upgradation of this high school into a good college. In future, we can also think of opening an Agriculture College here."

Everybody rose upon his feet and gave him a lusty cheer.

Pavanbhai said, "This is an excellent contribution from you, Mayur. You have already taken a major project on your shoulders. Concentrate on the *Krishi Mandi* work first. We will take care of the upgradation of the high school and the Kasturba Hospital. We will also do the preliminary work for opening of an Agriculture College here."

Basant adde, "Thank you Mayurbhai. I want to assure you that we will not lag behind. We will help you in all these plans. I will arrange the necessary local support with the help of our people here."

Sanjaybhai's eyes were moist. He said, "I have a strong desire to upgrade this school into a good college. Opening of an Agriculture college is also a very welcome proposal. We will always remain obliged to you for your contribution."

Pavanbhai asked Madanbhai, "Madanbhai will you come forward to help in these projects?"

He replied, "Of course, why not? Not only me, I believe everybody present here will participate enthusiastically. It is for our benefit."

Pavanbhai assured, "We will take the initiative for upgradation of the school and opening of an agriculture college here."

Sanjaybhai said, "Sardar Patel is our idol. He stressed upon unity. We must work together for the success of these very useful plans."

Pavanbhai said, "I have something to suggest."

Madanbhai asked, "What do you want to suggest Pavanbhai?"

Pavanbhai said, "Mayur should take all these steps only when we promise to strengthen our unity, only when we forget all differences of religion, caste, province and language. We have assembled under the shadow of the famous Vallabh *Vad.* We should take a solemn pledge here to work for a united and strong India, for making India asuperb nation which is loved and respected by all. "

He paused and asked, "Do you agree to my proposal?"

"Yes," the people responded.

Pavanbhai reminded, "But remember, it will be extremely difficult to implement all these projects if we are not united. No body will come forward to invest in a place where the work cannot progress smoothly."

A man from the audience rose, "I am eager to take the pledge."

Sanjaybhai reminded, "Don't take the pledge if you cannot honour it. Remember, people of this village faced serious consequences but they did not break their pledge."

The young man did not reply. He came forward, kissed the tree and went back to his place. A number of people followed. Soon the entire audience formed a long queue. Every volunteer was cheered.

Madanbhai said, "Every week we will meet here, under this historic tree to discuss our duties towards our country as desired by Sardar Patel."

He continued, "I want to tell you one more thing. Sardar had visited several parts of Gujarat where he had worked during the *satyagrah.* He came to Ras also and proudly showed this tree to Shri V. Shankar and other persons who accompanied him. He specially mentioned that he was arrested under this tree. He affectionately remembered it. Are we not lucky to be here?"

Several people nodded in affirmation.

A young person from the audience stood up and asked, "May I suggest something?"

"Yes," Madanbhai said.

"We have taken the pledge to work for unity. We all know that unity is strength and a united and strong India will prosper quickly and will earn the respect of all. We must thank our brothers who have come to Ras. They have shown their love and affection for us and are going to invest here in a big way. The *Krishi Mandi* will bring many opportunities to us. We also hope that our dear school, where most of us have studied, will one day become a good college."

He paused for a while and said, "We should be grateful to our brothers who have come to Ras. But we should also assure them we will honour the pledge. They are leaving tomorrow. Can all of us show them our spirit of unity by cleaning the streets of Ras tomorrow morning. Will you join?"

"Yes," the audience shouted with enthusiasm.

Sanjaybhai said, "Honour your pledge in the manner our forefathers had done. Work for strengthening India's unity wholeheartedly. This is the best tribute to our great leader."

Pavanbhai shouted, *"Sardar Patel Kee Jay.**"

The audience responded, *"Sardar Patel Kee Jay."*

✪✪✪

* *Long live Sardar Patel*

Annexure

हिन्दी :

पेज न. 27

सारा नसीब, सहजानंद स्वामी अंतर्यामी

पेज न. 41

जय जय शम्भुकुमार, शोक सदा हर्ता
देव विशेष विचक्षण रक्षणंकर्ता

पेज न. 44

जाग्या तान थी सवार
अच्छा काम देर से भी किया जाये तब भी अच्छा है।

पेज न. 47

जय गणपति प्यारा, जय गणगति प्यारा, विघ्न विनायकमूर्ति, सुखदायक सारा

पेज न. 52

लोभ सिवा शोभ न होये पन जाजा लोभे लक्षण जाये'
अर्थ : बचत के बिना मस्ती नहीं हो सकती, पर लोभ तो तुम्हारे चरित्र का पतन कर देगा।

पेज न. 58

सोना जेयों ससुरुं पण पीयर जेयों नहीं!
अर्थ : ससुराल का घर सोने का हो सकता है, पर पीहर जैसा नहीं हो सकता।

पेज न. 59

तमने तो गमीज हशे!
अर्थ : तुम बहुत खुश हो!

पेज न. 67

चोर पकड़ाये, चटुं पकड़ाये, खोटा बोलू ना पकड़ाये।
अर्थ : चोर पकड़ा जा सकता है, मछली पकड़ी जा सकती है, पर झूठा नहीं पकड़ा जा सकता।

पेज न. 98

चपटी भरी चौखा ने घी नो छे दिवडो
हे श्रीफल नी जोड़ लई ने हालो हालो पांवागढ़ जैई ये ने...

सामे नी प्रोळ थी मालिडो आवे....
ऐ गजरा नी जोड़ लई ने हालो हालो पावागढ़ जैई ये ने...
चपटी भरी चौखा ने घी नो छे दिवडो...
सामे नी पोळ थी डोसिडो आवे...
ऐ चुंदरी नी जोड़ लई ने हालो हालो
सामे नी पोळ थी कुम्भारी आवे...
ऐ माता नो गरबो लई ने हालो हालो पावागढ़ जैई ये ने...
चपटी भरी चौखा ने घी नो छे दिवडो...पावागढ़ जैई ये ने...

अर्थ : चम्मच भर चावल, घी का दिया और श्रीफल लेकर चलो पावागढ़। सामने वाले मोहल्ले से माली आता है, साथ में एक जोड़ा माला लाता है। उसे लेकर पावागढ़ चलो।
सामने वाले मोहल्ले से बजाज आता है, साथ में एक सुन्दर चुनरी लाता है। उसे लेकर पावागढ़ चलो।
सामने वाले मुहल्ले से कुम्हारन आती है, साथ में गरबो लाती है। उसे लेकर पावागढ़ चलो।

पेज न. 125
जुल्म-ओ-बेदाद की शिद्दत है मगर फिर खुश हैं
जोशी-तूफ़ाने-शकावत है मगर फिर खुश हैं
हाँ मुसीबत पे मुसीबत है, मगर फिर खुश हैं
जानते हैं कि भलाई से भला होता है
सब्र वालों का मददगार खुदा होता है

अर्थ : अत्याचार की तीव्रता है, पर खुश हैं, निर्दयता के तूफ़ान का जोश है पर खुश हैं, मुसीबत पर मुसीबत है, पर खुश हैं, जानते हैं कि भलाई से भला होता है और धैर्य रखने वालों का मददगार ईश्वर होता है।

पेज न. 132
जागने जादवा कृष्ण गोवालीया तुज विना धेनुमां कोण जैशे?
वणसेंने साथ गोवाल टोले मल्या, वडोरे गोवालीया कोण थाशे?

अर्थ : जागो ओ कृष्ण, तुम्हारे बिना गायों को कौन ले जाएगा? टोले के 360 ग्वाल-बालों में बड़ा गोवालीया कौन बनेगा?

पेज न. 142-143
रणशूर रास

ठोकाय जंग थाणां, हुशियार ग्राम रास तुं,
पूजाय वीर व्हाणा, तैयार ग्राम रास तुं।

शरणाई घोर बाजे, ने आत्मघेरुं गाजे
वीर ने वीरत्व छाजे, पड़कार ग्राम रास तुं।

एक दिन राष्ट्र नामे, झुकाव्युं जुल्म सामे
तुज कीर्ति ठाम ठामे, सरदार ग्राम रास तुं।

भानु सलिल खेंचे, वर्षा अधिक छे,
उन्धी राजनीति व्हे छे, निज धार गाम रास तुं।
स्वार्थ सदैव धूमी, रहीं कीधी भूमि,
सत्याग्रही झझूमी कर, वहार ग्राम रास तुं।
लड़ी सत्यनी लड़ाई, दफनाव दंड शाही
हो साच ना सिपाही, रखवाल ग्राम रास तुं।
शुद्ध आत्म शक्ति, वेरीदे वादड़ा विखेरी,
कर प्राण ने वधेरी, उद्धार ग्राम रास तुं।

वायु सुगन्धी वाशे, यश गान देव गाशे
ते धन्य धन्य थाशे, अवतार ग्राम रास तुं।

दे रंग ल्हाणां, किरतार ग्राम रास तुं,
ठोकाय वीर थाणां, तैयार ग्राम रास तुं।'

अर्थ : रणशूर रास

ओचतुरग्रामरास, तू संघर्ष करने के लिये विवश हुआ। जिन वीरों को तूने तैयार किया, सर्वत्र उनकी पूजा हुई। संघर्ष की शहनाई बजी, तूने रणभेरी गुंजाई। चुनौती को अतुर रासग्राम, तूने वीरों में वीरत्व जगाया। एक दिन के नाम पर तुमने जुल्म के सामने सर उठाया। ओ सरदार ग्रामराम, तेरी कीर्ति पूरे विश्व में फैली। सूर्य की तपन बढ़ी, फिर अति वृष्टि ने तंग किया, राजनीति भी विपरीत हुई, फिर भी ओ रास तू अडिग रहा। स्वार्थ नचाता रहा, स्वार्थ के कारण भूमि सही न हुई, तब सत्याग्रह का अवलम्बन लेकर, ओ रास तू अग्रसर हुआ। सरकारी दंड को दफ़न करने के उद्देश्य से सत्य की लड़ाई लड़कर, सत्य का सिपाही बनकर ओ राम, तू रखवाला बना।

शुद्ध आत्मशक्ति एकत्र कर भय के बाद बिखेरने हेतु प्राणों का बलिदान कर, ओ ग्रामरास, तू उद्धार कर। चहुँ ओर सुगन्ध बिखरेगी, देवयश गान गाएँगे, तब ओ अवतार ग्रामरास, तू धन्य हो जाएगा। ओ किरतार ग्रामरास, तू इस जंग को भी रंग दे। ओ चतुर ग्रामरास, तू संघर्ष करने के लिए विवश हुआ।

पेज न. 142–143

हिन्द युद्ध घंट वाग्यो, संग्राम बोरसद तुं,
जय शंखनाद गाज्यो, बहादुर बोरसद तुंय
चाल्या रणे शुराओ, सरकार जुल्म सामे,
नीति युद्ध आदर्युं, रणशूर बोरसद तुं।
तुं युद्ध नो रसीलो, तुं त्याग नो भरेलो,
स्वातंर्त्य ने वरेलो, मशहूर बोरराव तुं,
तुज ऐक्य मुग्ध करतुं, भूमि हिन्द छेक आजे,
तक छे मली अमोली, शूरवीर बोरसद तुं।
तोपो मशीनगनो थी, सरकार छेक भारे,
करतो न पाछी पानी, बहादुर बोरसद तुंय
जोने करे जमीन, आजे ज खालसा ते,
के तोप थी उड़ावे, डगतो न बोरसद तुं
विजय पूरो बनी था अमर बोरसद तुं।''

अर्थ : बहादुर बोरसद तुं

ओबोरसद, तूने हिन्द– युद्ध का घंटा बजाया। ओ बहादुर बोरसद, तूने जग में शंखनाद किया। सरकारी जुल्म का सामना करते हुए शूरवीर रण को चले। ओ रण शूर बोरसद, तूने नीति युद्ध आरम्भ किया। तू युद्ध में प्रवीण है, तू त्याग से भरा है। ओ प्रसिद्ध बोरसद, तूने स्वतंत्रता का प्रण लिया। आज भी हिन्द–भूमि में तुम्हारी एकता मुग्ध करती है, ओ शूरवीर बोरसद, तूने अनमोल घड़ी उपलब्ध कराई। सरकारी तोपों और मशीनगनों के सामने भी तूने अपनी पीठ नहीं की। सरकार जुल्म करे, जमीन खाली करवाए या तोप से उड़ा दे, फिर भी डटा रहे बोरसद तू। पूर्ण विजयी होकर, ओबोरसद अमर बनो!

पेज न. 219-220

हे माँ री महीसागर नी आरे ढोल वागे से
वागे से, ढोल वागे से, माँ री महीसागर नी आरे ढोल वागे से
गाम गाम ना सोनिड़ा आवे से
आवे से हुँ लावे से,
सोना–रूपा ना घरेणां लावे से, हे माँ री . . .
गाम–गाम ना सुथारिया आवे से,
आवे से हुँ लावे से
मानी गरबी झमाझम लावे छे,
हे माँ री . . .
गाम गाम ना गोवाड़िया आवे से
आवे से हुँ लावे से,
आवे से घी दूध लावे से, हे माँ री महीसागर नी

अर्थ : मही सागर नदी के किनारे ढोल धमाके के साथ गरबा का आयोजन हुआ है। आसपास के गाँवों से कई सोनी इसमें भाग लेने आए हैं। वे अपने साथ दुर्गा माँ के लिये सोना–चाँदी के गहने लाए हैं। गाँव के कई बढ़ई भी आए हैं, जो माँ की सुन्दर सी गरबी बनाकर लाए हैं। कई गाँवों के ग्वाल भी आए हैं जो माँ की पूजा के लिये घी दूध भी लेकर आए हैं।

पेज न. 233

के डंको वाग्यो, लड़वैया शूरा जागजो रे
के शूरा जाग जो रे, कायर भाग जो रे
माथुं मेलो, हाचववा हाची टेकने रे,
हाची टेकने हो, हो हाची टेकने जी
गाजो खेतर भाड़ी ने गाजो गामड़ा रे

अर्थ : संग्राम का डंका बज चुका है, सभी शूरवीर जग जाएँगे और सभी कायर भाग जाएँगे। देश हेतु लिये गए सच्चे प्रण को जीवित रखने के लिये अपना बलिदान देने को भी तैयार रहना है। खेतों में काम करने वाले किसान और अन्य ग्राम वासी भी इस संग्राम के लिये आगे आएँ।

पेज न. 238

Sardar Patel Kee Jay!
सरदार पटेल की जय!

Glossary

Anna	–	1/16 rupee
Arzi Hukumat	–	Care taker temporary Government
Charkha	–	Spinning wheel
Chothai	–	25%
Hartal	–	Strike
Mahalkari	–	Government officer, Head of a Taluka
Mamlatdars	–	Tehsildar of a Taluka
Mukhi	–	Chief
Peepal	–	*A* sacred tree, Ficus religiosa
Ryot	–	Tenant
Talati	–	Village revenue official
Taluka	–	Administrative unit comprising of a group of villages
Taqavi	–	Government loan advanced to the farmers for agriculture purpose.
Veth	–	Begaar, forced free labour